ENEMY FIELDS

J. MARIE DARDEN

A

PUBLICATION

A STREBOR BOOKS INTERNATIONAL LLC PUBLICATION
DISTRIBUTED BY SIMON & SCHUSTER, INC.

Published by

Strebor Books International LLC
P.O. Box 1370
Bowie, MD 20718
http://www.streborbooks.com

ISBN 13: 978-1-59309-023-4 ISBN 10: 1-59309-023-4
LCCN 2003112284

This book is a work of fiction. Names, characters, places and incidents are products of the author's imagination or are used fictitiously. Any resemblance to actual events or locales or persons, living or dead, is entirely coincidental.

Distributed by Simon & Schuster, Inc.
1230 Avenue of the Americas
New York, NY 10020
1-800-223-2336

Cover Design: www.mariondesigns.com

First Printing August 2004
Manufactured and Printed in the United States

10 9 8 7 6 5 4 3 2 1

Acknowledgments

Giving praise, honor, and glory to Christ, who supplies my every need, according to His riches in glory.

To Zane and Sara, who read my work, believed it, and offered their professional support.

To Granddaddy, whose singing rings on in my heart. To my Mama Sammy, who taught me the whole world from her front porch. To Nana and Papa, who speak for themselves. To Grandmother, who will always be the prettiest woman in Lexington. To my mother, who sacrifices herself every day in favor of the ones that she loves. To Daddy, who is, unquestionably, the smartest person I have ever known. To my sisters and brothers, who are my best friends, and who know me intimately and love me anyway. To all of my parents, who do not let circumstances stand in the way of their intelligence and love. To my extended family whose support keeps me resilient. To a rocking host of prolific, radical, and brilliant friends who are in it for the long haul. And to Ann and Frank Westbrook, whose contradictions, ultimatums, and nightmares of black grandchildren help give birth to stories like these.

PART I

Bourbon County, Kentucky, 1971

CHAPTER ONE

No in between here. That what Grannie use to say. Everything either black or white. Me, I'm black.

When I'm on the porch sometime, or up in Timmie and Albert room, I think about my Grannie. Seem like what she say always running through my mind. Stories she would tell and all. Mama say she make most of them up. Grannie say Mama claim that so she don't have to think about truth. But Grannie say ain't no sense in to run from it, and ain't no in between with it, cuz truth is truth.

The weather miserable today. Didn't have much winter before the weather turn plain hot. The air hot and thick as cocoa. Feel tight around you like outgrown sleeves. Hard to breathe. You could smell it, too. Smell solid. Seem like a mess of dirt, damp clothes, syrup, sweet honeysuckle, and rain all mix together. Real sticky.

Nobody feel like doing nothing but fan and drink lemonade. Wasn't no wind neither cuz the air too stiff and stubborn. But, bad as it was inside, seem like it was worse outside. At least you stay dry inside. Outside the air melt on your skin and stick to you like butter. Dribble down your legs like they cobs of corn. The fan don't help none. Those blades have to struggle to stir the thick air, but they can't move quick enough to make a breeze.

Pam Elizabeth come running down my street. She kick up dust that stick to the molasses air.

"Ooh, Sister! Sister, you not gonna believe! You wait!" She holler when she get excited. Then a smile rip across her face to show white horse teeth. She still pretty, though.

"What you got good to say, you simple fool? Screamin' like you crazy," I tease her. Pammie and me can joke because we close.

"Girl, you won't believe!" Pammie leap up the porch steps and plop down on the wooden swing Papa make.

"Naw, I sho won't believe less you tells me already!" I'm anxious since Pammie looking tickle at whatever it is.

"You know that big ole house? The one cross the field back of your house? Political man own it or somethin'. Well, my brother Edward say he hear from his boy Skeemo that folks is fixin' to move in Friday!" She smiling like she ain't said it all.

"That your news?" I play like I don't really care, but really I'm curious. That house so big and mysterious. Been empty ever since I can remember.

"Here's what else." She hitting me with the punch. "They's white folks, what's fixin' to move in!" She beam, satisfied that she drop me.

"Naw, sure enough? They's *white?*" I pronounce the word real clear, and my eyes get wide because I'm sure enough surprise. No white folks never come to our part of town even to visit. But to live?!

"And they rich, too. Got to be to afford that ole place. Skeemo say it need some work, but it real big. It got something like eight or ten bedrooms in it. And land for miles and miles. They say part of that field back of your house really belong to that house. Wonder how they gonna tend all that land, Sister?" The swing is old and the paint is chip and crack away. Pammie use her long skinny fingers to peel away layers of the paint.

"Quit pickin', Girl! Spose they ask some of us town folks to help them. Wonder what they comin' here for? Plenty of fine houses closer to town. Why they gonna live near us? Grannie say white folks is trouble."

"Spose she was right. I reckon we have to wait and find out for sure. You miss your grannie?" Pammie lift one foot up on the swing and use the other to sort of push and make us go.

"Yeah. Sometime it don't seem like she really gone. So much of what she say always runnin' round in my head. But she better off now, I guess." My Grannie pass last winter. She was 86.

"I miss Daddy, too. Seem like the people you love the most the ones that die first. Least he got to see me finish school. He always want for us to finish."

"Grannie, too. But she pass before I finish."

"Do your mama ever cry about Grannie? Mama, seem like she cry all the time. She a little better now that she teach piano again. Use to be she just sit around and cry. I guess she lonely."

"Mama don't cry. She pray. Me, I use to cry, but not no more. I still get lonely sometime, though."

"Why you lonely? Your husband ain't pass."

"Yeah, but Grannie pass. And your daddy pass. I ain't got no daddy. And people pass. And I ain't got no husband. I don't know. Just seem like maybe somethin' missin', I don't know." I finger my springy-coil hair.

"Right. That's why I wanna get away from here. I don't think there anything here for me."

Pammie and me talk a little longer. She always saying she going but don't go nowhere. Pammie ain't even got a job yet. She don't know what she want. Say she got a cousin name Bluff live in Detroit. She say she going and stay with him.

Me, I ain't press to go. One thing I do know is I wanna sing. Ever since I's little, I be writing down words. You know, like catchy phrases. Then I add a melody to it. Call myself writing songs. When I go to Pammie house, I play piano. Her mama play at the church and she teach some, too. I never had the patience to take from her. She wanna make you study theory or some mess. I just wanna play what I hear and sing what I play. I do like to sing in church, though.

Soon Pammie get on her going-to-Detroit kick, and I get bored. I say I'm going in the house, and she walk on down the street to hers.

Chapter Two

It cramp at home. Whole bunch of us in one little house. We got a kitchen, bathroom, living room, dining room, and three bedrooms.

It ain't that bad. But it do get crowded. It me, my mama, my older sister, Ruthanne, her baby, Nakita, my younger brothers, Timothy and Albert, and sometime Ruthanne boyfriend, Peanut. Ruthanne and Nakita in one room, Timmie and Albert in another, and me and Mama share one.

Mama getting old, so she go to bed all early. She want the light out by 10:00. I can't read or write or sing in there. Sometime I can sit in the living room and write. Then sometime Albert come in with some fast girl from cross town, acting like they grown. Else Ruthanne down there with big-headed Peanut and don't want me around. Timmie only five, so he usually sleep. Sometime I go in his room and look out the window and think.

Timmie and Albert room face the back, so the window show the back yard and way out into the field. Sometime it real pretty out there. The grass all soft and plush like crush velvet. When you walk barefooted out there it feel kinda cool and wettish, and the air smell real nice. I like fall best. Then you can see the leaves on the sycamores blended in different patterns. Green, red, and gold all together. Look like the patchwork on some of Mama quilts.

When the moon bright and in the right place, kinda hazy and yellow-like, it make the meadow look like maybe ghosts is back there. It spooky. Sometime I pretend they really is ghosts back there, and I imagine what they like. Is they black ghosts or white ghosts? Do they come from the dead folks in our town or from that big house back there? Probably they's all kinds. I reckon don't nobody care what color you is when you dead.

In their room you can see the back of that house Pammie say white folks moving into. Ain't nobody live there since I was real little, and whoever they was, I don't remember them.

Not long after I hear the news from Pammie, I seen the new people moving in. Everybody in the neighborhood talking about it. Only time white folks come around is if someone take some of they property—they stuff or they women. Don't nobody here do that. We got our own stuff, and the men here ain't too particular for white women. Least that what they say.

One night I'm in Timmie room and I could see clear into those people house. Why they got windows all over the back? They don't want privacy? I could see the dining room and one of the bedroom. I seen three people in there: one old man with white hair, a fattish woman look like she Mama age, and a boy my age with wild red hair. Seem strange to put those few people in that big ole house whiles me and Mama and all of us is pile up in our house cross the field. White folks is crazy. That what Grannie use to say. I ain't really known none of them personal-like. Just some of the teachers back at Dunbar, but you can't count them. They ain't there to get to know; they just try to teach you.

The lights was dim in the dining room, but I could see into the bedroom where the boy stay. I can't see all that well, but I can tell he got a guitar. I couldn't hear him play, but it seem nice that he try. Wonder if he good? I use to wish I could play one of them guitars, but I don't got one. Plus it seem kinda hard—all them strings.

All week I hear people talking about them white folks. They say the boy sick or something. That his mama and granddaddy he live with. They name Mandarene. Say the mama got the house left to her by her dead uncle. That may not be true. Folks around here often make up what they don't know for sure.

People saying they looking for someone to keep the house and cook during the week. Don't nobody want to ask about it because don't nobody trust white folks. I'm thinking about going cross the field and see if they maybe take me. Maybe they pay good. And anyway, I ain't scared of no white folk no how.

CHAPTER THREE

Grannie say white folks is crazy. They can be as crazy as they wanna be when they pay me $75.00 a week to cook and clean they house. Mama figure these people must got money to burn.

The old man over there is name Norman. He don't spose to smoke, but I find his butts all over the back porch and in the yard, too. Mama is name Cordial. She say don't call her Miss cuz it make her feel old. She is old, so I call her Miss. Cordial a strange name anyhow.

Her son sick or something. He got cancer. Pale skin and wild red hair. Calls hisself "Ev-ee-in." His mama say "Ev-yin." But he always put that extra sound in the center. Me, I didn't call him nothing at first. No need. If he come up on me, I just answer his question and go on.

Cordial, she one of them artsy types. She set up a board by the window in the dining room and call herself painting. First few weeks I come, all I see her do is mix paint together, sometime with a stick, sometime with her hand. Then she wanna "get her own lunch." What that mean is she gonna leave oily prints and a big mess in the kitchen. I say, if she wanna get her lunch, what I come for? Never mind. She still pay me.

Mainly she want me to wash the windows. That and the baseboards. That what she call the thin wood that stick out at the bottom of the wall. Twice a week she got me using vinegar and newspaper on the windows and Pine Sol on the baseboards. I never seen such clean windows. Good thing they clean, too, cuz Miss love to stare out them. Some days she just stand and look for hours, seem like. Make me chuckle. If I had time, I stare out them, too. Me, I'm too busy cleaning them to stare out of them.

One thing I do know, white folks ain't much for work. Miss hire somebody to do everything. She call it sending things out. Use to be I clean the sheets and they clothes, but for long she send them out. Sure enough on Wednesday morning, I gather up the laundry and set them by the door. Then Jefferson son come from the cleaners and pick them up, return them on Saturday. I ain't around on Saturday. Least not at first.

Evian, as he call hisself, talk on the phone a lot. He talk in a high-pitch voice real slow and drawn out. It don't sound like Kentucky, neither. More like Tennessee or something. But when he laugh, he cackle. Whoever he talk to must really tickle him, because he always laughing. That and play the guitar. He sing some, too. Singing don't sound like his speaking, though. Sound more like cranberries: sweet, cold, and tangy. I hum along sometime. Sometime I don't know the words.

One day I'm cleaning his bathroom and he in his bedroom playing Marvin Gaye and Tammi. Where he get Marvin, I wonder? He playing it real loud, so I start singing Tammi part. This time I know the words. Next thing I know, he at the door singing Marvin part real strong. We sound kinda good, but I act like I don't notice. Just keep singing.

When the record go off, he spin me around and say, "Hey, now! I never knew you could sing like that, uhh...ahh...What is your name again, I'm sorry..." Evian look shame.

I answer quick. "Don't make no difference. Folks call me Sister." I don't look him in the eye.

"Sister, you got a mean contralto! You like to sing real low, don't you?" Evian lean against the sink. His wild red hair matted in the back.

I'm surprise he interested. "Yea. I can sing up high or low, but I like it best when it settle somewhere in my chest."

Evian get real excited, start talking with his hands. "Cool! I love to harmonize. I love the way you people sing! I wish I could emulate it."

Right there I start tuning out. What he mean "you people?" I maybe clean the house and cook the food, but it 1971, and I'm 18 years old, a full women, and King done died, and I don't feel like conversating as one of "you people." I turn away and sprinkle Comet in the tub.

He don't take the hint. "...I have so many records. Old stuff. Newer stuff. You like Ray Charles? Oh, oh, and how about James Brown? Double threat—dances and sings! Aretha, the Beatles..." Evian chatter on, don't notice I ain't hardly listening. "Who are your favorites, Sister?" He cross his feet while he lean on the sink.

"I disremember. I...I think I better finish this here tub." I try not to be rude. He ain't worth losing my job over or nothing. One hand, I wanna talk to him. Don't nobody love Aretha and music like me. Other hand, what he wanna talk music with "you people" for?

Evian turn to leave. "Oh yeah. You're busy. Like my mom is too busy to clean her own toilets. I'm in my room, mostly. Come by and say hey sometime. I wanna know who your favorites are." He scratch his head in the back as he leave. He need to comb his hair.

He puzzle me. You people. Cracks about his mama. He setting me up? And I don't see him rushing to clean his own toilet.

Soon after that, Evian get sick. Miss leave me in the house some days with the old man. She say Evian be going to the doctor a lot for a while. She say I don't have to clean his room or his bathroom, neither. Okay with me.

But I still gotta vacuum. So, I hear him in his bathroom being sick. I'm out in the hall with the vacuum. I go in the room next to his and pull the door to. Don't seem right to have someone hearing you be sick. So first I sort of dust. But really I'm finish in there, so I turn on the vacuum and just sit a minute. Next I hear him go in his room and shut the door.

While I'm vacuuming the hall outside his room, something sort of sink down low in my stomach. He so young to be so sick. Next thing I know, I hear Dinah Washington singing "Unforgettable." Something jump up in me then, same thing that had sunk before, and I knock on his door.

Hear him rustle on the bed. "Yea?"

"I like her, too." I say through the door.

"Come again? Sister...?" He turn the music down a little.

"I say, I like Dinah Washington, too." My heart pounding some.

"Sister. Come in. Open the door." He sitting on the edge of the bed , hair breaking off and skin more pale.

I scan the room slow, like I don't never seen it before. It got carpet, but he also put down these wild color rugs on the floor. He got a painting of a bird over the bed, got its head stretch up and its wings half-spread.

Evian half-laugh, half cough. "She is my absolute favorite. Gotta be in the right mood for Dinah, though. She's better than some of them, I spose, like Billie Holiday." He not looking at me. He looking at the bird.

"Yeah. She take you down some place you don't intend to go." I sing along to "Willow Weep for Me." Evian sort of hum along, too. Then the record stop and all you hear is breathing. Mine shallow and his seem like water running through it.

"You ever get tired, Sister? Sometimes I'm so tired." He lean against the back board of the bed and cross his feet Indian-style.

"Sure. After working all day or walking around with Pammie." I answer without thinking.

"Yea, but I mean deep down in your bones tired. And sick. And sick of being tired. I mean, what is this about, anyways? All these trips to the doctor and therapy. Doesn't seem like I'll ever get better. And it makes me tired." He rest his head against the back board. Small tears run down his cheek.

I don't know what to say. What I got to be tired for? Sometime things get on my nerves, like when it crowded at home and I wanna write or just think. Or the way white folks look at you in Woodsons downtown like you dirty. I gets tired of that fast and want to go home. Bone tired? I don't know. I notice a pile of Negro spirituals on his desk. "Precious Lord" and "Deep River." They two of my favorites. These the ones they always let me lead at church.

"At home, it ain't no room to breathe. They's a bunch of us in there. I get sad sometime for my grannie. She pass a year ago. Those times I sing. You know. Out on the porch, just swing a little and sing till the heavy part slip away. You know this?" I hand him "Precious Lord."

Evian take the page. "Hand me my guitar, will you?" He let his right leg dangle off the side of the bed.

First he tune. He put the music on the bed in front of him. Then he strum soft. Close his eyes and strum around the melody. I don't never hear nobody play spirituals on the guitar before. Sound so soft on the outside, like when raindrops fall off the tree in the front yard and bounce on the window.

He rock a little and strum. Seem like some of his sick and tired, some of my dirty looks from Woodsons, and some of Grannie's "no in between" splash together and land at my feet. I start to sing.

I start at the center and move out. Through the storm. Through the night. By the time I'm back at the beginning, pleading to the Lord, Evian singing, too. We sound kinda sweet together.

Chapter Four

"So, what it like over there? Do they got marble floors and gold-plated everything? What about they clothes? Where do they come from—Fields? Gimbles? She got furs, Sister?" Me and Pammie in my room. Both us on the bed with a bowl of popcorn between us. We love us some popcorn. Pammie make it better than I do. She got a bigger pot. It don't never scorch over to her house. Pammie painting her nails. I'm filing mine.

"Girl, they not like that, I'm telling you. They house is big, though. They got real thick carpet everywhere. Cept the kitchen. Look like I spend most times vacuuming. That and cleaning the windows. They got plenty carpets and windows." My nails don't grow long like Pammie. I don't usually add no color to them.

"Do she got furs? What you be cooking over there? They eat strange food?"

"I ain't seen no furs so far. She always wear flower skirts and tee shirts. And bare feet. But they got two refrigerators. One really a freezer. That where they keep the meat and ice cream and all kinda dessert. Miss love dessert, wit her fat butt self. I cook chicken or steak or fish. Evian love fried fish. She got cookbooks, but I don't usually look in them."

Pammie better-looking than me. Her skin even tone and caramel brown. She got long, thick hair fall away from her face and turn under in fat hunks. Big brown eyes and full, heart-shape lips.

Me, my hair curly. It come down and coil back, look like rusty springs. Reddish brown, sort of. My skin ashy-looking. Not real brown, not redbone. Just plain. Pammie got a round butt and hips. I go straight up and down like a boy. I ain't ugly. Wholesome, that what Mama say. That her word for nothing special, I guess. Pammie always tell me I look pretty when I fix up, but usually I don't.

"Dang, Girl! You lucky! Wha you gonna do with all that money?"

"Give part of it to Mama; you know—help out. I spend some on clothes and records, and I'm thinkin' bout getting a guitar." I slip that in casua-like. I ain't ready to tell her about Evian and how he say he teach me how to play, maybe.

"And you gonna spend a little taste on your best bud, too, right?" Pammie giggle while she fan her nails.

"Girl, you know we gonna hang. Go to movies and stuff. You know that's right!" We slap five in the air.

"Maybe I could work, too. Save some money. Something. Edward say he going round there, too, but he never do. Say he hear they need somebody cut the grass and all." Edward Pammie older brother.

"I told Miss he comin;. Be nice to have him around sometime. Maybe then I feel more comfortable." I tell Pam how it is all day with white folks. How you feel kinda strange and don't know what to say. Truth, I feel kinda okay around Evian. Me and him seem like we can understand each other some. But in the back of my mind I know I got to be careful cuz he may be crazy, like Grannie say.

Weeks pass and Evian seem like he feel better. He got his hair so short he almost bald. Talk on the phone again. He got a cousin name Blister from over to Georgetown. First I think that a strange name for somebody. Then I seen him and understand. Big red face and fat sausage fingers. Look like he ready to pop. Got a fat butt, too.

One week he come over from Georgetown, gonna stay the weekend. He come on Wednesday and stay until Sunday. Miss have me set up the room next to Evian. All I gotta do is turn down the bed and put out towels and stuff.

I don't know what to make of me and Evian. All the time he call me in his room and we talk. He tell me about when he live in Memphis and he got sick. He got to stay home a lot and have a tutor come and teach him. Stay in the house, mostly, and play guitar and sing. Blister, he play guitar, too. They like to sing together or plan out how they gonna form a band and be stars one day.

Tuesday before Blister come, I'm rubbing the baseboards with Pine Sol. Evian call me in. He got James Brown playing on his record player. Don't seem like he ever listen to nobody white, cept the Beatles.

"Hey, Sissy!" He took to calling me that few weeks before. "You ever get tired of cleaning Mama's floors? I mean, you are so talented! You sing as good as Aretha, easy. What you got planned for yourself? You 18 yet?" He on the floor flipping through crates of records.

When he talk to me, I want to lean back and ease off, like with Pammie. But something catch in the middle and I can't. Maybe cuz he a little older and he a man. Maybe cuz when he smile I get a tightness in my shoulders. Mainly cuz he said, "you people," and I ain't forgot. Why he wanna know what I do?

"I be 19 in September. Anyways, I like to clean. Ain't nothing to keep a place clean, Ev. Plus, your mama treat me nice, and if I don't work here, how I get to know you?" I look at him silly and stick out my tongue.

Ev swat me on the leg. "You best keep your tongue in your mouth, Sissy, or someone might come along and snatch it out." He wink at me.

He do that and something buckle at my knee. I sit down for a minute.

He say, "My mama is so backwards! She acts like she lives in the dark ages or something. I mean, she claims to be such a liberal, but the closest she gets to Blacks is the people that she hires to run her house. That's so played out!" A vein pop out at his right temple when he get mad.

"Parents always seem backward. My mama still blame me if the kitchen ain't clean even though I ain't at home all day. Plus she don't like me to go nowhere less it with Pammie or something, like I'm a baby." I don't wanna say nothing about his mama. Where I come from, you don't talk about somebody Mama, especially when they your boss.

"Whatever. I guess you just lose your sense when you get older. Me, I'm never gonna lose my sense, cuz I'm never gonna get any older! Not with Mama around! She is so protective. Like she doesn't want me to go anywhere or do anything. I might break, or something. She doesn't want me to die, so she won't let me live. It's crazy. But, hell, when I go, I go. I can deal with that. I do have to live a little, first. Otherwise, what's the point? You gotta listen to this, Sissy." He hand me an album by Joan Armatrading.

"Your mama would love to know that I's back here listening to records while she pay me to clean. Specially when your cousin comin' and stay and I got to fix up his room."

"Oh, so you don't have time for me, Sissy? You so busy, right, you can't spend a minute with an old friend?" He tickling my leg, moving up to my stomach and sides.

"I'm ticklish, Ev. Don't! You make me..." I'm too laughy and nervous to talk.

"Make you what, Sissy? Huh? What does it make you do?" Evian tickle my underarms near my chest. He up in my face. Smell like Dove soap.

He pin my arms down so's I can't wiggle, face right up next to mine. Seem like my legs go to Jell-O. I start to slip down. He catch me around the waist and hold tight. Then he brush his lips against mine, and I feel his fingers on my back.

We kiss.

Seem like the walls fly out and we standing in outer space somewhere.

Feel like a balloon filling up in my chest and I can't breathe.

Seem like whatever he got on his heart he trying to push down my throat and into mine.

He got his hands in my hair. "I been wanting to do that for a long time." He looking at my eyes.

I can't say nothing. Seem like he took my tongue all for hisself. Then he put his finger on my lip and give it back to me.

"Ev... I gotta.... we better.... let me go tend to the cleaning. Miss be back from the store soon..." I lean away from him, but don't no space come between us.

"Sure, Sissy. You can take the album with you. Let me know what you think about it."

I head on down the hall thinking, "Damn. What I'm gonna do now?"

CHAPTER FIVE

What I decide to do is act like it don't matter. What I care if some white boy with cancer gonna make like we friends and stuff and kiss me like that? Big deal. So I shake my hair some, like I wanna get a bad smell off me, and then I go back to the room set up for Blister. Everything in order there. Smooth down the sheets and fluff up the pillow. Spray a little more daffodil air spray. Truthfully, I don't never smell a flower that smell like this junk, but Miss seem to like to use it. She keep it in every room.

But, much as I don't wanna admit it, it do seem like I got a little spring in my step afterward. Miss still in town and I done finish the list of cleaning to do today. Scared to go back in Evian room. So, I go to the kitchen and pull down one of Miss cookbooks. I look at desserts first. They got recipes for cobbler in there and banana pudding. Who need a recipe for that? Me, I just get down the stuff from the cabinets, like the peaches or the bananas. Then I just add a taste of this and a taste of that. For you know it, you got dessert. Now, I can't make some of the stuff Mama and Aint Nelly make. They can throw down, sure enough. Aint Nelly can make pound cake and pecan pie like you don't believe. Mama, she big with sweet potato pie. I don't mess with no sweet potato pie too much. Don't seem right to be putting vegetables in pies. But I do like me some cobbler.

So, for a treat, I decide to make Miss some apple cobbler. I like peach better, but she don't have none in the kitchen. And go to the store? No, I don't feel that special. So I'm peeling apples and sifting flour and the like. I got the radio on, and I am listening to the Jackson Five. For long I got a big pan of it ready to go in the oven. I put some in a small pan, too, so's I can take a little taste home with me.

I'm just finishing up cleaning the cobbler mess and done stashed my separate pan in a bag inside my tote, when Miss come in. She got old Norman behind her. He got a scowl on his face, same as usual. He notice me and smile a little. Seem like he kinda sweet on me or something. He always smile and say something when he see me. Specially when I'm in the kitchen. Miss, she always got the sound of the sun in her voice. Like God set her up with a picnic smack in the middle of the world, and now all she gotta do is kick back and enjoy. Sometime she sort of get on my nerves.

"Sister! Don't tell me you took and made a cobbler!" Miss always accusing me of "taking and doing" something. "Girl, you know the last thing I need is some cobbler! But, sure nough, I was thinking just today how I would like to have some with some ice cream. Had a sweet tooth all day. I must a been inside your head, cuz I took and brought some home. Ice cream, I mean. Vanilla—that soft kind." She start unloading her packages all over the counter.

Norman, on his way out to the back porch, which is where he stay most of the time, or in his room, laugh out loud. "Cor-jul, you got nothing but sweet teeth in your head. Wonder they don't all fall out. Just like your mama. One of these days you gonna take me round to that doctor and have to stay for yourself. Why in the world you eating all that sweet stuff when sugar was your mama's demise is beyond me. And you, Sister. Always her accomplice. For shame!" He wink at me and pick a little edge off the crust. The cobbler ain't been out the oven more than five minutes and he already picking. He look like warning Miss. "Well, I'm off to greener pastures than these. Sister, you have a safe walk home, now, hear?" He shuffle hisself on out the back door.

"Daddy is a real nuisance! Like I don't know that he smokes and drinks and God knows what else. Mama was diabetic, but she died from her stoke. Plus she was 74. And anyway, he ought to be more careful than he is, too. He is getting up there, you know."

I just sort of nod my head. Miss ain't looking for no comment, no way. Just talking to hear herself, really. I'm helping Miss put away the groceries even though it time for me to go. So, I figure I better say something.

"Bless his heart. He don't mean no harm. I guess that his way of letting you know he love you. Like my Grannie use to say, you gotta die of something. Might as well have fun while you doing it." I put the eggs in they special compartment.

Miss sigh deep. "Well, it is about that time, Sister. I guess Daddy could go any time now. Then I really will be alone. 'Cept for Ev-yun. And he is so grown these days. Doesn't want to hear anything I got to say." She put a stack of corn ears in the refrigerator. "That reminds me. I will be going into Louisville on Friday. I will be staying with my girlfriend, WilleMae. She has gotten us tickets to the symphony, and she has another male friend she wants me to meet. Folks are forever trying to fix me up! Since James died, I have dated more men. None of them hold a candle to my Jimmy..." She trail off. I hope she don't choke up. Jimmy her husband that died in Vietnam. Been dead since 1968, she say. He Norman son. She related to Norman by marriage, even though she call him daddy.

"Might be good for you. You never know who you may meet. Sound like a good time to me." I am being sincere, though I don't truly care. Grannie say don't get too sentimental for white folks. They sure never sentimental for us all these years. But don't nobody want to be alone, I reckon. So I think she might want to go and meet someone.

"Yea, well, we'll see. Sister, I am going to be gone til Sunday after church. I know you are normally off on Saturday, but... Would you mind coming over and checking on things? I worry about Ev-yun. And Daddy can handle himself, I guess, but... I'd just feel better if you looked in on them and maybe cooked something for their supper. And you know Blister is gonna be here, too. He can be so wild... Do you think you could come?" She look at me helpless.

"Yeah, Miss Cordial. I come by Saturday. No problem. Don't you worry. These men will be okay." Now I got to come round here on Saturday, too. What Miss thing they gonna do, anyways?

"I am much obliged, Sister. Maybe you want to take Friday off, since you're coming on Saturday. This way you don't feel overwhelmed. Of course, I'll leave a little extra for you this week. I don't know what I'd do without you."

"That'll be good, Miss. I can get some things done at home on Friday. Matter of fact, I guess I be getting on back now. I need to fix supper and all." I rinse my hands off at the sink and then move toward the kitchen door.

"Of course. I lose track of time, don't I? Running my mouth. Get lost already! I'll see you tomorrow." Miss smile and start humming a song I don't know as she move to the sink and look out the window. Always looking out the window.

Back home I flop on my bed and think. I don't mean to, but look like I can't help myself. Crazy stuff running around in my head. Like do Evian love me or do he mean to trick me or something. I think back to everything he ever said to me and every time we be together. What it seem like? I don't think he mean-spirited. Seem like he sincere. But all tricksters seem sincere, don't they? Otherwise how they gonna fool somebody? I don't know. I do know it feel nice when he messing in my hair and breathing so close. And I like to sing with him. I like the way he talk to me and listen if I got something I wanna say. I usually don't. But if I do, I think he listen.

I start to fantasize about him and me. You know. Walking some place or just sitting close and listen to each other think. What do he think about, I wonder? Me, it's always what Imma do or be. Pammie, she always saying she got to leave from around here. But I don't know. Leave and go where? Everything I know about is right here. Mama and my family and everybody. Plus, I don't wanna leave Mama. Seem like she need me, even though she don't act like it. The house is paid and all, but I do help around here. Pay some of the bills and buy some groceries. Keep the rooms clean and stuff. I don't know.

Evian cute to me. Didn't especially think so at first. But he grow on me, I guess. He got these strange color eyes. Not blue. Not green. Just pastel, sort of. Look like they got plenty water in them, but they clear and...I'm not sure what else. Patient, maybe. And he got fat lips for white people. Used to be so thin, but now it seem like he pick up a little weight. Miss say he getting better and they don't see tumors no more. But they still got to watch him. I pray that he be okay. I don't know why. I just don't want to think of nothing bad happen to him. Seem like he been through enough.

I put on the record that Ev let me borrow. This woman, Joan Arma—whatever can sing. She sing deep like I do. I look at the words on the back of the album. She write pretty, too. I listen and try to hum along even though I don't really know all these songs yet. I can learn right quick, though. Ev right. I do like her sound.

I lose myself somewhere around the fourth song. Just floating out in space somewhere. I know I need to see whether Mama fix supper or not, cuz I'm hungry. But something make me just sit there and think. Mostly about Evian and how he kiss. I like it. Thing that worry me is, I hope he kiss me again. Real soon.

CHAPTER SIX

When I went around there that Thursday before Miss leave for Louisville, Evian already gone. He downtown somewhere with Blister. I peek in Blister room to see what I can tell from what he got with him. Miss on the front porch with a magazine and some iced tea I made and let brew in the sun. It taste so good that way. But she out of my way, like I like it. So I snoop a little.

He got a guitar, too. And tons of what Evian call sheet music. All it is where the person wrote down the notes and chords they be playing. I can understand the piano ones. But some of them also got these funny marks. For the guitar, I guess. He got a bunch of tee shirts and what seem like army pants. Clean underwear. A notebook and some colored pens. A copy of *Lord of the Flies*. I read that at Dunbar. It was okay. But in the corner of his suitcase he got a plastic baggy with home-grown inside. Those boys from Georgetown always smoke corn. It must grow real well there. Pammie and her brother have a little in their back yard. They smoke it sometime, too. Me, I get real silly with that stuff. It don't agree with me, especially. Every now and again, me and Pammie and her brother smoke a little and act simple.

So, I cover all the stuff on Miss list for the day, same as usual. I try not to think about Evian and his kiss. Maybe he forgot about it. He don't seem like he too worried about it to me. Off with Blister somewhere. I ain't worried neither.

I'm about to put the dishes away and head home when I hear them in the driveway. Blister drive a VW bug. It got different colors all over it and got a Confederate flag in the side window. Blister wearing some jeans look real fray at the bottom and flare out. Evian wearing those baggy shorts, barefoot, and carrying a stack of albums. I guess they been to the record store.

They come busting through the back door that lead into the kitchen. I am standing at the sink about to drain the water out from the dishes. Dry my hands on a flower towel.

"Hey, Sissy. This here is my cousin, Franklin. But everybody call him Blister. Blister, this is Sissy. She's a friend of the family, comes and helps us out around here." Evian get two glasses out of the cabinet and set them on the table. "I'm gonna get us some tea. You want some, Sissy?"

I shake my head no.

"Hey there, Sissy. I heard about you! Evian done told me you was a sanger. I sang a little myself, me and Evian. Glad to know you." He squat, too bulky, over a chair. Drink a sip of tea. All teeth and pink skin like popped balloons, smiling at me.

"Yeah. Blister is pretty good, actually. Better than me on the guitar. But he can't sing so great. Though he thinks he sounds like Paul or John, or something." Evian tease his cousin. I guess they got it like that. "You should hear him play, Sissy. He does all these riffs and shit that I can't do to save my life. Blow you away." He wink at me and smile.

My stomach shift when he wink. "I bet he would. Pleasure to know you, Franklin. But Evian, you make me out to be more than myself. I like to sing and everything. But just for fun, you know. It ain't like you spose to be taking me serious and all." I act modest. Really it ain't much of an act. I know I can sing okay, but I ain't boastful or nothing.

"Puh-leez! Let Evian tell it, and you a regular Joni Mitchell or something. Reckon I just have to hear for myself and see if you sing as sweet as you look..." Now Blister wink. This time when my stomach shift it don't feel the same.

"You'll see. Sissy, you coming round here Saturday, right? Me and Blister fixing to barbecue. Ever taste my barbecue, Sissy?"

He know darn well I ain't. "No, Ev, I can't say as I has."

"Oooh-wee, Sister. Now you missing a treat! I can make some barbecue make you wanna slap your mama! Sure enough. You just come on out and see Saturday. And if my ribs and Blister's riffs don't make you wanna sing, I don't know what will." He grinning all over. Me too.

"Hey now! The party is on. Imma be practicing all day tomorrow and make sure my plucking is primed for your sangin'. We'll have us a regular ol jam session." Blister seem like he really excited about all this.

"Good, then. That's settled. Oh, Sissy, Mama asked me to show you something in the back room. Will you come back with me before you leave out?" He already heading for his room.

"Okay, but I do gotta be getting' on. Please to meet you, Blister. I spose I see you sometime Saturday." I follow at Evian heels.

"I spose you will!" I hear Blister say from half to Evian room.

Evian pull me in his room and press against me real gentle. Then he kiss my cheek, my lips, my ear. He say, "I'm glad you're coming on Saturday, Sissy. I been waiting to show off your singing to somebody. Be selfish to keep you all to myself."

My heart pounding like I don't know what. What if Blister come back here? What if Miss or Norman hear? "Go on! What you wanna flatter me like that for? Plus, ain't you scared? Bringin' me back here to kiss and all...?" Truthfully, I wish he kiss me two times more. Once for me to feel, and once to think about later.

"What I got to be scared for? I like you, Sissy. You're sweet and smart and got good sense—nothing wrong with that. Saturday my mama's gonna be gone, and we can get to know each other some. It'll be fun." Evian hold onto both my hands and stare at me.

"Well, Miss did ask me to come and check on y'all. You think she be mad if I stay and eat barbecue? I mean, I do all my work first, of course."

"You worry too much. What she got to care for? We both got to eat. And me and Blister'll walk you home if it's dark when you ready to go. You be my guest, Sissy. Don't give me a problem." He tweak my nose and open the door again. "So, I'll see you Saturday, okay?"

"You ain't gonna stop worryin' me til I say yes, so I be here." I follow him out the bedroom and go round to the kitchen door to go home. Miss in the kitchen with Blister. They both sitting and drink iced tea. I wish Miss a safe trip and say goodbye to both of them.

I got a little extra jiggle to my walk as I shuffle through the field to my house. First thing I think is, I gotta tell Pammie. She gonna be surprised I ain't already told her about how it is with Evian. Which make me think. How is it with him, anyways? What he mean when he say we get to know each other? What do he have in mind? I mean, I do wanna be with him sort of. I like to spend time and have him talk about how I could sing and brag on me. It feel good when he do that. And when he kiss me. But something tell me Miss would have something to say if she knew we back in his room getting close all of a sudden. Wonder what everybody gonna think if they knew?

Too soon to tell, I guess. Maybe I get over there Saturday and Ev done change his mind. Or maybe I change my mind. We just have to wait and see. But I know that when I get in the house, I hope nobody ain't on the phone, cuz I need to talk to Pam. See what she got to say about all this.

CHAPTER SEVEN

"So you round to the Manderenes' kissin' white boys and don't wanna tell nobody, huh? Should have known you was hiding somethin'. Ain't talk to you in almost three days. But you know you askin' for trouble, right? It ain't like we ain't in Kentucky, up in Detroit or somewheres where they be doin that stuff..." Pammie talk real breathy and fast. Sound like she filing her nails while she talk. She spend more time on her nails!

Now I'm almost sorry I tell her. But not really. We so tight. If I make a mistake or something, Pammie always the first to let me know I done it and let me know it ain't gonna kill me, too. "Girl, I know. It ain't like I plan it or nothin'. Just sort of happen that way. Too late to worry about it now. Plus, Evian say there ain't no cause to worry." I'm in my room, and I pull the phone in with me from the kitchen. We only got one in there and one in Mama room.

"Now you quotin' this boy, too? Sister, please! You so simple. Just cuz this Evian say it don't mean it is true. Do his mama know y'all is... What are y'all doin? And do she know?"

"Naw, I don't guess she do. But she bound to find out if we decide to keep this up."

"Keep what up? You sleepin' with this cracker?" I hear Pam stop filing her nails.

"No! But I do work with him. And he do want to be my friend."

"Girl, you work *for* him. And his mama. Don't forget that." She add a little "hmmph" sound at the end.

I get quiet. What do she mean by that, I work for him? "You don't have to be so mean-actin'. I'm just tellin' you cuz you my friend and... Pam, you think he usin' me? That what you mean by I's workin' for him?" I start to bite my nail. Which I don't usually do.

"I'm sorry. I don't mean to be cold. Just surprise is all. And I don't want you to get hurt. See, we ain't use to these people. And they do have a history of hatin' us Blacks. Sometime they take advantage. SO. I guess I am sayin be careful, that's all. And inside of that, don't worry." Pammie soften the sound of her voice.

"Now *you* quotin that white boy!" I start to laugh, feel a little better.

"Right! That will be the day!" Pam cough out a laugh.

But what Pam say stay on my mind for a while after I hang up. She right. I do gotta be careful. But something tell me Evian not the one I gotta worry about. He so gentle and sweet with me. And we ain't the first to be interested in somebody outside our race. People done this before. Plenty. Just not around here is all. So, maybe I be a first in this town. It gotta happen sometime. Plus, time is changing. What did King die for if we ain't never gonna change?

So, I take it easy on Friday. I tell Mama I got the day off. She quick try to get me to do stuff around the house she could ask Ruthanne to do. I do it, but I also relax. I watch some TV and make some popcorn. Once again it ain't as good as Pam. I also wash my hair and try to set it. It look the same to me, except it a little more curl than usual.

Then me and Ruthanne and the boys decide to play Monopoly. It's fun. We all live here, but seem like it take a big Sunday dinner for us to all be together at the same time. When Mama come in, she in a good mood.

"Ain't this sweet! All my babies lined up all pretty playin' games!" She come in the living room and pick up Nakita. Nakita spoil. She almost two and don't never have to walk, practically. Someone always got her hoist up on they hip. But she so cute, don't nobody want to put her down. She got Ruthanne big brown eyes and head shape like her daddy. Peanut!

"Hey, Mama. I went and paid the lights today; I lef the change on the counter in the kitchen. You think you can spot me five til I get paid Monday?" Albert a hustler. Always out to see what he can get, what kinda deal he can work out. He not too bad though, for a man. He do help with the bills and can fix up anything in the house. He say he wanna be a engineer when he finish school. I bet he will.

Mama plop down on the floor in the middle of us. "Boy, you always after me for somethin'! Yes, you go keep whatever that change is you say is in there. And make it last til Monday so you don't have to worry me. Sister, you cook anything?"

Ruthanne answer. "I made lunch for all of us. You shoulda been here then! Fat burgers and french fries and everything. We was greasin' for real!" Ruthanne so proud of herself when she cook something somebody can eat rather than throw away. She ain't a champ in the kitchen. But she can sew real good. She make all of her clothes and Nakita clothes, too. One day Imma have her make me something pretty. She ain't done that for a while.

"Well, that's great, baby. But your mama is hungry now. Let me get in here and fix us something right quick." She get up to go in the kitchen.

"Good," I say. "I got the day off!"

Timmy follow right behind her. He love his mama, now. He always right up under her. And look just like her, too. Me and Ruthanne got springy red hair like Daddy family. Mama got slick black hair that don't half curl. Timmy got hair like that, too. Albert hair is curl, but he cut it real close most the time, so you can't tell. "Mama, I can help. I can make hot dogs and beans and potato chips and corn..." Timmy voice trail off as they go to the kitchen. He love hot dogs and potato chips more than anything. Figures he try to coax her into fixing that.

Sure enough, when Mama call us in to eat, she got franks and beans and chips. No vegetables neither. Timmy must have really sweet talk her into that one. As it turn out, Albert take two dogs and run out the back. He and Pammie brother, Edward, gonna hang for a while. What that mean is they gonna drive downtown and try to talk to some girls. Ruthanne going over Peanut house and take Nakita. Me and Mama and Timmy stay home and watch some more TV.

About 11 I decide to go to bed. It so quiet and I can hear Mama breathe, slow and deep. She sound asleep. I try to go, too, but can't. I keep thinking of Evian. Imma go around there late, after 11, so I don't seem anxious. Maybe I wear a little lipstick or do my nails. Maybe not. Maybe he think I'm taking this too serious if I do. But, I do wear a little lipstick sometime, no big deal.

Blister seem strange a little. I can't pinpoint why. Just seem like he smile too wide and look at me funny. Like he see straight through to my underwear. He make me feel uncomfortable. I could be seeing him strange cuz I don't know too many white folks. Don't know. Plus, he from Georgetown. Everybody know folks is simple in Georgetown. Least that what people say. I don't really know none personal.

Wonder what Evian doing now? They over there playing records and guitars, I bet. I go in Timmy room and look out the window. I can see the kitchen light is on, but don't look like nobody in there. The light on in Evian room, too. But Blister van ain't in the driveway from what I can see.

This field all overgrown. I don't know who spose to be keeping it cut, but whoever they is, they don't do it much. Miss say once that she need someone to help with her part of the field. But ain't nobody come and say they do it. Edward say he would do it, but he never did come around to ask Miss. Hope someone start to do it soon, cuz it look kinda bad. The grass so tall back there. I always make sure to watch where I'm walking real good when I come home from over there, make sure I don't fall or step on nothing slimy or living or dead. I could get absent and fall and probably break my hips. Then I just disappear in all that brush. Somebody have to walk right up on you to even know you back there. So much flowers and weeds and stuff. But in some ways, I like the way it look. It kinda mysterious and colorful. But in some ways it kinda scare me, too.

I get tired of looking and go back in me and Mama room to sleep. Really I lay there for another hour before I finally fall asleep.

CHAPTER EIGHT

Saturday morning come, and I wake up late. It feel good to be laying in the bed whiles everybody else is running around. I can hear Albert and Ruthanne fussing over the bathroom and who spose to have clean it. Timmy and Nakita watching those loud Saturday morning cartoons they love so much. Truth is, I like to watch them, too. Specially *Bullwinkle*. He tickle me. But today I don't want to watch. I don't hear Mama. She must be outside in her garden. She start to grow string beans and tomatoes last spring. She go out there a lot in the summer. But she always go out there on Saturdays and after church Sunday, even in the fall.

So, I enjoy just laying and not sleeping some more. But soon I get bored and get up. I don't feel like being bothered with my family today, so I slip in the bathroom real quick and wash up. Comb my hair a little and add a little orangish lipstick. I like the way it feel going on—smooth. I put on some yellow shorts and a yellow and pink flower tank top. I feel comfortable in this outfit, plus it look all right, too. I call to Ruthanne that I'm going to work and then out somewhere, so I be back later on. Walk across the field to the Mandarenes'.

I'm walking and I can see Blister and Evian set up next to the garage in the back yard. Really you can't tell what is their back yard from what is that field back of our house. Pammie say it all belong to the Mandarenes. But I say me and Mama and us is been there longer. And before us Grannie and Papa. So some of it belong to us, too, probably.

I can see over to Evian house. Blister is sitting on a wooden chair with a blanket next to him, look like. They got a cooler from what I can tell, and Evian at the grill, call hisself barbecuing, I guess. I don't wanna say nothing, but I doubt his barbecue all that good. Just don't seem like he be able to cook; otherwise why he and his people hire me? Blister holding a glass of something, and he got his guitar between his knees. I get closer and they still can't see me. These weeds is so high back here, specially out in the middle. I can hear them talking.

"Reckon you never gonna lose it if you don't just go ahead and do it. You be all dried up and sorry if you don't! Pecker might up and snap off, same as one of those old twigs out there." Blister chuckle and point toward the big tree out in the field. I wonder do he see me.

"You're so full of shit, Blister! Like you're some kind of Romeo, or somethin'. Just because I don't wanna jump on everything that moves. I'm not a hound like you..." Evian flipping steaks on the grill. Swish the smoke away with his hands.

"*...You ain't nothin but a hound dog, cryin all the time...*" Blister start playing and singin' like Elvis Presley. He don't sound half bad. But Evian right. He don't sing as good as Evian. "Never know, Ev. You might get lucky tonight!"

"You're in the wrong business, Blis. You shoulda been a comedian. I'm gonna go get the ribs. They been marinatin' all morning—they oughta be ready to put on the grill. Call me if Sister comes while I'm in there." Evian go in through the kitchen door. Few seconds later I walk up on Blister. He still playing his guitar.

"Hey now, Sissy! Didn't recognize you in those pretty colors. You all dolled up like a spring flower, huh? Look mighty pretty!" Blister stop his playing for a minute. Stand up from his chair.

"You always so full of compliments, Franklin. You flatter me. Keep your seat, now. No need to get up on account of me." I don't look him in the eye. Something tell me don't. Like he don't really need me to no way.

Blister pull a chair over next to his and point to it. Seem more like an order than a suggestion. "Take a load off, there, Sissy. Done walked all this way. How bout a cold drink?" He look at me in that wide-tooth way some more. He lean in a little when he talk to me.

"Thanks. I am a little winded, I guess." I sit down and sit back in the chair, try to keep my space.

"Don't tell me you winded from a little walk as that! Girl, like you seem like you in good physical shape. Real good physical shape..." He wink at me a little.

"I don't know what to say. You always say such nice things." I clear my throat a little.

"Well, I'm a nice guy. And you seem like a real nice girl. Real nice." Blister start to strum a little. He start to play a song I don't know about a girl look good enough to eat. He play that guitar real easy, like it attach to his fingers or something. He can carry a tune, too. But mostly he sound like talking sand paper. His voice real rough and scratchy almost.

"Hey, there she is!" Evian come out the house carrying a big pan of ribs. He got an apron on that say "*Kiss the Chef.*" I wonder do he mean it and decide to ask him about it later. "Go get yourself a glass, Sissy. Me and Blister is drinking Juleps. Bout the only thing Blister can make besides music is Mint Juleps. Try some, Sissy. But drink it slow. I don't want you to get drunk on me. Then I might have to take advantage of you." He narrow his eyes at me.

"Yeah. Me and Evian might have do something crazy, and you wouldn't even know the difference." Blister laugh too loud and tip back his glass and gulp. Wipe his hand on his sleeve.

I don't never drink Juleps before. I thought people only drink those on Derby day. But I don't wanna act like I ain't with it. So I get a glass off the table they set up by the grill. Ev got some chips set out in a bowl and some napkins on there, too. The drink already mix together in a cover plastic pitcher. I put some ice in the glass from the cooler and pour some in from the pitcher. It taste real sweet, but I like it. "This is good, Franklin. Probably the best I ever had." I sit back down in the chair.

"Hear that, Ev? Sister says I'm the best she ever had! Drink up, now, girl. Plenty more where that came from." Blister keep leaning in and laughing in my face.

"Oh stop, Blister! Misconstruin' her like that. You watch how you talk to my lady friend. Might have to send you on back to Georgetown somewhere." Evian always coming to my rescue.

By time the sun start to set, all of us drunk. I don't know whether it the heat or the Juleps or Blister guitar, but those ribs was saying somethin'. Ev right, he can make some ribs, now! Something about that sauce speak to ya in a sweet Southern speech. I seen him put honey and lemon and look like molasses and some peppers and I don't know what all else. But when he drizzle it on those ribs, it make you wanna sing.

So, I did. Ev pull his record player out and put it on the kitchen table so's we can hear it out in the back yard. He crank up Aretha, and soon her voice ring out rich like church. What he wanna do that for? I love Ree-Ree, and if the spirit move me, I try to sing just like her, right along with her. On a normal day, I might just hum along, pat my foot some. But, these Juleps tickle with my head. And Ev look so sweet. Always got a smart answer for Blister when he mess with me. He got my back for real so Blister can't get to it.

Seem like Blister always there when I get up or turn around. I fix my plate, and here he come with some napkins or some extra sauce. Don't let my glass reach half way—here come Blister with enough to fill it again. Ice cubes if it look like it ain't cold, slice of cake "sweet as yourself" just in time for dessert. Make me feel uneasy. Like he make me take now so's he can collect on his kindness later.

Evian always right there behind Blister. He never let Blister lean in too close. And I like that. He like a watchful dog with me, and if it look like I'm in trouble, Ev bark. So, when Blister ask me can I show him where the bathroom at, like he ain't been staying here for two days and ain't had to go, Evian shove him on the shoulder and tell him to go on somewhere. Blister stumble in the house by hisself. That when Aretha start singing "Bridge Over Troubled Water."

Ev got his guitar strap on, and he start to play along with the organ part. He make the guitar hiss like water and whine. Real soft, like sizzling marshmallows. Seem like he melt hisself right in the middle of that record, blend hisself in smooth. Seem natural to me to sing. Everything so clean and quiet up in the sky—no birds, no clouds, just wide sky. Got a greenish glimmer in it, too, like a mirror hanging down over the grass. Between the moon, and the Julep, and Ev , and Aretha—so much green, something say sing. Because she right. Sometime evening do come too hard, and all you need is somebody to be there, too. Not stop the dark, not change the night or nothing, just be there and see it with you. Ev strum under me, and it make my voice a little heavier. And this song we make together rock like a baby and hum.

When the record stop, Evian just look at me. He got this look on his face—quiet and sad and satisfied, like when the cake all gone and you got to share the last piece. The record needle bumping up and down, and Blister don't never come out of the bathroom or wherever he at. I get up to change the record, but Evian catch my hand before I pass. He unhook the guitar in one slick move. And in the next move he got my whole self standing between his thighs.

"Sissy, you...you're something else." He web his fingers through mine, look up at me. I try not to shake or say somethin' dumb, so I just don't say nothing. But my knees too nervous. I can't be still. So, he lean forward and hold me on his lap.

A piece melt off from my thigh when I sit down. I can't move. So I sit there with him with my hands inside his. Just sit there. Keep my breath. Feel what seem like his secret thoughts pushing into mine.

This time when he kiss me, I am all open. I can taste the mint, the honey, the molasses on his tongue. His fingers in my hair tickle, feel like blades of windy grass all over me. And I don't wanna stop, and I don't wanna move, and I don't wanna go home, and I don't wanna take another breath.

I can hear Blister snore as we walk down the hall. Seem strange to be in this house in the dark; don't feel like the same place. The old man got the TV up loud in the room, and he snoring soft, too. Evian hold my hand as he walk me down the hall, to his room, to his bed.

Since the record player out in the kitchen, Ev turn on the radio. He find some jazz, sound like Miles Davis to me. He keep the volume kinda low. He got a stick of green incense burning in a wood holder on the desk, and the smoke from it wind up toward the ceiling in a blinking curve. The window open, and he got the light off. Just the moon jumping across the floor, and the shadow of tall, sharp grass from the field making pictures on the wall. Inside I am a little scared. Wish he say something to ease this up some.

But, what we got to say? What words gonna add something to that thing we just sat and gave each other in that chair? So, he put his arms around me, don't say a word. Don't have to. And his hands on me feel like warm chocolate. When I look at his eyes I see his mama holding him in the house and I hear when he was in the bathroom being sick, and I smell the Julep and the honey and the molasses, and feel him cackle when he on the phone, making jokes even though he sick. And I feel the strap of his guitar, and I wrap my legs around him and sing. And sing. And sing.

Guess I must of fall to sleep. Guess I don't wanna stop his even breath. Guess I wanna see his eyebrow twitch and think of what he dreaming. Whatever it is make the right corner of his lip lift up a little, and he smile in his sleep. Guess I don't wanna wake somebody who smile when they next to me even when they sleep. But I ain't so grown as to stay around here all night long. Don't seem right. So, I pull my shorts back on and yank down the flower top. Slip in the bathroom to look at my face.

Do it look different? Could Pammie or Ruthanne or Mama tell? Still creamy brown. Still spring-coil hair, sticking up a little at the back of my neck. I stick my fingers through to smooth it out. My lipstick gone. Just a short trace of orange at the corner. I wipe it away with a piece of tissue. I'm sorta scared to cross that field in the dark, but I tell myself this simple-minded. Been knowing that field since the day I was born. Been seeing the grass thicken and dance and get chopped down. Been seeing the ghosts dance, too. But I try not to think about that when I slip out the sliding-glass door that face the field, the ghosts, the field that separate Evian from me.

CHAPTER NINE

Something don't surprise me when I see him brush up beside me, but I get a feeling of ice cubes in my chest, like I just swallow something really bad that taste awful and might kill me. I keep my back straight. My shoulder hitch up to cover this cold growing round my heart. I don't feel safe.

"Heard you and Evyun up 'err, creakin' like some kinda pigs." His breath stink, and I can feel it move from his nose and leave a hot moisture on the air. He had put on some cut-off shorts with thick strings hanging from the bottom. His tee shirt barely cover his belly. His leg flesh all squishy, look like the inside of a rotten peach. He laugh low. "Ol Ev done popped his padiddle, sure 'nough." He lift his eye brow up and squeeze out a wink. I don't want to share what I do with Ev with him. So I don't say nothing.

"Heard you naygra girls—that what you like to call yerself, right? Naygra? Heard y'all are hot to trot. Heard y'all take it between those dark thighs and squeeze till it runs dry. That true, there, Sissy?" When he say my name, my special name that Ev call me, it hiss and make me wanna spit. I just keep my head up. "Thank you for walking me home, Franklin. Pleasure to know a gentleman like you." Try to sound sweet and gracious. That what Grannie say—always be gracious to white folk—they need that. If they think you ain't grateful to them for something they did or didn't do, Grannie say they apt to be trouble.

"Didn't seem like you thought so while I's busy making sure you had plenty of my whiskey to drink or plenty of my ribs to eat. Never wanted to show me no mind when I's complimenting your voice and all. Naw, sir. Just looking up at Evyun like he some kinda Greek god out of Athens or someplace. Never did wanna sing for me." He half-smile, half-snap at me.

I think to myself, ain't no Greek gods in Athens no more, and *Evian* invite me to eat ribs—they wasn't Blister ribs. "Yes, you was real sweet tonight. And I thank you for looking out to give me a special time, always making sure I got enough to eat and to drink. You a real good host, Franklin." We ain't even halfway cross the field yet, and Evian asleep in his bed seem real far away. I can see the lights is off at home, and I wonder if Albert home. I wanna get in my own house and lock the door and think about Evian. What he give me, and what I must have lose.

Blister breath heavy as he walk next to me. "Naw, Sissy. You ain't right. Evyun always braggin' about your sangin', an I barely hear you sing a note. What, you only sang for him? Don't got no song for me, do ya?" He stepping so close I feel his sticky breath in my hair and near my face. He catch my arm and pull me next to him. All I see is crack lip and sharp, wolf teeth. "You gonna sang for me, Sissy? Tell me you sang like a bird. Give me a tune, there, Sissy." He grind hisself into my middle. "Everybody's always sweet on Evian. Just cuz he's sick, everybody always wanna sang and fuck for him. But, you gotta song to sang, Sissy, you gonna sang it for me!"

I can't breathe. I try to back away. I want to scream, but won't no sound come. I try to look over his shoulder, but all I can see is wide blades of fat, green grass, milkweed, buttercup, dandelion, wild onion.

He pull the cut-off shorts down in one rip. Got me down in the dirt, and I feel the grass wiggle on my shoulder, and it don't tickle like Evian fingers in my hair. It burn. I can't think straight. I keep my hand up over my chest, one over my pants. He keep pushing at my clothes, and his hands feel like farm tools on my skin. Private push, that private push, and I rip inside and scream. He quick with the hand over my mouth. "Yes, now you gonna sang. Sang real pretty, there, Sissy. Sang one for me." I close off every piece of me that is on the inside, try to force him out. He jab right, jab left, where Evian touch me. Stabbing me in my Evian place. I fight like a mule to push him out. I clamp my legs together as tight as I can and feel hisself splash on me like mucous from the flu.

I feel smoke in my nose, and I am mad enough to kill. I start pulling up grass and sending brick-hard blows to his backside. And I am trying to scream, but the sound come out like empty tea kettles. He try to put his snot in my Evian place, and I rather make him die than let him get away with it.

I am wet with sweat when the old man pull him away from me. "Ya outta yer mind? Are ya outta yer Goddamn mind? Carryin on like an animal, like you never seen the inside of a church or a school or any other sacred place. Get outta here! Take your backwoods shit and get the hell out of here!" Norman come up to pull Blister off out of nowhere.

"Try to tell Cord-yul you just an ornery elephant, born and bred with triflin' elephants, none of you fit to wipe this woman's ass. You stay away, you hear me, Franklin? You stay the hell off of this property, Goddamn it. I own this fucking land, every blasted piece—not your mama, not your redneck daddy, not none of ya but me. I'll shoot you right in the head, and you know I got the aim to do it, and when your daddy comes to look for you, by God, I will shoot him, too." He pointing the rifle at Blister, pushing him away from me and out into the field. "You get your nasty shit, you hear me, and you get the hell away from here, and don't you bring your backwoods shit around here again, or I can promise you two bullets straight center in your skull. If I get back and see you here, you better have a talk with Jesus cuz you will surely see Him soon." He don't look again at Franklin when he lift me off the ground. He hold my shaky middle while I straighten up my clothes, rifle in his other hand.

"Crazy ol nigger-lovin' fruit!" Blister mutter, but he get away from there quick.

"Some of us ain't that way, Miss. I can promise you that some of us ain't that way. God save that boy, Sister; his father is a sheet. Are you all right? Can you walk, or shall I call Evian to drive you back?" He stand with me and look sorry. He don't move to hold me or to take away the pictures that Blister plant in my head and in my private. He don't seem to know about the mucous snot that Blister spat on me from his nasty-hard self. He hold onto my arm, as much to support hisself as to help me, and he lead me on across the field, use the rifle as a cane.

"Sister, can't nobody change an elephant to an eagle. Try to tell Cord-yul that. Best to break way and leave it alone. I am sorry this had to happen to you. Evian tries to see the sweet side of everything; he acts like he don't know that his daddy's people are cross-burning idiots. Maybe he really doesn't know. He'll stay away, Sister. I can assure you of that. Anyone who knows me can tell you, if he comes around these parts again, I will kill him myself. I can't spend these last days holding onto ornery ignorance from the backwoods." I do not know what Norman talking about, but something let me know he telling the truth and I can believe him. He take me right up to my own back door. He look again at me, sorry.

"You go be with your people. Let me take care of mine. If anyone ever, ever bothers you again, you tell me. You come and tell Norman. I got nothing to lose, Sister. I lived a long time, and I ain't afraid to die, and if they try to bring the backwoods onto my land again, I will kill them. I'll send Evian around tomorrow, Sister. I am dreadful sorry." He stand outside and watch me close the door, pull the latch, turn on the light. He watch for a minute as I hold myself and cry. Then he light a cigarette and head out across the field to the other side, lean on his rifle like a cane.

CHAPTER TEN

If I tell, everything in my world change. Albert hunt down Blister, probably take Edward and some others with him. Come up on him and shoot to kill. Next thing you know me and Pammie got no brothers; Mama pray to God not to give her more than she can bare. No job because Miss Cordial likely to side with her people, and Ev probably take they side, too. And I'm the one sticky from *his* mucous, pushed on, ran through. Norman say he take care of his people. I hope he do, cuz if I tell my people, half my people get locked up and kill, and won't be none left to take care of. So, I hold myself and cry.

In the bathroom, I look at me again. Got grass on my head. Got what look like red clay on my neck, down my arm, and cake under my nails. Look like someone in my head light matches so now my eyeballs melt out and puss up at the lids. And his thick spit somewhere inside me.

I run the water hot enough to boil. I don't even wince when I yank myself in. Sit. Close my eyes and pray. I don't want to touch me with no soap, and I don't want to touch me with my hand. Seem like nothing down there really belong to me. Now it belong to everybody else. Best part belong to Ev. Rest belong to Blister. And Norman. And Ev daddy people and they sheets. Don't none of it belong to me.

Next day I don't even wake up until 10 a.m. Mama come look at me on her way to church, put her hand on my forehead to feel if I'm sick. I guess she satisfy I am, cuz she don't wake me, and she don't ask me why I don't get in the bath and get ready to go, too. Usually just me and her and Timmy go. Pammie claim she don't wanna wake Nakita, but usually she already awake. Albert ain't usually get in til real late on the weekend, so he don't get up and go. Sometime I bathe Nakita and put bows all over her head, and she come, too. But mainly just me, Timmie, and Mama. Today, just Timmie and Mama, cuz I ain't fit to go. Too filthy dirty, too slow and sad and full of nasty spit. On a normal day, I pray when I feel poorly. Today, the prayer don't come. I don't want God to see me and feel sorry for me. Don't want to think or dream, just sleep, and maybe I wake up and it be Saturday, and maybe they ain't no Blister, and maybe just me and Ev sing together and eat ribs and be quiet and think. I fall to sleep and my dream is weird.

That field out there is red and purple and light shine here, then over there, real quick. I'm out there caught in the middle, can't see which way to go. Then the vines climb up and catch me at the ankle, drag me down. And when my head hit the ground, molasses pour out slow and full of worms. When the blades of grass strap over me like chains, and they flying down my mouth and choking my throat, I hear Ruthanne over me.

"Sister! Girl, wake up! Yo spose to go round to white folks today? Cuz one of 'em out there by the door looking for you. You bes get yourself up and talk to him, cuz he won't leave, and I don't feel like being bothered with no white folk." Nakita swinging from her hip, still got her pink pajamas on. She say, "A-da-da-da." And she smile, offer me her bottle.

Ev. How I'm spose to look at him? All that he give me ruin now and full of spit. "Tell him I see him some other time, Ruthanne. I ain't feeling myself today." I turn and face the wall.

"Don't look like he fittin' to leave nowhere soon, Sister. Been out there for over half-hour waitin'. I done tole him you was sleep, but he say you bound to wake up for too long. Must be important. Must be his Mama ain't home and he hungry. You know white folks can't cook. Starve to death if it weren't for some of us to cook they meals." She look like talking. She can't half cook herself. She switch out the room, satisfy she have the last word. Ruthanne big on having the last word with me, since she older.

"Sissy, is that you? Why won't you come out and talk to me? Sissy...let me come and...I don't know. Sissy?" Ev outside the window at the side of the house. He standing next to the window, but he don't look in. Like he wanna respect my privacy even though he know I'm in the bed half dress.

I don't say nothing. What I'm spose to say?

"I am so sorry, Sissy. Blister is a damn nut; I should have known that. They never fall far from the tree. But I thought I could explain things to him, make him be different. Make him see how things could be if he just opens his mind up. Look, Pap told me what he tried to do to you, and...shit, Sissy. I wanna...Let me hold you and I promise I will...This is all my fault..." He make a sound like a cough and a gag.

I peek out from the quilt and lean up a little. He lean on the side of the house and shake. What I do to make Ev shake? I lean up and pull the quilt around my neck, open the window a little more. "You make good ribs, Ev. Please don't shake for me." It's all I can think to say. If I think of him inside of me and picture his guitar and remember being on his lap, I can feel almost clean. I wish I could put those feelings into words so he don't have to shake for me.

He reach his hands through the window, brush his fingers on my face. When did I start to cry? He put his fingers on them like he can make them dry away. And we stay like that for a minute, me on the bed against the window, and him outside with his arms push through.

"Sissy, Norman tried to kill Franklin. Sure enough, I was really scared. Pap has a rifle, you know, and he knows how to use it. He's a sure shot. It took me a while to figure out what happened, but I was up all night piecing it together." Ev hold my fingers in his hands and look in my eyes when he talk. Seem like all the color out of his face, and his lips straight and hard as cement.

"You don't have to worry about Franklin, Sissy. I can guarantee that he will never come around here again, not if he values his life. Did you...did he...hurt you? Did you talk to...Sissy, I love you, and I will help you, whatever you want to do, Sissy..." His eyes is cool blue, and his lashes thick, fire brown and curl. He got his face lean into the window, and I want to reach out and pull him in. But all I do is cry.

He come around the front and find his way to my room. I don't care that I got on an old shirt of Albert, underwear and no shorts. I don't care that Ruthanne probably look at him strange when he walk through the living room, like we always entertain white folks. When he climb on the bed, I wanna curl around him and breathe deep and stay. This time his hand at the back of my neck is steady, and he hold my middle up tight against him. He move with me when I cry, like he got an answer for every one of the tears. I cry til the filthy pit on the inside of me dry. I want it to be empty, but I do not think it will ever be empty. If he go to move, I quick close up the gap that come between us. I feel safe as long as he next to me, but if he move, I choke on grass and fire and spit.

"Mama is staying in Louisville tonight. She and Miss Willie Mae are making fried chicken, and some of her friends are coming over, and they wanna play bridge. Mama doesn't wanna drive in the dark. Sissy, will you come and stay with me? Let me hold you? I can't take what he did away from you, but, I just wanna be with you tonight." He hold my cheeks in the palm of his hands. I see him and I think I might somehow come clean.

"You tell her about...?" I look down at my thighs and remember his spit.

"I told her he and Pap got into it and Pap told him to take his backwoods ass home. Mama can't stand daddy's people. She only puts up with them for me. That's why she always leaves if ever Blister comes out to see me. She won't miss him, Sissy. And neither will I."

"Can we have ribs again? And listen to your records?" I say this into his shirt, because I wanna breathe at his chest and smell his Dove soap.

"Anything you want to do, we will do it. I love you, Sissy. You make me feel right inside of myself. I wish I never fell asleep and I wish you never even left last night. Why'd you go and leave? But let me...Sissy. Let me hold onto you. Let me make you safe." He fold me in his arms, and this time I move with him when he cry, hope I can find an answer to all his tears.

CHAPTER ELEVEN

First I get up and go to the bathroom. Me and the bathroom getting to be close friends. I soak so long last night that my skin almost scrub off. But I can't take a rag to my inside, where can't nobody see that I got nasty backwoods spit. I sit on the toilet and cry. Don't look like I can do nothing but to cry. One hand, I feel like I got it better than ever. Ev say he love me. Wonder do he mean it? Wonder what it mean? But, he say he do, and he hold me like that, and he shake for me. Other hand, inside I feel awful. Feel like I won't never be private no more. Ain't nothing no more that belong just to me that somebody can't walk up and take if he strong and if he want to. Make me wanna die. But if I die, then I can't stay over to Evian house. And I wanna stay over to Evian house bad, because he say he make me safe, and I wanna be safe.

Next, I go to the kitchen and call Pam. Her phone ring and ring, and I remember she probably at church wondering where I am. But, I gotta talk to her before I go round to Ev house, because Mama think it strange if I don't go to church and don't be at home all night. Pammie gotta cover for me, give me some time to think. I look in the fridge. Orange juice, butter, bread, eggs—all of it look like spit. I close the door and go back in my room.

Ruthanne come in and plop on the bed like she own it. She got a puzzle-worry look on her face. "Sis, what chou got into? You all right? I seen white folks round here looking' like a sad dog, and you not dress and ain't go to church. You all right?" She sound concern. Me and Ruthanne don't see everything the same way, but she do love me. Think she know everything because she two years older, but she do try and look out for me. What I'm spose to say to her? I think for a minute and pray.

"I'm all right. Round to the Manderenes' late last night is all. Evian, he who you call white folks, he all right. You know he be sick sometime. Sometime he like to talk to me, you know. His mama don't listen and he ain't got friends around here yet. So, sometime he tell me his trouble. No thing…" I try to sound truthful, not sure if I succeed. But some of it true. He do like to talk to me. Just when his lips ain't moving that he seem to say the most.

"Please. He live in a big, fine mansion, got help to come in and do everything for him, and *he* wanna talk to *you* about trouble? White folks don't know what trouble is, specially if he keep sticking his arms in your window and laying on your bed." Ruthanne look at me sly. She know what the deal is.

"Ruthanne, you don't know so much as you think. What you know about Ev? Just cuz you got a big house don't mean you ain't got no trouble."

"*Ev*, huh? Mmm-hmm. Look like you better watch yourself, or you both gon' find some trouble. Do his mama know he like to 'talk to you,' as you say? Or do she got trouble and wanna talk to you, too?" She swing her slipper-foot off the side of the bed.

She got real skinny ankles, and don't seem like lotion wanna stick. Always got ashy heels and ankles.

"Look. I know it seem strange, but I like Ev. He listen to me. He nice to me, and he my friend. It be all right, Ruthanne. You sweet to worry." I sound convincing, almost believe it myself. Truth, I ain't never been friends with no white folks, as she say, and I don't know if it really be all right. But seem like if I say it and believe it, I make it true.

"You watch yoself, Sister. Wasn't ten years ago they found some of Aint Caroline people back of the park half-dead, and you know wasn't none of us got to 'em. And you know Aint Caroline people love them some white folks. Where is white folks when we in the park half-dead, Sister? You think of that while you strikin' up with your white folks what got trouble and need to talk." She seem like she wanna shake me or something. Why she so upset?

"I hear you, Ruty. I'm going round to Pammie house and spend the night.

We probably listen to music and watch TV. Tell Mama if she ask after me."
I get up off the bed and start to straighten up the quilt. Mama say why I keep the quilt on when it get warm, she don't know. But I'm always cold.

"Mmm-hmm. Pammie my foot. You grown. You do what you wanna do. But I done tole you already, Sister. Watch yourself." She scoop Nakita up off the floor and switch out. She learn to switch when she turn 17. Mama say that why she got Nakita now.

CHAPTER TWELVE

I go back in the kitchen and call Pammie. She answer on the third time, out of breath.

"Sister! Girl, why you ain't come to church? You all right? Edward say he seen white folks papa outside with his gun late last night. He say Bernie and her people seen him out there, too. You get into trouble around there last night?" I can hear her running water, probably bout to make coffee. She drink two cups when she get home from church. Then she start to do the ironing for the week.

"No, no trouble. He got mad at Evian cousin is all. But I gotta go round there again today cuz Miss staying in Louisville. Ev don't wanna be by hisself—you know he been sick before. So...Imma tell Mama I'm round to your house..." I just breeze this information out cool, and hope Pam don't press me just now. I think I explain to her, but I ain't ready today.

She pause for a minute. "You round there freakin' white folks, huh? And don't wanna explain nothing, and don't wanna say what it feel like to be with white folks, and want me to cover your ass, too? Sister...!"

I cut her off. I can't stop and talk about this now, because Mama and Timmie be home soon, and I don't feel like running into Mama. I see her tomorrow. "Pammie, girl, I...let me talk to you tomorrow, okay? I promise I come around there tomorrow, and...we talk. But I gotta go right now, okay, and I am really okay. Okay? Cover for me, Pammie. I do it for you. Shit, I done it for you!"

"Yea. You better bring yo white folk-freakin' ass around here tomorrow, sure 'nough. I am ready for you." She hang up the phone.

In my room, I grab my long nightshirt, my toothbrush, and that's it. What you need to have when you stay round to white folks' house where you spose to work but now you also sometime sleep? I sure don't know.

When I look out at that field, my throat close off. Ice cube poison back in my chest, and the feeling of filthy spit. How I'm gonna get cross that field and not suffocate and die? I step out the back door. My feet freeze and stick in the ground. Can't move. Can't breathe. I can see Evian in his window on his bed. I wanna get over to him, but I am scared. Then I see it. Few feet away where the grass bend up and curve away from each other. Just enough space to hold someone between the blades. He crouching there, and the wind make his pinky thighs shake. He got a cigarette between his teeth, and he waiting for me. Lord. Lord, Lord, Lord. With his spit, with his sheet and his backwoods spit. I remember when he pull on me and poke in Evian place and take away what Evian give me and fill it with filthy spit. Before I ain't have no power, no right to scream, but today, Ev say he love me and make me safe. This shadow leap up and reach for my heels, and this time I make noise like cast iron on glass.

I feel hands on me. I scrape and scratch and try to make him bleed. He can try to kill me, but he can't have no more of me. If I got any left, I am gonna keep it or I am gonna die. But these arms on my shoulders is warm. I hear a voice saying, "It's me, it's me, you are okay, Sugar. I promise, you are okay." Ev got his arms around me, and he talking in my ear. I open my eyes and see us standing in the field in front of my back door. I got the toothbrush clinch in my hand like a knife. And a yellow cat looking at me, like he heard I'm crazy and he come over to see for hisself.

"He come back for me, Ev. He come back. But this time I kill him myself. This time I am ready to kill him for myself." I fall on him, so tired, like I barely got away with my life.

"No, Sissy. Oh. I thought that was you standing out there. Saw you from the window. I kept expecting you to come across, but you were just standing. So I came out to get you. Sugar, please don't be scared. This is your home.

You shouldn't have to be scared in your own home. Blister ain't nowhere around here. I promise he ain't." He put my right arm around his middle and we start to walk slow. I pick my leg up real high with each step because I know there is worms and molasses and peachy fat skin in every step. Ev hold on to me and force me ahead. I keep my eye on his window and the soft light I see inside and there I go, pull my leg up, force it back down, pull my leg up, force it back down, all the way cross that field.

CHAPTER THIRTEEN

Wish I can always stay over to Ev house. He treat me so sweet. First thing he put my things in his room, and he tell me I can sleep anywhere I want—with him or in the room next to him, or anyplace. When I stay at Pammie house, only one place to stay, really, that in her room with her. She do got her own room, but ain't no extra room to offer when I come. We take turns in the bed. One time I come, she sleep in the bed; one time I come, I sleep in the bed. If it real cold, like that time I stay for the whole blizzard, we both sleep in the bed. But, Pammie wild when she sleep, arms and legs all over the place, and cover all wrapped up under her like she don't have company that get cold.

Ev got four extra rooms, and I know they clean cuz I clean them myself. But that night I don't want to sleep alone. I don't want to wake up with weeds and molasses and spit choking me. He smile when I say I rather stay in there with him. I put his smile in a bottle and drink it all day long.

Sometime I get this chill climb up my back. I freeze up and stare off. Ev come and put his arms all around me. He kiss my shoulder. He hold onto my hand. Then that cold thing fly off somewhere.

Ev make us some more ribs. This time he got potato salad to go with it, and he got a big green salad, too, in a Tupperware bowl with a wrinkle top. This stuff smell so good, and I wonder where he get it from. I ask him.

"Mama doesn't want me to do it, but I love to cook. I love to try out new recipes and stuff. McCall's and all, they got pretty good stuff. I mean real food, though. You won't catch me baking. Now, I am no good at cakes and stuff." He putting plates on the table and filling tall crystal glasses with lemonade. I get out napkins since I know where they stay, find forks and serving spoons.

"For real? Why you have me over here slaving away when you know how to cook?!" I try to tease him some, but only half-heart. Something drag in me and won't let me really laugh.

"That's Mama. She loves to hire people to do this stuff. She calls herself being philanthropic or something. Really she's kinda clueless where running a house is concerned. She has that temperamental artist mentality. She can really only focus on one project at a time." He put the top on the Tupperware bowl and shake it around. "Plus, we need you, Sissy. You lend us... continuity." He look at me soft, like he mean more than he say.

"Oh, like Pammie mother. She was never one for keeping the house. But she never hire nobody. She got Pam and Edward for that. And she just play the piano or sew or build something. She and Edward love to build stuff—models, you know. Pam like to do the housework, though. She like me. Only she complain the whole time how she could be doing something else." I wonder what do "philanthropic" mean. I guess it mean you don't like to cook and clean.

"Is Pammie the one who sits on the porch with you? I seen her a few times. She has long hair and walks fast." Evian is careful to put the forks in a certain place, the spoons in another, the knife next to that. He put some ice right in the pitcher of lemonade. At home I do that, too.

"What you looking at Pammie for? She been my best friend since...I don't know when. She do walk fast. Talk fast and act fast, too." It make my stomach jump to hear him notice Pam. What he gotta notice Pam for? All my life people always notice her.

He cut his eye up at me and smile. Just on one side. "Ooh, Sissy! You jealous? You look so cute when you're jealous!" He swat me on the behind, but I don't say nothing. "What Pammie don't know is I love *you*. See there? What you got to fret about? You got the prettiest teeth I ever seen, Sugar. Smile for me while I fix you up a special plate of ribs. If these ribs don't make you smile, I got something to give you that I bet you will." He kiss my cheek. Give me that look he give me before when I sing for him private.

But all of a sudden I feel like I be sick and gonna cry and wanna scream at the same time. I close my eyes and cover my ears. I try to force the tears back in my head. He trying so hard to make me happy and make me...forget. But I can't. It all jumble up in my head. What Ev and me do and what Blister do to me. They the same, but they ain't the same at all. And one make me think of the other one. I wanna be happy when I think about me and Ev, but now I also feel like I be sick. I look out the back door and see where we sit and sing with Aretha. Where we eat ribs and drink Juleps and play guitar and laugh. And I see where *he* sit and look at me and give me so he collect later. I will be sick for real. Down the hall, in the bathroom again, and shut the door. I hear Ev at the door.

"Oh, Sugar. I know you're scared. But you can't let that crazy nut take anything else from you." He sound like he kick the door. Why he so mad?

"Look, I'm gonna run and get you a towel and washcloth, hear? I'll be right back." Hear him fast down the hall to the linen closet and back. I splash water on my face and sit on the toilet. Mama hate when one of us sit on the toilet like it a chair. She say it ain't made for that, and next thing you know we got to get a new commode, and do we think she made of money when we got perfectly good chairs in the kitchen.

Ev knock before he come in. He reach around me and run warm water in the tub, test the temperature with his fingers. He drop two red balls in the water, look like beads from a necklace, and they foam up and give off the smell of flowers. In my stomach it feel like rocks and spit and bad breath. I keep thinking, what if he come back, what if he come back, what if he come back. I don't wanna move.

Evian kneel on the floor in front of me. He take my hands in his, and mine feel so small and wet. "Sugar, listen. You know I get sick, right? But do you know it feels like some kind of an alien is inside of my body? Every time I get so scared, like it finally is going to take me off somewhere with it. But I ain't ready to go yet, see? I just ain't at that point yet. So, instead I get mad. I gotta get real mad. Mad about having to puke up my guts and lose my hair and have to lay in the bed and stare at the walls and wonder if Mama will ever let me up again if I get better. I gotta get mad, see?" He is looking deep at my eyes, and he got this crazy dance in there, like he dare somebody to mess with him.

"But, Ev, I ain't sick. I mean, I…I just. All I feel like I can do is cry."

"Listen, Sugar. You gotta stop crying. Crying is for babies, and you ain't a baby. Like Ecclesiastes. There is a time for tears and everything else, okay? But then you gotta stop crying and, and live. Now, I wish I could make this thing go away. I wish I never heard the name Blister, and I wish I never even gave him the pleasure of knowing that you exist. But I never wanted to believe that shit Pap says about them is true. And I am sorry." He look over my head like he talking to the mirror and the sink more than to me.

"I know it ain't your fault, Ev." I blink to make the words come out clear.

"I ain't so sure, and I will have to live with that. But I am sure of this. It's mean out there, Sissy. And it will kill you if you let it. Blister helped himself to shit he had no right to—no damn right. Just like cancer helps itself to me—I never asked for it. But I can't let it have everything, totally characterize my life, okay? I am more than this thing. And you cannot let him have the rest of you. Sissy, listen. You gotta have something inside you that can't nobody touch, you hear me? Long as you scared, and long as you cry, and long as you throw up, then he got everything. You better get mad, Sissy, because that's the only way you'll be able to fight." He got his hands on my knees, and he gripping real tight. "You get yourself in this tub, and wash every piece of that son of a bitch off of you, and take it back, because it is yours. Everything you got on you, inside you, belongs to you—you take it back." He unbutton my shorts and lift off my shirt. He hold my eyes in his, and it make me step out of my shorts and all and get in that tub.

"You got a special song, Sissy?" Evian sit on the toilet and soap up the rag real good for me. I just stare at the tile and count colors. Five black, then three blue, then five black, then three pink.

"What you mean? Like, my favorite song? You know I love *Troubled Water*. Anything by Aretha." I answer without looking at him. In the bathtub, naked, with flower-smell suds, around to the Manderenes'.

"Yea, those are good. But, like, I have one song that I sing to myself when I feel like…you know…when I wanna be close to God. Sometimes, if I can't sing, I just say the words in my head. You ever do that?" He rub my back with the soapy rag and lift my hair so it don't get too wet.

"Like Grannie. She use to say the 23 Psalm. I know we trying her nerves when she say the 23 Psalm. She say, 'He Preparest a table in the presence of mine enemies, mmm, mmm, mmm!'" I laugh to think of it. Think of Grannie at a table set with her cut crystal and fried chicken while that woman sing soprano in the senior choir sit and drool. I think she dead now, too. Or move to North Carolina. That woman jealous, Grannie say, cuz she can't make fruitcake as good. She the only enemy Grannie have. Everybody love Grannie. Why somebody be jealous of a fruitcake, I don't know. Seem more fit for a doorstop then to ate, if you ask me.

"Exactly. With me it's *Amazing Grace.* You sing that one?" He scrub my legs with the soapy rag. I flex my foot so he can get the ankle, too.

"*How sweet the sound*? I ain't too particular about that one."

"No, the one that says *Amazing Grace shall always be my song of praise, for it was grace that bought my liberty*...you know that?"

I start to sing. "*I do not know just why my Savior died for me. He looked beyond my faults and saw my needs*..." We sing the rest real loud. Ev take this moody harmony underneath of me. While we sing he scrub my face, my neck, my stomach. He stop just below my belly button.

"Sister, listen. This is yours, darlin'. It's warm and it's sweet and it's yours—yours! Don't let Blister take it from you. Wash him off and let him go, and next time kill him dead—do you hear? Kill anything that tries to take you away from yourself." He hand me the rag and turn his head. "You get yourself dressed and we gonna go walk in that field. We gonna go right back out there and claim that field, Sissy, because you can't be forever scared and fighting ghosts. This is our home, and we gonna go right back out there and reclaim what belongs to us. You wash yourself and get dressed. I'll be waiting right outside the door for you." I hear him leave and close the door.

I just close my eyes and scrub. *Take your raunchy spit. Take your spit and your cake and your guitar and your farm tool hands and your stank breath, and your spit, and your spit, and your spit! And go to hell where you come from. This here is mine. Evian told me so, and...Grannie told me so, and Mama and Ruthanne, and...and me. I say so.*

When I pull the plug and let the water go, I let those tears go, too. Maybe they come back sometime, but right now I let them suck themselves down the drain and go.

CHAPTER FOURTEEN

But soon as I set my foot out the door, seem like I wanna crawl back in the tub and scrub or sing or cry. Evian give me an old shirt and shorts to put on. They smell like chlorine bleach. I put my Keds back on without the socks, too hot for socks. Everything still all over the kitchen table—the salad, the ribs, the lemonade with the sweat all over the glasses and the pitcher. The silver that Ev took time to place just so. The old man, Pap, as Ev say, been in his room since I come over here, ain't come out or nothing. But I walk up to the sliding-glass door and stop.

"Come on, Sissy. We goin' out back for a while. J'ever here of a technique called *flooding*? Psychology term. When I got sick the first time, I never had the chemo before, and was afraid to go back to the doctor. As far as I could tell, it was the doctor that made me sick, made me lose my hair and all. So, Mama had to take me back there kicking and screaming. One day we stayed there all day, and she wouldn't take me home until I stopped carrying on. Worked like a charm." He grab my hand and pull me out the door.

"I keep tryin' to tell you, I ain't sick, Ev. Don't everybody get sick like you, and anyway I ain't you." I dig my heels in when we get to the edge of his cut grass where the blades change from short crush velvet to wild root and molasses.

"That's where you're wrong. The whole world is sick. Hurry up and believe me when I tell you that. The war that killed my daddy. The ignorance that makes Blister think he's entitled to you because of who he is. All that *is* is sickness. Plenty of it out there. I'm blessed to be able to take something for my sickness, and maybe it will realize it can't come back. There ain't a cure for what Blister and daddy's people got. Except whatever you and me create together. Now, quit your stalling and let's go." Evian start to sing *His Eye is on the Sparrow*. I don't join in like normal, even though it one of my favorites, too.

I walk like the dead to the middle of the field. Evian stop walking and turn to face me. He reach down and get a big stick somebody crack off one of the trees back there. He hand it to me.

"You satisfy now? I come out in this field with you in the middle of the night. I done it now, okay? This flooding thing you preach about, we done it. Now, let's go..." I turn toward his house, but he catch me on my arm and hold on tight. I get mad and start to panic. "Damn it, Evian, you turn me loose, turn me loose!" I got the stick in one hand and twist from his grip with the other.

"You mighty strong, ain't ya, Sissy? Makes you angry to have me hold you when you don't want it, huh? Makes you good and mad, don't it?" He hold onto my wrist even harder. "But you mad at Blister, not at me. Fight him, Sissy. Fight him and win." He keep his hand like a wrench around my wrist, and I start to feel smoke in my nose.

I stab at the ground with that stick. "You get your fuckin' hands off me, Goddamnit, off me. Off me! Who do you think it is here, anyway?! Somebody you can push down and run through? With your filthy backwoods spit and your sheet, and can't half sing no way, and your filthy spit from the pit of hell—get off me, get off me, you hear? Don't you fuckin' touch me! I kill you—you ain't no good host and you ain't no gentleman, and I ain't gonna sing for you, and he *is* a god out of Athens to me, and you can't have me, you can't have me, you can't have me!" I sweat and stab and cry and murder the ground until finally the stick break. I force the rest over my knee and crack it in three places. Then I throw the pieces far ahead of me as I can.

Evian got this look on his face, like he caught between a cry and a cheer. He put his hands on my sides and he breathe real hard out loud. "There you go, baby. You can lick any of 'em. That's my baby." He wrap his self into me, and we both breathe.

We sit down right there in the middle of the grass. I don't think about the spiders and the mosquitoes probably in my clean hair, sucking me dry. I'm busy look at Ev eyes. Ever seen a cornflower? Like that. And he look at me like Nakita look at me sometimes. Like she glad I wanna be with her and play creepy mouse, like she don't care if somebody see how happy she get just to look in my pockets for something I got her at the store, or just to sit on my lap and laugh when I tickle her in the sides. I thought only babies look at you like that. But Ev, he don't seem to care if somebody know he can look like that and feel like that, too. I pull off the tee shirt he give me, unhook the white bra. Maidenform. I don't fill up the cups. Mama don't seem to get it, but I ain't big-busted like her and Ruthanne. She don't have to pick up C-cups when they on sale for me, cuz they just gonna sit there empty.

"Part of it mine, Ev. But part of it belong to you. I mean, if you...if you want it, I mean." I slip off the shorts, too.

"I think I would take anything that you gave me, Sissy. Anything at all."

"You remember in the kitchen before, that stuff you say? You mean it, Ev?"

"One thing about the Mandarenes, Sugar. We don't lie. Let me show you what I mean, hear?" He pull me on top and grab my backside.

Ev use his fingers and his tongue like he playing the guitar on the inside of me, making melodies like what I make in Timmie room when he and Mama asleep and Ruthanne around to big-head Peanut house. When I sit on him and rock and he got his hands on my hips and he bend his knees so I don't slip off and I pull up grass cuz it feel so good, and Ev say, "Yyea, yea, yea," I start to hum deep in the middle somewhere, and with his slow-whistle yes, it feel like music, sure enough.

I look around that field. Pammie say it belong to the Mandarenes. True. But part of it belong to me. And this part here in the middle belong to us, me and Ev.

CHAPTER FIFTEEN

Part of me think I ain't got no more business over to the Mandarenes', lay up next to Evian, than a Black man in the White House. Mama use to say that, about Black men in the White House, til Grannie got on her about it. Mama, she backward about stuff. That why Albert keep his hair so short. He wanna have a natural, but his hair real slick. Mama say what he wanna ruin his hair for, when one of the best thing he got to say for his family is good hair. So, he keep it short. When it stick up just a little, nobody know whether it good or bad. To me, that stuff is stupid, good and bad hair. If it grow out your head, then it good, far as I can tell. Some folks have it to grow out they face and they legs, like Pammie mama. She got a mustache and would have a beard if she didn't pick it off with tweezers. I seen her use her fingers and just yank. To me, hair all over your face when you a woman, *that* is bad hair.

Evian shift, and I put my left leg over his. He smell warm like donuts. I ain't sposed to know that. Something tell me I don't spose to be close enough to no white boy to know he smell like breakfast sweets. Here I am in his bed, and his mama don't know, and his granddaddy don't seem to care. He pass by the door on the way to the kitchen, I guess, or out back to slip and smoke, and he seen us on Ev bed watching TV. He just nod his head and say, "Evenin', Sister." Keep on down the hall. After that Ev close the door.

But I like to be close enough to smell him.

His sheets stay cool, too. Maybe cuz it a big bed and we stay huddle in the middle. When I reach out my hand to the edge, it always feel cool. I like that. He let me light incense and read any book on his shelf, too. Not that I like all his books. He like science fiction, but me, I like stories about real people. Biographies. Always have. I learn biographies in the fourth grade. Did mine on Lincoln. Miss Taylor say he the one freed the slaves. But when I read about him, I find out he wasn't too particular for the slaves, really. He just wanna save the union is all. Miss Taylor say I'm real smart to find this out, but she don't give me a "A" on the report. Book reports on famous people. Always like to do those.

Junior year I did one on Kennedy. He was cute. He Catholic. That why they had all them kids. John-John and who knows what all else. Use to say it was like Camelot when he in the White House. Whatever that mean. Guess cuz he look like a prince, and Jackie look like a princess. But one book I read say he use to sleep with other women and Jackie didn't know or care or something. Mainly Marilyn Monroe. Why he wanna sleep with her, I don't know. She look cheap. But Jackie, she a princess, sure enough. I like how she dress. She got pumps in all kinds of colors and pearls. And how she make her hair stay like that? She the prettiest white woman I know. What she think, I wonder, if she knew white boys lay next to they cooks down in Kentucky? Probably she don't care, if she do know. I wonder if she still sad because her husband dead. I know Pammie mama still cry over Mr. LeRoy. And he just a factory worker. Everybody cry when Kennedy die, since he was President. I guess Jackie still probably cry sometime, too.

I look around and get mix up. First I'm so comfortable to be next to Ev, watch him sleep. Then, I get butterflies and feel like I better sneak out and go on home. Then I remember...what happen before when I slip out. Feel like I better stay where I am. Until he wake up or I go to sleep or something. Then I get hungry. We never did eat those ribs Ev make me for dinner. Mouth start to water when I think of that lemonade and salad and rolls he fix. House quiet. Wonder would Evian mind if I go get me some? Should I wake him? Naw. He got this little lift at the corner of his cheek that he keep when he sleeping and he smiling at the same time. I just run and fix up a plate, and maybe he be awake and want some when he wake up. He ain't eat, neither.

TV still on in Norman room. Wonder should I call him Mr. Norman. Really, I don't have many times to call him something at all. Just say hi. Answer his question, laugh at his joke. But he say if anybody bother me, come to him. Strange thing is, I think I would. He seem like he like me. I don't hear him snore, but I guess he in there sleep. Tip on down the hall to the kitchen and turn on the light.

I put the potato salad in the fridge. I ain't big on potato salad tonight. Really I want some ribs, some lemonade, and something sweet. Miss got ice cream in the freezer, and I wonder do they still have the brownies I make on Thursday. No. That ain't true. I make a cobbler, and I know Miss and Norman—Mr. Norman or whatever—done finish that. Can't keep cobbler around for more than a day or so. I take the ice cream out and put it on the counter. I like it to get soft. Miss say this brand she buy is already soft, but it ain't really. You gotta let it sit for a while for that. So I think, I just sit right here and eat some ribs, and by time I get finish, the ice cream be soft, and I take some back in a Dixie cup, and maybe Ev be awake and eat some with me. If not, I eat it by myself.

My heart stop when I hear the sliding-glass door creak. There stand Norman with half a Pall Mall in his hand. He barefoot. Norman got skin that stay real tan all the time, and plenty hair on his chest. I know cuz he keep his shirt unbutton down to the fourth hole. Miss say button that shirt before you catch your death of pneumonia, but Norman say he gonna die soon and he specs what he wear ain't got nothing to do with it.

"Nothing like a midnight snack, eh, Sister? You like me. Don't want to eat at dinner but get ravenous in the midnight hour. What ya got there?" He don't ask me why it is I'm in his kitchen, why I got the ice cream out, why I'm around to they house real late on a Sunday. All he wanna know is what I got to eat. He don't wanna ask no question, and I don't really have no answer. So I act casual.

"Ribs. Evian make ribs tonight, and I didn't have much appetite, but now..." I ain't real good with casual, so I just stop talking.

"Yes, Lord! Evian can cook like his daddy. Bout the only thing his daddy did worth something. Naw, that isn't exactly true. He could tie a cherry stem with his tongue. Make folks laugh at parties. That and cook— those were his claims to fame. Let me get me a plate before you eat all the barbecue up from me. Hah! I can see you got a real big appetite, big as you are!" I ain't big at all. Seem like he kidding me, but I ain't sure, so I don't laugh hard. He get a flower plate from the table, the one Ev set for hisself, and he plop down two big slabs. "Thought I saw Evyun make some potato salad—you done ate all that up, too?" Now I know he teasing me. I point to the fridge.

"Didn't want it to go bad, so I put it away. You want some salad, too? And I know you need some lemonade. Can't nobody eat a slab a ribs without some lemonade." I take the other glass and pour him some. I feel like I can joke with him, don't know why.

"You right, Sister. Lemonade makes men strong and virile. Forget what they say about whiskey—that stuff'll kill you. But lemonade, now, that's the drink of a champion." He get ice from the freezer. He spot the ice cream on the counter. "I see you planned ahead for dessert, huh? You're a smart woman, Sister. Never trust a woman that eats her ice cream hard, straight from the freezer. Speaks of mental illness on the paternal side of the family tree. Ice cream belongs soft, see? Good for the soul." He chuckle when he get down his bowl.

I laugh out loud. I thought me and Mama and all was the only ones let the ice cream sit. I laugh out loud. "Amen to that!" We about to eat, and I go to say grace. I say it silent to myself when I ain't at home. But when Norman see me bow my head, he grab my hand and bow his head, too.

He say, "Lord, you seen us through another day, and again we come away unscathed. I wanna thank you. Sometimes we let the world come from behind us and try to spoil our equilibrium. Knock us on our butts and muddle up the water. But you always come in the nick of time and restore the peace. And I wanna thank you. Thank you for giving us a cool spell and allowing us to keep a roof over us. Plenty good food and good company to share it with. Special prayer for my friend here, Sister, and hers across the way. Lord, send your angels to protect her as she walk across this here field. Give her the strength to fight when she needs to. She's a real blessing to us and to Evyun. You gave us another good friend. And I wanna thank you. In the name of your precious son. Amen." He squeeze my hand a little before he let it go. Then he break apart a rib and dig in.

Norman think I'm a good friend. Somethin' in what he say make me feel safe and glad. Wish I could pray like that. "I bet you be glad when Miss come back tomorrow." I ain't sure what all to say to Norman, Mr. Norman, who I just find out is my good friend.

"Cord-jul needs a life. She's always up under me and Evyun, and we don't need it. Call herself being helpful. Biggest help she can give me is to leave me be. Seems like she feels guilty anytime she leaves the house. Truthfully, I am glad that she is gone. Do her some good, have some fun." He pour hisself some more lemonade, wipe his hands on a towel I use to dry dishes. I make a mental note to change that towel first thing tomorrow, before I clean the kitchen.

"Sound like she having a good time from what Ev say. Playing cards and going to concerts. Maybe she making new friends, too." I don't know if Norman know she went to meet a male friend. Maybe he be mad if he knew she out there dating somebody when her real husband, his son, dead.

"Hope so. She never got over it when Jim died. No good son of a… scuse me, Sister. I loved my son. The Lord knows I did. But he was an ignorant son of…pardon my French. Different minds, that's all. I guess. Jim and me never agreed on much. Cept Cord-jul. I knew he had a sound woman when he met her. What I couldn't figure out is what she saw in him in the first place. " He burp out loud and say scuse me again.

"So, you think she still miss, ah, her husband?" Don't seem right for me to call his name, him dead and all, and his daddy talking bad about him, sort of.

"Yep. Poor thing. She and Evyun alike that way. Never can see the truth of things, never wanna call a spade a spade. Jim was a smart man, now. In his way. Took good care of his family. Dragged them all over the country with his assignments, and I never thought much of that. But he was serious about the Army, really believed all that bunk. Damn fool. Bless his heart." Norman dump his bones in the trash can and rinse off his plate, put it in the sink. Then he dish up a bowl of ice cream. Look like a serving bowl. Thought that belly he has was from beer, but come to think of it I never seen none in the house. Must be he just like to eat. "Hand me your bowl, Sister. Let me get you some, too." I was planning to use a paper cup, but I get down a bowl and hand it to him, since he offer.

"But, Cord-jul is a young thing, really. Got plenty life left in her. She needs to stop chasing ghosts. Jimmy is gone. All there is to that. Made his choice when he went over there, and Lord knows he didn't have to go. He chose it. Made a lot of ignorant choices, if you ask me."

"You mean people go to Vietnam on purpose? Why somebody wanna do that?" I lean in now, because I never really understand Vietnam. What they over there for? People around here get drafted, and some of them get sent, if they was already in the Service, but why somebody would choose to go, I don't know.

"Well, Sister, that's hard to tell. Some people need the benefit of an organization, you know? Somethin' to believe in. That's the way I see it. Military folk don't have to think for themselves; they just do what they're told to do. And if the Army says we got to fight a war, and if the Army says it's our job, and if they say we need strong, smart people over there, well, people like Jimmy leave their sick boys and their wives and go. Never mind they don't want us over there. Never mind they know their soil way better than us and got appropriate weapons and all that there, never mind. Jimmy was one of those 100 percenters. Either he did it all the way or he left it alone." Norman stare at his bowl of ice cream when he eat, like he seeing the words bout to leave his mouth in there before he say them.

I don't see where this stuff he say answer my question really. I just wanna know why people go to a strange place across the sea if they don't have to. "Oh. Like when my friend Pammie wanna be on the Pom Squad. She say they throw the best parties and have the cutest boyfriends." I stop talking, because Pammie did get on the squad, but she still alive. Norman son dead, so I guess it ain't really that similar anyway. I eat my ice cream.

Norman look up at me and smile, like he think I am really something. "Yes, Sister, it's exactly like that, only worse. People join up with a group to make themselves feel like something. Never mind if the group is a backwoods mob with sheets, and never mind if they start trouble in countries they got no business in. See? My Jimmy was like that. And my brother, too. Always going along, even when it don't make sense. You tell your friend she better look at herself and love herself and worry about Pom Squads later."

He point his finger at me. "Don't you ever go along with the crowd, Sister, unless the crowd makes sense, you hear?" He scoop up the last of his ice cream. Push back his chair.

Ev come running through the door. "Sissy! Girl you scared me to death! Thought you snuck off or God knows what else. And all the time you're out here with Pap, eatin' ice cream without me." Evian sit in the chair next to me and seem a little nervous.

"You like your mama, Evyun. Always wanna worry about something. This young lady can take care of herself, though—no need to worry about her anymore." He give me a quick wink and squeeze my shoulder. "Well, Sister, I thank you kindly for your company, but now I am going to bed. Evyun, your mama say when to expect her tomorrow?" He wait for an answer while he rinse his bowl and put it in the sink.

"No. She'll probably leave early, though. She doesn't like to drive in the dark."

"Spose you're right. Y'all young folk can keep your strange hours, walking around the house like raccoons, but I am going to bed." Norman laugh to hisself as he walk down the hall.

"Good night, Pap. Sleep tight." Ev and I look at each other and start cracking up so loud Ev get up to close the kitchen door.

CHAPTER SIXTEEN

Ev sleep with his arm up under my back. It ain't really comfortable after while, but I like to know he want to be close, so I don't move. I fall asleep with a full belly and heart. No dreams. But seem like I sleep better than I do in a while.

When I wake up, sun is poking through the blinds even though they close. Ev on his back, and he looking at me. He got a serious look on his face, like if he study it, he can remember my face line for line to tell the police later. Like he wanna get every little crease right. I say, "Mornin this mornin. How long you been awake?" I turn on my side to face him.

"Not long. Just a minute or two. Sissy, you are so beautiful when you sleep." He reach out to touch my hair, like it something to save for later.

Usually if somebody pay me a compliment, I get bashful. But not today. Ev say this stuff so quiet and truthful, I don't feel shame. "You, too. You know you smile in your sleep?" I wanna hold his hand, but he already know that and put mine inside his.

"Mmm. Got a lot to smile about, right?" He push closer and put his arms around me. "You hungry? You ever have my French toast? With syrup and plenty butter—honey, hush! I feel like I could eat about six pieces about now." He talk into my ear and into my hair, and I feel his breath tickle my neck.

"That do sound good. You know, Ev, your mama gonna be home soon. Maybe I better get dress and go home." Much as I love to lay in his bed and feel his tickle breath, feel the sun fight through the close blind. Much as I want that toast he talk about, which he know I never had since he ain't never made me nothing so far but ribs. Much as I wanna act like there ain't no Miss and there ain't no windows and bathrooms and baseboards, I know I better go.

"So? Mama knows you gotta eat, and Mama knows how well I fix French toast, too. And Pap. You and Pap get along famously now, remember? Up til all hours like the raccoons eating ribs and such! Shucks, Sissy—you a part of the family now!" He says this like it only half a joke. But something say don't go eating this toast just yet with Miss.

"I ain't been home and ain't got no clothes, Ev. I gotta clean up and… my mama…well. You know. We eat toast together another time, okay?" I can see shades pull over his eyes when I say this stuff. Like he really don't want me to go. I get this rush of wind in my stomach, and I don't wanna go neither.

"Fine. Go. Who needs you anyhow? Go on home—that's just more French toast for me. Because I'm gonna make some sausage, too, and then you'll be sorry! Using me for my ribs and leaving me alone…" Ev start to tickle me in my sides. Can't help but laugh, him being so dramatic and acting simple.

"Better not let your mama find out you cook so good. Next thing you know I'm out a job, and you the one washing them baseboards!" I giggle, but Ev stay quiet.

He scoot to the edge of the bed and swing his feet to the floor. Put his head in the palm of his hands. "You know, I mean it when I say I love you. I mean, these baseboards or whatever—who needs it? Why do you do it? I mean, you can work anywhere in the world you want, or go to school, or become a singer, you…" He turn and look at me lay on his bed.

"I like it, Ev. It make sense to me to keep stuff clean. Ain't hard. I can think. And I get to see you." I shut up quick, because I ain't ready to say what I may truthfully feel about Ev. I wanna talk to Pammie first.

"You know something, Sissy—*you* make sense to me. You really do. I mean, you can see me no matter what you decide to do. I just don't want you to think that I…I don't know. You're more than just someone to clean the baseboards or whatever. You know?" He rest his chin on my shoulder like he don't know what all to say.

"I know that, Honey. I already know that." I kiss him on his cheek.

"*Honey*. You called me *honey*! You know what that means, right? When a girl calls somebody honey..." He start to tickle me again. "...means she's done for! Had! Ha ha—now I got you where I want you—you are mine!" He slobber me with wet kisses.

"No, Sugar. It mean you got me where you *need* me. So really, *you mine*." I don't know what I mean when I say that, but it feel true. So I kiss him on the lips and run to the bathroom.

Ev say he tell Miss I come and clean Sunday so I can have Monday off. He know I need to get some stuff straight in my head before I look in his mama face. I don't know how I get this stuff straight, but one thing I know I do is go over Pammie house. And play like normal with my mama and Ruthanne. Give me a headache and a heartache to think about all this. How my life seem to change in two days.

Ev give me a shirt to put on and say he walk me cross the field. I say I walk this field all my life and I ain't gonna stop walking it now. He smile hard when I say that, like he won something. He still watch me all the way cross. I look at the spot where me and Ev...you know...and I get a hot flash somewhere down there, but I keep walking. Look straight ahead. Keep my eyes peel for sticks, just in case. Ev wave to me when I open the back door lead to the kitchen. He give me a thumbs-up sign. I blow a kiss before I close the door.

CHAPTER SEVENTEEN

Sposed to be just another day, but something in it feel different. Seem like the house got a glare to it wasn't there before. Like I should go through here and clean out the old stuff that don't belong. I don't know. Maybe I spend too much time at Ev house, because now stuff around to my own house look dingy. Which is crazy, cuz me and Mama and Ruthanne is good housekeepers. But when was the last time I took some Pine Sol to my own baseboards? Haven't done that since I don't know when. Truthfully, I think Miss have me do it so much just to make sure I got something to do every day. Come to think of it, baseboards don't really need cleaning every week. So, once I remember that, I start to feel better.

Next thing I go to the bathroom, make sure I don't look strange. Something say don't say nothing to Mama or Ruthanne about...well, Evian and all. I maybe tell Ruthanne, since she always in my business, but Mama? Not yet. She ain't ready for this. In the bathroom, I pull the door to and look at my face. Same old me, I guess, but I do have a zit coming up near the left side of my nose. Always get them there, but they don't last long. Pammie say don't pick at it, or you leave a mark, but I always do anyhow, and don't no marks come. I'm busy picking at this zit that ain't fully there yet when Ruthanne come in.

"Well, if it ain't Little Miss White Folks! Glad you could make it back to our humble home. What, you get tired a being around to that mansion and feel like slumming, or did White Folks finally get some sense?" Ruthanne got a bite in her voice, like she trying to kid me, but really she mad. I ignore the mean sound and go with the kidding part.

"Yep. Evian look up at me all of a sudden and he say, 'Gra-yut day, Sister—you Black! Get on away from he-yah now!'" I put on my best plantation voice, and I sound so simple that I laugh out loud. Can't even imagine Ev talk to me that way.

"Ha, ha. Sister, you sleeping with that boy? Tell me for real, now, no fooling." She got her hands on her hips again, like she dare me to lie about it. She seem like she scared or something.

"Umm. Well. We don't just do that, Ruty. We good friends, too..." I don't want to really admit nothing to Ruthanne. Seem like what I do with Evian sposed to be private. Maybe it lose part of the magic if I tell her about it.

Ruthanne cross her arms in front of her chest and shake her head. "Sister! You better think long and hard about this, hear? I mean it. Ain't just you over there to White Folks when you busy 'making friends.' It all of us—me, Mama, Timmie, Albert, and everybody! I mean, for real, you think it so easy, and y'all got so much in common, and he wanna talk to you and all, but...his people ain't like your people..."

Now I get mad. "What do you know about his people, Ruthanne? You said yourself yesterday that you don't feel like being bothered with no White Folks! What do you really know about them anyway? Plus, his family like me—they treat me real nice, most of them..." I stop talking when I think of Blister and what he do. My chest tighten up and get cold.

"Yes, but do they know you sleeping with they son? Cuz I guarantee you, they ain't gonna treat you so nice when they know what's going on. They can be real nice, long as you working for them and keeping separate. But when you act like you trying to be one of them...I don't know, Sister. This just don't feel right. I ain't playin', neither."

She may be right. I don't know. What she mean, trying to be one of them? I don't feel like arguing about what I ain't for sure about. "Ruty, I know what you trying to say, okay? It ain't like I don't think about that stuff—I ain't stupid. But, I just...I don't know. Maybe it be a problem, but then again, maybe not. We just have to wait and see. Meantime, I wish you wouldn't worry so much. I really can handle it. I promise." I look at her serious for a minute.

Ruthanne just stand there and don't say nothing, shake her head. "Mama thought it was me that was fast, always getting in trouble, just cuz I have Nakita, but you...Sister, ain't nothing to have a baby. Mama can handle that, but this White Folks thing...I just don't know! I hope you know what you doing."

Then Nakita wake up from her morning nap, and Ruthanne rush down the hall. Nakita learn how to climb out her crib a long time ago. She can get into more trouble in those few seconds after she climb out her crib before you come get her in her room! One time she got out the crib and pulled the humidifier down off the dresser on top of herself. By time Ruthanne got in there, she was soaking wet and scared to death.

I turn off the light in the bathroom and go get the phone in the kitchen. Better call Pam Elizabeth. After all I been through, I gotta find out what she think of all this. Maybe she tell me what to do next. Probably she act like Ruthanne—tell me I'm crazy and asking for trouble.

I pull the phone in my room, so I can have some privacy. Albert at work, and Timmie at daycamp at the church, but I don't feel like having Ruty listening to all my business. She already worry enough about all this. No need to give her details.

"Hu-llo?" Pammie sound like she sleep. I forget she like to sleep in during the week. She a night owl. But she would want me to wake her up for this, so I don't feel bad.

"Girl, wake up! With your lazy self!" I plop down on the bed to get comfortable. I figure this call will take a while. But I hear somebody grumble in the background, and Pammie whisper something. "Pammie? You there? Do Eddie wanna use the phone?"

Pammie clear her throat. "Girl, please! Eddie at work. You do love to wake me up, don't you? Everybody ain't into morning like you, Sister. Some people don't even get to bed hardly before the birds get up! You could let somebody sleep!" She laughing, so I know she ain't really mad.

"Who you talking to, then, if Eddie at work?"

"Uh-uh, Sister. No—don't be asking me shit first thing in the morning after you sleeping over to the Mandarenes' and got some love affair with the white boy and don't wanna tell nobody about it! *You* the one sposed to be answering questions, not *me!* When are you coming?" She sound wide awake now.

"I guess I could come, but I need coffee and breakfast. I feel like I could eat a horse!"

"You are too much! I'm sposed to cover for your ass and cook for you, too? I know what let's do! Let's make that coffee cake your grandma used to make! With the crumbs on top. You got any butter over there? I think we only got one stick. You bring the butter, and I start the coffee. I see you soon, girl!"

She hang up before I can say anything else. She always like that—seem like she tell more than she ask. But she my best friend, so...Most time I go along with her. When was the last time I make that coffee cake? Leave it to Pammie to remember that stuff. She been friends with me so long, seem like she part of the family. I quick take a bath and grab the butter, tell Ruthanne I'm going over to Pammie house, this time for real. I be back for dinner, though, cuz I ain't seen Mama in a while.

Pam got the fan blowing on high when I come in. She don't like it to get too hot, which ain't hard to have happen in the kitchen in the summer. During the day, she keep the windows open and the drapes close, which I don't like, cuz then the sun don't come in. But last thing Pammie want is the sun to come in. Number one, she don't wanna get no darker. She seem to think there some kind of good in being lighter than other folks. And number two, she don't like to sweat.

She playing Mahalia Jackson. Pammie love gospel. She got the record player set up on the kitchen counter, and she already pull out the flour, the sifter, and the mixer. Pammie real organize, so we can get along good making stuff together. She like me. Mama, she fly through the kitchen like a hurricane coming and she wanna get done with dinner before it get too wet. Leave all kind of dirty pots and grease and spoon marks on the counter. When she cook, I just stay out the way and plan to clean it up later. It like this: we take turns cooking and cleaning. If she cook, then I clean, and the other way around. It ain't even, though, cuz when I cook, I leave the kitchen clean, but when she cook she leave all kind of mess! Oh well, she cook better than me anyway, so I guess I don't mind. And I don't have to clean the rest of the house, cuz Ruthanne do that.

"Pammie! Nobody told you, you don't be leaving your guests alone when they come to visit? Come on, now!" I get the apron out the drawer under the sink. I don't like to get flour on my clothes. Pammie always wear the pink and black check one. Me, I wear the plain white one with the pockets. We always use to cook stuff together. She teach me how to make cookies, and I teach her how to make biscuits and stuff. Sometime we make dinner for her whole family, just cuz we wanna try something new. Most time we cook over to her house, cuz Mama funny about having other people in her kitchen. I get a warm feeling over to Pammie house, been coming here so much for so long.

When she finally come from upstairs, she got a smile on her face. She miss me when we ain't around each other for a few days.

"Aw, sooky-sooky, now! Sister done got her this high-paying job and fancy white boyfriend, and can't come see nobody no more! But I got something for ya! I remember you when you didn't! I knew you when you couldn't half keep your bathing suit on down to Kentucky Lake cuz your boobs was too small, and ain't much bigger now, so please! Don't get too big for your britches!" She teasing me. Hand me the measuring cup and the flour.

I assume we making two cakes, cuz she got so many people around here, and I measure out four cups, set it in the extra bowl. "You ain't right, Pammie. Anyways, Evian don't like big chests no how, so there!" I sift each cup of flour into the mixing bowl. Granny say sift it twice if you want tender cake. Mama say it the other way around—sift it once for tender, twice for coarse. I go with what Granny say, since it her recipe.

I notice Pammie got a purple mark on her neck, just above her shirt line, but I don't say nothing yet. Pammie don't like a lot of questions. She tell me everything, but she do it in her own time. Usually I don't bother her about it less I'm real curious.

She got a paring knife, and she cutting the stick of butter in small chunks, for the topping. You got to cut it cold, else it won't stay separate when you try to make the topping. Cut it in chunks and put it back in the fridge til you ready. "So?! Don't you got something to tell me? And don't be leaving stuff out, neither, cuz I done waited long enough for your secretive ass!"

"Well, you know Evian, right? He know you, cuz he seen you on my porch before and notice you walk fast. But anyway, he so sweet, girl! You can't believe! When his mama, Miss Cordial, went to Louisville last week, she ask me to come on Saturday and make sure they got enough to eat and all. Norman, he Miss father or whatever, old, and she worry for him. But Evian say he make ribs and gonna have this cousin over, and, well...that's when it happen. I mean, the first time." I pause for a minute, because I remember Blister. Do I tell her about that, too? I ain't decide about that yet. Maybe if I think about it, I get too scared like before. I get the eggs and cream out the fridge.

"His cousin? Norman? You call this man by his first name, Sister?" She full of questions in her eyes. "Do he be there all the time, too, or just, what's his name, Evian?"

"Norman live there, and I don't really call him nothing, you know, cuz it never really come up. But he nice to me mostly, least so far. And can eat some ribs, too! He like his ice cream soft, too, Pammie. He seem sweet."

"Okay, so, what is going on, girl—enough of this Norman already!" She use the other stick of butter to grease two pans.

"You can put the mixer up, cuz Grannie say you got to cream the butter and sugar by hand. She never would use a mixer with this cake. She say it taste better that way. Anyhow, one time me and Evian in his room, and I notice he got all this sheet music, you know. And he listen to Dinah Washington and sing and stuff, so one time he ask me to come in and..." I cream the butter while I tell her all about Ev and how he play his guitar and maybe teach me, how he sing to Aretha and love Marvin Gaye, how we eat ribs and what happen after in his room, and how he say he love me.

When I say that, she like to have a fit. "Say what, now?! Love you! Girl, y'all barely know each other! Please! You think he mean it?" Pammie a soft touch. She love all that romantic stuff—cards, flowers, poems, and anything else connected to love. She get a soft look when I answer.

"He seem for real, Pam. I don't know. Like, one time when I'm sleeping, he just stare at me, you know? And he put his hand on my face and look at my eyes. I think he for real, Pam." I crack the eggs in the butter mixture and start to stir. She hand me the vanilla.

"Wow. Well. What do *you* feel like? You busy talking bout him and how for real he is—are *you*?" She mixing flour and cinnamon for the topping.

"Yea, girl!. He real sweet! And can sing! And when he hold me, I don't know...it just feel like...like can't nobody bother us or something. I don't know. His mama don't know, though. Unless he telling her right now, like I'm telling you." I pray silent that he not.

Pammie squinch up her brows. "Umm. Well. She bound to find out sooner or later. You think she gonna...I don't know what! White folks get crazy when they think you overstepping, Sister. You could lose your job or anything! You thought about it?"

"Yea, but I don't know yet. I mean, I don't care that much about the job—I got this one, and I can sure get another one. But I do care about Ev and what happen to him, and to us. Guess I just have to see, and be prepare for I don't know what."

By now the topping finish, and I finish mixing the cake. We pour half the batter in one pan, and the rest in the other. Pammie sprinkle the topping on each one. You gotta have a light hand here, cuz if the topping sink too far, it bake into the cake and turn the whole thing brown. But if you do it right, it end up like a crumb cake, with the cake moist underneath and the topping buttery-crisp on top. Add some coffee with plenty cream, and honey, hush! Breakfast is on!

CHAPTER EIGHTEEN

We take our coffee in the living room while the cake baking. She turn off Mahalia Jackson and unplug the record player. Next thing she pull the wooden box out from under the couch. I know what that mean. She and hers always got home-grown laying around. It grow real well in back of their house, and don't nobody pay these houses back here no mind. For real, I don't smoke much, but sometime it fun when I be over to Pammie house. She can be so crazy! Seem like everything crack us up when we smoke corn. She got a special tray she use to roll johnsons on. She do it quick, too. She got nimble fingers. I learn that word in fourth grade. *Jack be nimble. Jack be quick.* It mean you do something smooth, with ease. Pammie do a lot of stuff like that, but specially johnsons. She roll up two quick as you please, pass one to me, light the other.

After a few minutes, I got some questions of my own. And she ain't said nothing yet, so I ask, "So, when you gonna say something bout that mark on your neck? Are the mosquitoes that bad this year, or you seeing somebody new?"

Pammie start to giggle. "You sitting down? Cuz you not gone believe this one." What do she mean, am I sitting down? Here I am right next to her on the couch! We both start laughing.

"You would like this one, Sister. He nice. Got good hair. Always keep a job, nice to his mama. And he remind me of you." She all the while grinning, like she ain't said it all. She like that. She wanna build you up and then drop you later.

"Why he remind you of me?" I am curious, sure enough. This suspense stuff always work with me. She know me too well.

"Umm. I don't know. Seem like he could be in your family. His mama go to church and all, and he grew up around here. He like the same stuff we like. He even watch that movie you love, you know, with the lawyer and the little girl and the man who rape the white woman and all—we check out the book a few summers back, about a bird, remember? He like that movie, too. Did I tell you it was on Friday?" She look at me from up under heavy eyelids, and she still not being straight.

Pammie can be with some dingalings, for real. She don't have no sense when it come to men. All she wanna know is do they have a car and can they take her out and do they have good hair. Never mind if they stole the car, and never mind if they work making license plates around to the county jail—do they look good, and do they dress right is all she wanna know.

But then the timer go off in the kitchen, and I jump up off the couch and scream. This make us laugh even harder than before. Next thing, Pammie start looking for her shoes, lifting up the skirt on the bottom of the couch and sticking her head under there. She crazy. "Girl, why you need your shoes so bad? Let me go get this cake before it burn up!"

I laugh my way into the kitchen.

I turn off the oven and put two towels down on the counter, so the cakes can cool. They fall apart when you cut them hot. I put each one on a towel. I'm about to get me some more coffee when my brother, Albert, come walking down the steps from upstairs. He stop for a minute when he see me, then he act casual and come down. Albert ain't slick! He probably got somebody up there with him. He and Pam brother real tight, and they always into something. He probably brought some girl over there and don't want me to know what he doing. I don't say nothing about it. Figure he stay over here with Eddie last night and ain't made it home yet.

"Hey, Sister. What chou cookin'? Umm! I know that ain't Granny coffee cake!" Albert love him some sweets. He stick his face down next to a cake and breathe in, then he pick some of the topping off one.

I swat his hand. "Stop, now! Let this cake cool, Brother! You can have some when it get cool." I shoo him out to the living room. I'm getting cream for the coffee when I hear all this whispering going on out there. I get quiet, but I can't make out the words. I go on in, and there is Albert with his arms around Pammie and his nose press against her neck, like he so glad to see her.

I stop in my tracks. What in the world??!

Pammie break away from my brother. "Sister, 'member when I say that this new guy remind me of you and could be in your family? Well, guess what..." They both look at me and smile.

"Oh please! Albert? My baby brother? Pam, you must be out your mind! He a year younger than you, Pammie! And besides, I mean, I don't know! What chou talking about?" I am so shock, I plop down on the couch and almost waste my cup of coffee.

Albert sit on the couch next to me, and Pam sit at his feet between his legs on the floor.

"Why don't you stop trippin', Sister! You should be glad for me. You never think I have nobody worth nothing, and you accuse Pam at the same thing. Now we both got something good." Albert pull Pammie hair, and she say, "I know dats right!"

"OH PLEASE! Oh my goodness, y'all are a mess! I know you ain't for real about this! How long have y'all been...what y'all doing, anyway?"

Pammie stop laughing and look at me serious. "Same thing you and... anyway, we is for real, too, Sister. It ain't like with everybody else, you know? I mean, Albert is like...family and stuff." She rub her cheek on his leg. YUCK.

"For real, Sister. We straight. Pammie got me reading the Bible and stuff, and she taking me wid her ta church next week. She a good influence on me. You'll see..."

Now he really tripping. Albert don't never go to church. "Why *she* gotta take you? We go to the same church, and you don't never go with Mama, but all a sudden you wanna go with Pammie? Oh my goodness. Now I seen it all!" I just shake my head. Weird. I mean, I don't wanna be jealous, but, Albert always would be with Edward, and me and Pam the ones was tight. Now this. How I'm sposed to act? I sure don't know.

"Well, look like this summer full of surprises, huh?" Pam look at me and wink. I know she won't say nothing to Albert about Evian unless I say for her to, so I guess I better get straight with this new Albert thing, too. She trying to support me with my craziness, so I guess I better support her in hers. And, believe me, this is craziness.

Albert all familiar over to Pammie house! This time he get the wooden box hisself and roll one up. Next thing you know, Pammie bring the record player in from the kitchen, and we play records and sing. I forget Albert can sing. He don't never come to church, and he don't sing in the youth choir, but he should! He got a smooth sound, you know? Sound like melted chocolate. Higher than mine sort of, but thicker or something. Nice. Pammie play the piano like her mama, but she sing a little, too. Most time she just stare at Albert like he got some answer she been trying to figure out all day written in his eye.

One hand, I'm glad for them, cuz I love both of them. Pammie like family, and Albert *is* family. But, for real, I can't understand what do she see in my baby brother? He the same little boy as always to me, nobody to date or make a fuss over. I mean, I guess I just don't see him like a real man, but he is. He almost six feet tall. He got short wavy hair and clear skin like me, light brown. Strong arms and soft eyes. He cute! I guess I never notice that before. Look like Marvin Gaye.

And if I didn't remember that he could sing, I did know that he the self-appointed leader of the local revolution. He so militant, as Ruthanne say. Nothing is what it seem like, far as Albert can tell. Everything tied to something else and connected to how the white man scared of the black man. Truth, I get tired of hearing about it and don't half understand none of it no way. But Pammie must don't realize how long-winded he could be when it come to this stuff, so she get him started. But this news they talk about, I ain't heard yet, so I'm interested, too. A lot can happen when you over to Ev house for a few days!

Albert say, "Eddie tell your mama bout last weekend yet?" His eyes get narrow when he about to get real serious.

"He don't talk to me about this stuff, Albert. Like he think he can't trust me or something. So I don't know if he said nothing yet, but I kinda don't think he has, cuz Mama ain't said nothing neither." Pammie climb up on the couch next to Albert, got his hand between hers. (Oh please!)

"What? What is Eddie into now and ain't told his mama?" I move to the other end of the couch, so I can give these two lovebirds some space.

"You ain't told Sister?" Albert turn to look at me. "You know last weekend, Eddie had the car, right? So we went to Georgetown and stuff. Just messin' around, you know. Pick up Virg and Darryl, got some beer—no big deal. So, we had stop at the park for a while, and some fellas was playing ball, but it was about to break up. You know Georgy? Davita and Alice brother? He and all them from east end. They was going up to Chicago next day, say they was ready to roll out. So, it was still early, and Eddie don't never have the car, so..." Told you Albert can talk when he get started.

"Tell her what happen, Albert! You see she ready to explode!" Pammie nudge him in the side and look at me. Who she to talk? She always draw stuff out, too, don't never wanna come right out and say it. Maybe they *are* meant to be together!

"I am! But see, we was kinda tipsy, you know? Not too bad, cuz me and Eddie don't go in for that too much, but Virg—I don't know. He can knock em back. But dig, we decide to go look at them new houses on North Vine. Oh my goodness! Those are some bad houses! One got windows all over one side, and somethin like three floors and a circle driveway. Don't nobody live there yet. So, Virg get the idea to stop and look up close, you know, see what it look like inside. Not a good idea." He stop there, like he finish.

Now I really am gonna explode. "What happen, Albert? Y'all in trouble? What you drinking beer for? How you get beer and just 17?" I got these questions and a million more, but he cut me off.

"Please! Don't nobody know or care how old I am, Sister. Nobody trying to worry about some beer. Specially since they want us to stay drunk so we don't half know what's going on, and dats why I don't mess with it no more. Anyway, it was all right until we started making noise, I guess. I was saying how it don't make sense to have the living room face the back where the kitchen sposed to be, and me and Darryl was arguing about it and acting silly, and dats when the man rolled up." He pull his hand out from Pam, like he pissed to think about it.

"Man?! What man? The one that live there?" Oh no. I can just see this man drive up and all these black boys outside his house looking in—Oh Lord!

Pammie start to laugh. "Girl, you could be so simple! The *man*, girl. You know, the cops."

Albert explain how the man wanna know what they doing looking in the window, and do they have a license, and this private property, and they breaking and enter. He tell me how Virg always gotta seem like he in charge a things and don't wanna take no flack from nobody, talking smart to the police.

"Virgyl so crazy! Why he gotta act up wid the cops, Albert? I mean, damn! Why he couldn't just say he sorry and get his black ass back in the car and go? He always make trouble! I wish you stop messin wid him!" Pammie shake her head.

"I know. Virg do got a attitude. What happen?" I sit with my knees pull up to my chin and wait to hear.

Albert say how they took them all downtown. They could a had a warning, but Virg wouldn't keep his mouth shut, saying how the man always in the wrong place asking the wrong questions when there's real criminals they oughtta be worrying about. He right, but he need to shut up!

"Yea. They say we was disturbing the peace. I call Uncle James, because I ain't wanna tell Mama, and he come down and all. Me and Darryl just got let go, but Virg, he got hisself in a mess. Come to find out he on probation. And Eddie, well...They check his license. Look like he got four speeding tickets he ain't tell nobody about, and now he gotta pay a bunch of fines. With money you know he don't have. So, he gonna have to say something to his mama sometime. And we can forget about getting the car anytime soon!"

Albert twist his hands and frown like he mad. Sometime I worry about him, because he so serious. He always look close at stuff, wanna figure out who and what and why. Especially when it come to the police. See, where we live, everybody know the police don't like black men. They look for a reason to mess with them. Every time Albert hear about someone he know that they mess with, he remember. And the serious look he already have get older and deeper.

"How much do Eddie owe?" If it ain't a whole, whole lot, maybe his mama won't be too mad. I cross my legs up under me. The fan blowing right on my toes.

"One-hundred fifty dollars. He could make that much if he save. But he acting like he don't want to work round to the gas station no more. He say Gus mess around with the paycheck and don't never wanna give it up on time. One time when he try to cash the check, wasn't no money to cover it, and he had to wait three days. But dats what he get for working for the man!" Albert get on my nerves with this stuff sometime. What he gonna think when he hear about me and Ev?

Even though I don't feel like having him around to the Mandarenes', I remind them that Miss had want someone to keep they lawn during the summer. I know she pay good, cuz I work there. And Eddie could make this money he owe pretty quick, so his mama don't get too mad. Albert say that sound all right, and he gonna tell Eddie when he see him. They gonna be painting houses with Vincent and his crew later today.

"Dat could be tight. Imma tell Eddie today. But, I need to roll out. Gotta take the bus downtown and meet Vincent and them. Imma see you later?" Albert pull Pammie off the couch, and they walk together to the back door. I stay on the couch. I done had enough of this smoochie stuff from my brother and best friend for one day.

When Pam come back, she got a smile all over her shoulders and face, like her whole body on fire. She sprawl out on the other side of the couch.

"Girl, ain't love fun?! You know, I don't never do the...you know...with Albert, neither. You would think I would. But he so...I don't know. He say he wanna wait and get to know me, or even be married. He so decent." She shake her legs out in front of her and shake her feet, like she got water on the floor and don't wanna get her feet wet.

First I am quiet and don't know where to start. Then I ask a bunch of questions fast.

"Why Albert? All the other people in Kentucky, and you gotta hook up with my little brother? I mean, why? When? How y'all get to this point so quick? I mean, shoot, I ain't been out of it that long!" I am so surprise. What do she be doing when I'm at work anyways?

She just giggle. "Girl, I don't know! He always be over here, I guess, with Eddie and stuff. And you would think they with girls and stuff, but most time they read stuff and talk. You know Eddie met this guy from East End, and he in this group. They give him all this mess to read about Vietnam and how to go into business and all this other stuff, and they talk. Girl, they make it seem so...important or something. So that's how come I got interested in Albert." She look at me like this the most normal thing in the world, her messing with my baby brother.

"My baby brother?!" I just can't get passed it.

"He ain't a baby, Sister. Timmie the one who a baby, and I ain't trying to be with him." Now she sound defensive. "Anyways, you out there posting with white boys trying to tell me! Girl, I ain't even done that yet! And ain't trying to. Dag, Sister. I mean, I really like Albert." She start to pick at her lip. She do that when she feeling sorry for herself and want sympathy.

Hmm. Life strange. But no stranger than me over to the Madarenes' eating ribs with (Mr.) Norman. So I try to understand and back off. "Yeah, all right. I hear you. But guess what?"

"What now?" She look at me like she don't wanna hear no more news.

"I ain't a virgin no more!" We both bust out laughing. We always knew Pammie would be the first, because she act so fast. Always into boys, since we was 12. But it turn out to be me, and a white boy at that. So you never know.

"Yes, so now that you a experience woman of the world, what you gonna do?"

"I guess I stick with it. Unless the Klan come after me."

CHAPTER NINETEEN

Round about 3, I know I need to go home. Been a couple days since I seen Mama, and I miss her. The thing with Mama is, seem like she always know everything. I don't like to lie to Mama. Something about it don't seem right. But how I'm gonna tell her about this one, about Ev and all, I don't know. Wonder if she be mad at me? Wonder if she tell me to stop? Wonder if I *can* stop. I mean, I don't wanna make her mad, but I really like Ev. He make me feel special. I don't know. It sound corny to say. I wonder should I tell Mama that, and would she understand. Anyways, I can't stay gone forever. Time for me to go on home.

Pam give me a plate to take home one of the cakes. She say she got to keep some here for Albert, cuz he like sweets. Like I don't know that! Like I ain't been knowing Albert all his life and don't know he like sugar. Not to mention that he live at my house, and I'm taking cake home, and he can eat his sweets there, if he like sugar so bad, but I don't argue. Not that I care if she keep the cake, but for her to say she looking out for Albert. This will take some getting use to.

I come in through the kitchen door, and I can tell Mama home already. She don't usually get back this early. I put the cake down and go in the living room. She got her feet prop up on the table, and the bottom of her hose is ripped. Look like she had a hard day.

I sit down next to her. Mama work for the state, has for years. She don't like her job, but she good at it, though. Everybody say so. If somebody got a question, they come to Mama. She say she quit if she could think of something else to do. But look like after you do something so long, change don't come easy. I pat my Mama on the leg and smile.

"Hey, Mama! You home early. Look tired, too. You all right?" I take off my sandals and put my feet on the table, too.

"Baby Girl! These folks is running me to death! Lord! You think the state of Kentucky would fall down and perish if Jeanine Radley didn't make a point to wear me out every day—asking me for stuff she need to learn how to do herself. Worry me to death! But I been working with this one account for three weeks, coming in early and staying late. So, today, I took me some comp time. Left early, and tomorrow I'm going in late. Turn things around for a change. How you feelin', Sister? Look like you was feeling poorly yesterday. You back to yourself, now?" She always find a minute, in the middle of complaining, to ask after me.

"I'm all right, Ma. Just, you know, that monthly thing. And I ain't sleeping so well, next to this heat. But me and Pammie made Granny's crumb cake today, and I brought some home, too." I don't wanna get into nothing yet with Mama. Too scared.

"Nakita got a doctor's appointment today. Hope Ruty remember to take her. Seem like she might have a head cold or something, but we wanna make sure. I don't feel like foolin' with no sick children. Where Timmie?" She rubbing her ankle. Mama feet swell. Sometime it get real bad, and she can barely put on her shoes, but she still wear pumps every day. I never will understand it, but Mama has her ways.

"I bet she do remember. Last time Nakita got sick, Ruty cried all through it. Every time Kita cough, remember? Tears start rolling down her cheek. She ain't gonna forget. But Timmie don't come home from church camp until 4. On Mondays, they do arts and crafts. Hey! You remember when we made those sand-dollar necklaces? Used paint and sparkle on them and all that? You still got yours?" Every year when I was young, I went to camp over to the church. Mama say it keep us out of trouble. It was fun. You do arts and crafts, sing songs, learn scripture. You get to play softball or badminton, and some days they take you to the park or to the pool.

Mama laugh when I mention the necklace. "Girl, you got a memory! Course I got that necklace. Bless your heart, that necklace had some crazy patterns to it! Pink and purple and a little bit of orange. Specks of black-Lord! Sister, what was you thinking with those colors?! Didn't match nothing in my closet! Remember I wore it to church that Sunday, and I got all kinds of compliments on it. Look around the congregation, and all the grannies and mamas got on these crazy necklaces! Pastor say, 'Lord, must have been arts and crafts day at the camp!'" She laugh at that. "Thank goodness you learn to cook, Sister, cuz I don't think arts and crafts is your calling." Teasing me.

I don't get mad. "But Timmie good at it, though. You see that cabin he built last week? Never thought you could do so much with macaroni! He even paint the doors and stuff with finger paint. He something else." Truth, Timmie is good with his hands. He can paint and draw, too. He got a picture he drew of the lake hung over his bed. Pretty colors and stuff.

"Macaroni is something we better leave to use with cheese, but he did do a good job. Sister, tell me bout this job you got, over to those white people's house. How they treat you over there?"

I try not to get tense. I knew she would ask about the Mandarenes sooner or later. "They treat me proper, Mama. Cordial, I call her Miss, she nice to me. She a little strange, though. She paint and stuff all the time, talk on the phone. She live with her father-in-law and her son. He the one got cancer." I don't mention Ev name, even. Don't wanna call no kind of attention to him yet.

"Mmm-hmm. I know her people. Seem like some of them had some trouble some years back. Disremember the details. That why they left the place all those years. Never thought they was coming back. Understand the daddy dead." She get that wondering look she get when she trying to figure things out that happen a long time before. Sometime it take a while, but eventually she do remember. "Mandarene. She got people in Georgetown. Family got plenty money. Plenty money. Seem like they breed horses or something. Can't place the rest. What she got you cookin' round there?" Mama pick up the sports section of the paper and start to fan right in front of her face.

"Usual stuff. Chicken. Fried fish. Sometimes roast or pork. Miss ain't too tough on roast, though. She like her meat cook real soft and red. I don't know where she get that from. I gotta pull the steaks out way before they look done to me, but, hey—she gotta eat it. Not me." Truth, she want the meat blood red. So it don't even look dead yet.

I tell Mama about how Miss have a sweet tooth, and how her father love cobbler and soft ice cream. When I mention his name, Norman, she lift her left brow at me. She don't say nothing, but I know she notice I call him by his first name. After I talk a few minutes, Mama start to stare somewhere over my head, like she only half listening. She do that a lot. She get bored quick. Really, she keep to herself a lot. She say people can wear her out.

"Yes. Mmm-hmm. Seem like some of them got red in their blood. Caused a mess a few years back. And all of them got bad tempers. That happen when white people get a lot of money. They think they above the law. You be careful around there, Sister. Do what she ask you to do, and no more. Nice little job for you. Convenient." By now she has already got up and left, in her mind. Soon she say she going and change her clothes, do some gardening before the kids get home.

Wasn't too bad. I don't never have to say nothing about me and Ev. Yet. But I wonder what do she mean when she say they got red in they blood and have bad tempers. Ev and Cordial just as mild as butter. Norman, he got a little fire in him, but he so old. But for all I know, Mama mix them up with somebody else she heard about. She don't know them personal, just think she remember.

I go on to my room, take advantage of Mama being in the garden. Mama don't like for us to sit on the beds. She say it make them soft. So, I get out my thought book and sit on the floor near the window. What they doing around to Ev house? I turn away from the window. Can't see round there from here no way. But I don't know what to write. I wanna take what I do these past few days, me and Ev, and Pammie and Albert, and Virg and the man, and put it somewhere small where I can think it out and have it make sense. And Blister. What about Blister? Forget Blister. Nothing I can do about Blister.

Am I crazy? I don't feel no different than I always do. But Ruthanne, she make it seem so strange that I would like Evian and his people. Some people do be with other people outside they race, though, I know. The Andersons, live downtown, all of them got blue eyes, and they sure don't get them from they mama. Something must have happen, and they still faring pretty well. But, what about Blister?

Blister. I try and don't think about him. What he do. About Norman and what he say about Blister and his daddy and they people. And Norman brother. Right now, after what Evian say about keeping myself and killing whoever take it, I don't feel scared. But what I do if he try to do that again? If anybody try to do that again? I don't know. Hope I don't never have to find out. And why I gotta spend my time thinking about that crazy sheet, as Norman say. I did have some self before I even knew Evian and his people. Seem like they all I think about these days. So, I think about other stuff for a while. This song we learn last Sunday in church. Me and this girl Linda singing lead. I think about the words to that song. "Keep your lamps trimmed and burning. The time is drawing nigh..." It mean that we don't know when Christ gonna come. We gotta be ready. Linda sing real loud and high. We don't balance at all. Really, I don't know why Miss Jackson put us together. We don't blend. Linda could just sing it by herself, if you ask me.

Blister. Blister. Don't think about it.

What would Christ think if he seen me and Ev together? *If!* Like he don't see everything! I think He smile. I guess He don't like it that we...you know. Cuz we ain't married. But I don't think He mind that Evian and me two different colors. I think Christ love all of us the same. I really do. Then I remember. I ain't talk to God in a while. All this He seen me through in these last few days. Was He there when Blister put his spit inside me, private? Is He the one call Norman? Maybe He speak in a quiet voice to Norman, and that why he come. But he old, and he don't get there in time. So, I quick close my eyes. I tell God thank you. I say thank you for letting Norman get there after all. And for giving me Ev. And for making me be able to sing. Then, I do something strange. I start to cry. Because it don't go away. Not the sex. I can wash away the sex. But the rest of it hit me all of a sudden, and it make me cry.

Blister hate me.

Why? Why Blister do that to me? He don't know me. Why he don't wanna know me? At first he act like he did, when we was eating ribs and drink Juleps. Then he change and get mad and remember he hate me. It hurt. Not just the thing he did, but the reason why he did it. Inside of me, I don't want nothing bad for nobody. For real. And I always think that everybody feel like I do. But Blister, he different, I guess. He hate me. Then I cry some more. Why do he hate me? He like Evian, and me and Ev got a lot of stuff the same. Why he like Ev and don't like me? I sing, just like he do. I like some of those songs he mention. I drink Juleps, too, but not the whiskey he pull out later. I read that book he got, *Lord of the Flies*. But he hate me anyway. For some reason, the thing he did don't seem as bad as the fact that he don't know me and hate me anyway. I feel like I cry for two days about this. But after while, I stop. Don't everybody hate me. Just some people, like Blister.

I get up and blow my nose. Sometime when I think of it, the world seem like a cold and mean place.

CHAPTER TWENTY

I don't know what to expect when I get round to Ev house next day. I know he say he love me, and he don't care about his mama and all, but, me, I ain't so sure. So I plan to get there right at 10, so there ain't no extra time before I get started. Sometime I go early, and Miss wanna talk while she drink her tea. Use to like those times. But today, I ain't for sure after so much happen, I figure I get there right on time. After my shower, I dress and walk over. March across that field and make sure to keep my mind blank. No sense in remember and then act crazy like before.

Miss at the table about to rinse her cup and put it near the sink, like she always do. She drink out this one cup all the time—got a gold rim and real light color flowers on it. Miss like flowers. She got her hat on the table, and her gloves. She got pink nail polish on her fingers and toes, and she wearing high-heel sandals.

"How-doo, Sister! I see you kept them outta trouble for me while I was away! I thank you kindly! Came back, and everything was in order. Windows just as clean, and linens crisp and put away. You are such a blessing to us, Sister. I wish I could visit with you this morning, but I have gotta run..." She got a broad smile on her face, and when she grin like that, she look like a horse. Plenty teeth show when she smile this way. Seem like she got something else she wanna say.

"You flatter me. Just doing my job, Miss. No problem at all for me. Where you heading out to this morning, so dress up?" I ask cuz it seem like she wanna tell me, all grins and everything.

"Well. You know my friend Willie-Mae introduced me to a gentleman this weekend? His name is Griffin Howard. He escorted me to the symphony. Such a nice man! Now he took and asked me to a benefit at his church. Seems they show all kinds of plants and flowers that the ladies have been growing, and you can bid on them and bring them on home with you— the flowers, not the ladies! My goodness, can you imagine if they auctioned the ladies?! What kind of a price could they get for them! But, his sister belongs to the Rose of Sharon Club, and so he thought I would enjoy this event. So, off I go!" She busy putting on her hat while she talk, and she got the hat pin in her teeth while she listen for my reaction. She seem so happy.

"Well. Go head, now, Miss! Got a suitor and all dolled up in pink, no less! Sounds like a good time to me! Maybe next time you take some of the flowers you been growing. You got a green thumb, too." Not really. Mama flowers and vegetables would put Miss ones to shame easy.

"Oh, Sister! I imagine these annuals I grow would seem like weeds to these ladies. They are serious with their gardening. Me, I just piddle, you know. I am going to meet Willie-Mae at her house, and then we'll meet Griffin at the church. I think I'll be gone a few hours, but not overnight. I miss sleeping at home. There is something so comforting about sleeping in one's own bed." She pick up her bag and head for the door. "I understand Franklin got into some trouble while he was here. Daddy had to ask him to leave. I hope he didn't give you any problems, Sister. I explained to Evian and to Franklin's father that he will not be asked back. There are limits, you know, to how much one can take!"

Why Miss keep saying "one?" I don't never see her act like this before. So confident and directed. Usually she just wander around, sort of, like she don't know what to do next. I just tune out when she mention Blister. I ain't prepare to think or talk about him with Miss. "Yes. You have a good time, and drive safe. Maybe I have something special for you when you get back."

"No-no! No more sweets for me for a while. I had trouble getting into this skirt this morning. I need to watch it now. Let me run, before I get there and Willie-Mae has taken and left! Bye-Bye!" And she flutter out the door and drive away.

No sweets, huh? Miss must be serious about this new fella. Glad to see it though. Something about a woman change when she got a man. I think about how true that is with me and Ev. I say I don't feel different, but in some ways I do. Like something inside me is fresh at having met him.

Speak of the devil. Who come walking in the kitchen with no shirt on and baggy jeans, barefoot. Got a big smile on his face, hair all over his head like wild grass? Ev. I chuckle to myself. And this the man who I think I may love?

He grab me around the waist and lift me off the ground. Plant wet, sloppy kisses all over my face, taste like Crest toothpaste. "Sissy! Thought you was never coming around here again! Thought me and Norman must have run you off for good." He collect up all my hair in his hands when he put me down, and he press his face against my neck. "Mmmm." He whisper. "You smell good. You miss me?"

His fingers feel like hot stones rolling down my back. I feel so warm when he touch me. And at the back of my knees. I can't think quick enough to say something smart like I usually do. When I see him, I just want to be close, real close, and hear him breathe. "Yes. I miss you." I put my arms around his neck and pull him closer to me.

He lean me against the back of the sink, rest his hands on either side of me. He just rubbing his cheek against my face, and neither of us say anything for a minute. When he close to me like that, and we don't say nothing, just listen to the breath rush out from both of us, I *know*. It don't make sense, and I can't explain it, but I just *know*. I look at his eyes, and I see them run over warm, and I know that he know, too.

"Yes. Absolutely. I agree with you wholeheartedly, Sugar." He put his hands on my shoulders and smile a little.

"What? You miss me, too? That what you agree with?"

"Yes, I do. But that's not what I meant. Yes, to the other stuff." He got that look like when he wanna bring my attention to something.

"What other stuff, Ev?"

"You know. All the stuff you were thinking and feeling just now. Me, too. That's what I mean." But then he stop talking. Seem like words can make things thin out. Sometimes it seem better to be quiet. "Yeah, so, what's on the agenda today? I gotta plan. You ever been to the lake? I think we better go to the lake today." He move away from me and reach in the cabinet for a glass. I feel sorry to let him go.

"Please! I done live here all my life, and you think I never been to the lake? Evian, I grew up on that lake!"

"No, not this part of the lake. I gotta take you to this one particular spot, and I gotta take you there today. Right this minute. So run on in my room and get you a shirt to change into. I expect that the one you're wearing will get wet. Just a feeling. And then come on out to the car." He gulp down the orange juice he pour while he telling me this crazy plan, and then he head for the back door.

"What?! I gotta work, Ev. I got cleaning to do. And I ain't plan to go to no lake..."

Ev cut me off. "Ahh-ahh-ahh-poo! Go get the shirt, and let's go. Right away!" He wink at me and slam the door. I stand there for a minute, shock. I see him start up the car, turn the radio up loud. He reach for something in the back seat, and I see he putting on a shirt. I think for a minute, then I run and get me a shirt. I take the one that say, "Anti violence. Not Anti violets." Whatever that mean. It smell like bleach, the way I like it. I roll it in a ball and run out to the car.

I don't never drive with Ev before. He got this Chevrolet from his dead daddy, and he say he don't drive it much. His mama hardly let him go out. But these days, since he feeling better all the time, he use it more and more. It got an 8-track tape player inside. He got two tapes. One with a bunch of people you never heard of singing other people songs. The other Mahalia Jackson. You know I gotta say something about that.

"You like her, too? Pammie crazy for her! What song you like off here? Do it got *Heaven*? She can sing that song!" I can't believe I'm driving down the road, in the front seat of Ev daddy car, listening to Mahalia.

Ev tell me he get this tape from Norman. He don't listen to it except when he in the car. Can't play it in the house, so that how come I don't know he like Mahalia. He say he use to go to the lake all the time before they move. And now that he back around this way, he try to go there whenever he can.

Sometime he walk if he don't think Miss would let him drive. It far, though, almost four miles, and he get tired these days. So now he just drive there.

He got a special place, though. You gotta walk out the path and back behind some trees to get there. Then the grass get real thick and green, and it only a few trees now and again. And just a few steps more, there a big rock and another tree, and that where we end up. If you sit on that rock and face the water, you can see clear over to the other side, the part that face the next county. You can see them, but don't look like they could see you. And the water is so blue back there. Deep and dark blue. You could sit on the grass, near the water, or move back in the middle of this clear, green space, and it seem like the whole world is far away.

Ev brought his guitar and a notebook. He got a satchel full of color pens and pencils and chalk. He call it his ditty bag. When he hike back to this place, I take off my shoes and let them dangle from my fingers. He got his guitar strap slug around his shoulder, and the guitar keep slapping his back as he walk. If we step on a stone or over a stick, you can hear the strings vibrate and make a jangle chord.

I'm busy thinking about this place, how green and soft it look, and I notice Ev start to breathe hard. I take the guitar off his back, and we sit down, right in the middle of the clear, green place that Evian brought me to, special. Behind the big rock. Away from the water. Evian put his paper and his bag down. He catch his breath. Breathe in real deep, exhale long and hard. When he start to sweat, I wipe it off his brow with my hand. This make him smile.

"You got any blue pencils in there? I might would draw something, if I had some blue pencils." I reach for this bag and dig around. But Evian surprise me and snatch it out my hands.

"Wait! Don't go rooting around in there, Sister-God!" When he yank the bag away, some of the pens and color pencils fall out. And then I see what he don't want me to see. Fat sack of green and papers. Toke stone, clip, and a box of rosewood matches.

I start to giggle. Then I stop. Go in a different direction. I scrunch my eyebrow down and turn down my lips. "Evian Mandarene! What chou got in here?! All this time I'm thinking you a gentleman, a nice boy, and look!

You a stoner, aint chou?! I knew this was too good to be true!" I push the green sack away like poison and cross my arms in front of my chest. When he try to look at me, I turn away quick, so I don't laugh.

"Oh, Lord. Sissy, listen. You don't understand. When I get sick, I get really, really sick, and then I don't wanna eat, and...well...it's a really bad scene. I know you won't believe me, but this stuff is medicine for me. Really. Even my mama sanctions my using it." He quick collecting up the pens and his other stuff and put them back in his sack.

Sanctions? I was just doing it for a joke, but I forget that he get so sick, and now it don't seem funny no more. "Oh, Ev. I don't mean it. I don't care about that stuff, really. I done it myself sometime, over to Pammie house. I ain't much for it, but if it make you feel better when you sick, then I guess it ain't so bad. Do it really help?" I never knew it could help with, you know, cancer.

Evian tell me how the chemo make him throw up and how he can't eat and feel dizzy. He say it help in those times, but it also make him sleepy. I don't like to hear him talk about when he get sick.

"Sissy. I been feeling okay for a while. But I gotta say it. I don't know what will happen, you know? I am in remission right now. I pray to God that it stays that way. But if it doesn't, well, I want you to know..." He looking at me so serious, and what do remission mean, and I don't want to think about him being sick.

"Let's don't talk about it. You got mad, remember? And you took back yourself. And it's all there is to that!" I wanna change the subject.

"Yes. But, just like there's a part of Blister you can't get rid of, and I know it's true, because I can feel you, there's a part of this that maybe I can't get rid of, too. I mean, I can get mad enough to live, but I can't keep it from making me die. But I want you to know, I meant what I said the other day." He take my hands inside of his. "I meant it when I said that I love you. I knew it right away, from the first time I heard you in the bathroom singing to Tammi Tyrell. It felt like something was plugged in and turned on when I heard you in there. And that way you blow the hair out of your face when you work. I loved you right away, even then. And I always will." He rub the back of my hands with his thumbs.

What I'm sposed to say to that? The same thing, I guess. "I love you, too, Evian." So, we stare at each other like simple fools for a few minutes, and then Evian jump up and take off his shirt.

"Who wants to go swimming?!" He stand on that rock, and then he dive in. I look at him from the very edge, but I don't get in. I don't like to get in the lake. It got bugs and animals and stuff I don't want to be bothered with. But Ev swim around and splash and make it look like so much fun. I roll up my jeans and wade out a little. Not too far. Ev come up behind me and splash my face, but I don't get mad. After while, we get out. Just my feet and a little of my pants is wet, but Evian soaked. He strip down to his undershorts, and he put his pants on the rock to dry.

CHAPTER TWENTY-ONE

I wish we had a blanket, because I don't like to sit in the grass too long. Stuff start to bite you, and then you think about critters too much. But even the thought of critters don't make me want to leave from beside Evian, next to the lake, in this clear green space. He stretch out and put his head in my lap, so sweet. He got his foot prop up on his knee.

"So, what you do when you was little? I bet you was a mischievous thing!" I'm busy making parts in his red hair with my fingers. Close the part up and then quick make another.

Evian tell me about when he was in elementary school and he don't want to take gym. He say he was real pale and skinny, and sometime he get sick back then, too. Not like now, but sick just the same. And he never want to play soccer or freeze tag, because he get winded too easy, and then they get mad at him. I tell him how I can't catch the ball to save my life when we play basketball. Always miss. But I can dribble and shoot to this day. Wouldn't know it, though, cuz I can't catch the ball when we play. They don't bother to throw the ball to me, cuz I never will catch it. I get scared just before it reach my hands and drop it.

"Yes, so you and me will never be great athletes, huh? Can you imagine the kids we'd give birth to? Little klutzes that can't catch balls and get winded when they run. We could have a whole team of them—can you imagine? What a ruckous they would cause during PE!" He laugh to think of it.

"No, they wouldn't make a great team, but I bet you they could sing!

They be like the Jackson Five! You could teach them to play the guitar and all that, and I could write they songs. And teach them to dance! You couldn't do that, I bet, cuz everybody know white folks can't dance!"

Ev take offense. "You don't believe all that stereotypical bullshit do you? I got moves you never even seen, Sister! Make Jackie and James look silly!" He jump up and do this slide in his bare feet, wiggle his skinny bottom and spin around. He ain't too bad at it, neither.

"Well, wonders never cease! Let me find out that you can dance!" I start to hum, and Evian dance some more. Look like he practice this for a long time, like he been waiting to show somebody he can dance. I don't mind being his first audience.

"Lotta stuff you don't know about me, Sister, and you gonna find out. But, I been meaning to say something to you. About Mama. We gonna have to say something to her soon."

Oh, Lord. I knew this was coming.

"She loves you, Sister. And she knows you are good for me. And I don't want to slip around like we're doing something wrong, because we aren't. I wanna tell her about you. About us. What do you think?"

I close my eyes for a minute and breathe. Us? What us? I mean, I don't think of this thing me and Ev do, spending time and all, as "us." Shoot, we only been...whatever we been, for a little more than a week. Technically. Unless you count how he say he love me right away. In that case, it really been a few months.

"Evian. Let's wait, okay? Give me some time to...to...think. I don't know about all this, hear? I mean, I don't want to cause no trouble. Can we just wait?"

He don't seem too particular for this idea, but he agree to it, for me. Then he change the subject. He say he read where some folks been meeting every week at this old church downtown. Only it ain't a church no more because they got a new sanctuary last fall. He say they talk about politics, and government, and civil rights, and music and other stuff he interested in. He say they mainly black, but he think that maybe there some white folks there, too. And he want us to go round to one of the meetings. He say I can at least do that for him, since I don't wanna say nothing about us to his mama, since I act like I'm shamed of how much we in love. So, I don't think I can say no, and I agree to go. He say he will find out when is the next time they meet, and then we will ride out there together.

We been out there a long time, in this special spot at the lake, and I feel like we need to head back. I am hungry, and I need to get my work done before Miss get home. In the car, I sit real close to Ev, and we keep the windows down. His pants ain't completely dry, so he squish on the leather seat when he move next to me. In front of the house, he kiss me long and slow, tongue making wet circles around my own, and then he open the door for me. He say he working on a picture he want to get done, and he go on back to his room. I tell him I check on him before I go home, make sure he ain't forget about me, but he say he never would forget about me, even if I don't check, but he want me to check just the same.

I'm in the kitchen scrubbing down the cabinets when Norman come in. Miss like me to take a bleach wash and wash them down every other week. Her cabinets white, but they old, see, and if you don't keep them real clean, they look mighty dingy and yellow. I think she need to repaint them, for real, cuz the bleach wash only help but so much. But she ask me to do it, and I don't complain. Norman got a cigarette pack roll into his shirt sleeve, and he going out the back door.

"Afternoon, Sister. Evian take you round to the lake today? Bet he did, if I know my grandson. Does him some good to be out there, specially when it's warm out. Enjoy yourself?" He stop for a minute before he open the door.

I feel a trick. What I'm sposed to say? Admit that I been running around with Ev when I'm sposed to be at work? Lie and say I don't know what he talking about? I choose neither. "The lake is a nice place. I'm making croquettes for dinner today. You planning on coming back?" This way he can't say I lie, and I don't admit to it, neither.

"Mmmm-hmm. Make a plenty, Sister. I feel a big appetite setting in. I will be back—set a place for old Norman, because I won't want to miss it. What you got with it, Sister? Don't want to make any special request, but let's just say I hope it's okra. I'll be back presently." Norman shuffle out the door, unroll his sleeve when he get to the driveway. He walk to the bottom, look right and left, then he start walking slow to the left, toward the field and my house.

Okra. I don't think much of okra. Hard to work with, cuz it got this slimy film on it. You gotta batter it before you can fry it, and it take a lot of time. Oh well. Least I can do is make this man some okra, seeing as how he don't seem to care that I took up with his grandson. Two different skillets, two different sets of grease, and a pain in the neck, but I'll do it. Least I don't have to bake today, since Miss claim she watching herself for this new Griffin Howard.

Close to 4, and I done the cabinets, clean the bathrooms, and vacuum in the formal living room. Bout ready to head on home. I set three plates down on the counter and some water glasses. Silver for three, and cloth napkins. Miss like to use matching cloth napkins at dinner. I set the table and put the croquettes on top of the stove, uncovered. If you cover them while they still hot, they get soft, and Miss like to have them crisp. Me, too. But I put the okra in the oven on warm. I hope they come in soon, cuz otherwise everything be cold. The iced tea in the fridge. They can pour the ice in and serve it theyselves. No sense in to put it out and let it get warm.

Bout this time, Norman storm into the kitchen from outside. He got a wild look in his eye.

"They burn me up! Always with their balls and their sticks and whatever the hell else—who needs them? The whole lot of them are crazy, disrespectful hooligans! I told that woman, you keep your crazy youngins out of my way, or there will be trouble. I promise you that! Can't so much as stop to say good afternoon while they're busy ripping up my bushes and messing with Cordial's flowers." He drop his cigarettes on the counter and wash his hands in the sink. "Cussing like sailors! Who needs it, Sister? Who needs it?" He dries his hands on the towel I hang on the stove, but he fling it on the counter when he get done. He shake hisself like he want to get rid of cobwebs or something nasty fell over him.

"What you fretting about? Those Wilson kids messing up the yard again? I done told them about it myself. They hard-headed." Which is true, but they don't make me so angry. I just run and tell they mama to mind her children, that Norman will get after them if they don't stop. Usually that all I have to say about it. Maybe I feel different if it was my bushes and stuff.

"Lord have mercy, Sister. They trouble me so. It's their whole demeanor, you see. Their very countenance is disrespectful. They show it in their shoulders, in their backbones. It unnerves me! You don't go rooting around in others' greenery, for one thing. But even if you do, you show some respect when you're approached by an elder. Say you're sorry, and mean it. These hooligans, they just laugh and snicker and keep at it until you threaten to tell their mama. But, I can expect, from their behavior, that this woman is just as bad as they. Enough to make a man hungry, very hungry!" Norman get a plate from the counter and fix it up with plenty. Two croquettes, mess of okra, healthy portion of corn, and a big glass of iced tea.

When Norman sit down to the table, he bow his head and move his lips for a long time, like he got a lot to say to the Lord. He shake his head and rock a little, too. By time he say amen, his body change. He look more calm and relax, like his usual self. He take a big swig of tea and smile.

"Ooh-wee! What did you do to this tea, Sister? It's just perfect- perfect! Not too sweet, not too strong." He sip some more.

"That there is sun tea. My grannie taught me to make it. You brew it and let it sit out in the sun in a glass jar, good long time. Let it cool down to room temperature before you add the sugar. Something bout the sun and the glass make it taste just right. Glad you like it." Now I smile, too. The way Norman carry on about my cooking and all make me feel good. "You enjoy it. I tell Evian that dinner on, maybe he come out and eat with you. I'm fitting to go home." I walk back to Ev room.

I knock before coming in. I hear him put some stuff away, open drawers, before he say come in. He at his desk, and he still got his colors out. Got the lamp pull down close to the table, like he been working on something with details.

"Hey, baby. Figured it was you. Guess you're all done, ready to go home now, huh?" He turn around at his desk chair to look at me.

I explain that I make croquettes what's done and on the stove, and maybe he like to go eat with his grandaddy, keep him company. His mama still ain't home yet. He ask me to stay and eat with them, but I say I rather go home and eat with Mama and the others. I sit on his lap for a minute and tell him I like to go to the lake with him, and I like to see how he could dance. He laugh and say we gonna go somewhere sometime where he can really show off his moves. I'm fixing to go, got my hand on the door, when he tell me about the meeting.

"Oh, Sissy. We going to that meeting tomorrow? Down at the old church? They say it starts at 7, but lots of time people don't really show up until 8. They plan rallies and other protests, and sometimes they meet on campus at U.K. They have guest speakers and all kinds of stuff. They are really trying to do something positive, in terms of social change. I been hearing about it for a while, and now I know I have to get involved. You're in, right?" He say it like more of an answer than a question. And really I already promise him, so I say yes. He say we go on over after I get done tomorrow. He gonna pick me up in the car.

"Uh, Ev. Why don't I meet you over here? Then we go round there together." I don't know how I explain it if he come to my house and want me to go with him in the car.

"You're being ridiculous. It's one thing not to tell them that we are seeing each other, but I think you're being overly cautious here about us being friends. It's okay for us to be friends, Sissy. They can't stop us from doing that!" He talk kind of impatient, like I wear on his nerves.

But I don't give in. Mama won't buy that we just friends, and I'm going to some new meeting been around a while and ain't never show no interest in before. So we compromise. He walk over and meet me at the back door. Then we walk back to his house together and go. I figure out what I tell Mama about where I went later. I hug him again before I go. But he keep me from leaving again.

"Oh, another thing. Mama is pressing me about getting somebody to keep the yard. Didn't you say you knew somebody who might be interested? Long as we've been here, I still don't know too many people, and neither does she."

"Yes, I do. Pammie brother, Edward, he may be looking to work. I call

Pam when I get home and tell him what you say. Miss will want to meet him, won't she? Or do you think she want him to call, or should she take the number and call him?"

"Umm. I guess he can call her, let them work it out. Let me know what he says, and I'll tell Mama to expect the call."

I got the door open and ready to walk out, when he stop me again.

"One last thing, Sister. I love you."

I close the door again before I tell him that I love him, too.

CHAPTER TWENTY-TWO

"So, how'd it go? Miss White Folks come after you with a gun?" Pammie her usual playful self. I call her when I get home, see what she got into that day.

"Nah. Not yet. I don't say nothing to her. Although Ev say he want to. Pammie, he keep pressing me about it, too, like he think he die if his mama don't know what we doing."

"More like *she* die if she knew. She seem like she suspect anything?"

"No. I do hate this sneaking, though. It seem deceitful. But Ev and me went round to the lake today. He show me this special spot—real pretty. Girl, he so sweet to me! I wish you knew him, Pam. You would like him. Do you know he listen to Mahalia Jackson? Got a tape of hers in his car. He know all the words, but he sound silly singing it. Nobody sing like her, really."

"Mahalia? Really? My girl! Well, y'all keep up with this, and maybe I get the chance to know him. You seen Albert today?" Would know she ask me about him. I tell her I ain't my brother's keeper, and she probably know more about where he go than me, anyway. Then I remember about Miss and the yard work.

"Miss say she need somebody to keep her yard again. Will you tell Edward, so's he can call her? Be nice to have him around there some days."

"I'm sick of y'all with these fancy jobs and do! Don't nobody ask me do I want a job, and do I want to make some money. All this stuff I do around here, and Mama barely give me nothing. I'm thinking of going downtown, see if I can find me some work, too." She go on with her complaints and threats to work, but Pammie ain't for real. She like keeping house, and she like getting up and do it when she feel like it. Ain't nobody gonna pay Pam to sleep in til noon at a real job and make her any kinda clothes she want, like her Mama do. Plus a little piece of change every week, too.

I wanna tell Pam about this meeting me and Ev going to, but I don't know how. She seem so nervous about me and Ev and all. But I tell her anyway. "What you heard about that group been meeting round to the old church? Anything? Seem like they plan revolts or something. Anyway, Ev say they do a lot of good work and stuff, and he ask me to go with him sometime and check it out." I act casual, like I always go to revolts with white boys.

Pam don't sound too surprise. "Yes, I hear about it. Edward and them been going over there for a while. They the ones hosted when Newton was in town last year. They make a lot of booklets they be passing out on campus and stuff. They tryin' to start a breakfast program at the elementary school, too. They seem all right. You going?"

"Yea, Imma go, I guess. You think Edward be there? What if he see me and Ev?" He so militant these days, I don't know. One thing for him to work in the yard—I can just act like Ev somebody I work for. But if he see me at the church…

She say I have to worry about that myself. She say I should have thought of that before I start to sleep with him. She say Edward talk a lot of trash, but he not as hard as he pretend to be. I give her Miss number to give to Edward, and she say she wanna go eat. I do, too. Mama making chicken, and I like mines hot.

Seem like the whole family got fried chicken radar. When Mama cook chicken, all of us show up, right on time, at the dinner table. Kita only eat drumsticks, and Timmie only eat wings. Don't think Mama and Albert care much what piece they get, as long as they get some, but me and Ruthanne fight over the back. Best piece in the world, the back. Tonight she make corn muffins and string beans. All this sneaking and cleaning around to Evian house done made me hungry. I come to the table ready to throw down.

We at the table together for the first time in a few days. Albert say grace.

He go on and on, too, while the chicken getting cold. Seem like he got a lot to be thankful for. Wonder how much this gratefulness have to do with Pam.

Ruty got on a new dress she just make. It got a black background, white dots, and yellow flowers on it. The neckline square and trim in pink. It sound worse than it look, with all those colors. Really, she look cute. It real short, too, barely cover the top of her legs. She got her hair press straight and curl under. Yes, she cute. But she know it. Days like this, Ruty wanna put on airs at the table. She eat her chicken with a knife and fork. Please.

Timmie like to fill up on Kool-Aid before he finish his dinner. But Mama tell him he can't have no more til he finish all his string beans. He gotta whine about that. "Aw, man! How you gonna do me? I been playing in the hot sun for two hours, Ma! I'm thirsty!"

"Then you drink you some water til you finish your vegetables. You ain't drinking no more of this punch until they all gone. What you do at camp today?" Mama break up her muffins in a bowl with too much butter and eat it with a spoon.

"Kick ball. I was on Kevin team with Darryl. You remember him? He come and stay every summer with his cousin. He can play good, better than Kevin, really. And they barbecue today, too. Hot dogs today. No hamburgers." Timmie burp loud and don't say excuse me.

"Excuse you! Do Kevin brother still work around there? He usually run the grill and clean. He is sooo fine!" Ruthanne got a one-track mind.

Mama sound surprise at Ruty. "That'll be the day when little old Jarvis Lincoln is fine! Wasn't too long ago his mama campaigned like the president to make sure he got the Precious Baby Award at church. Shameful how she carry on over that child, asking for donations so that her baby would win. Bless his heart—he was a cute little thing back then. Now they tell me he fine! Ha ha ha!"

Albert eat his chicken, but he look serious. "Y'all remember that incident that happen at Kent State last year? Where they was protesting the war, and some of them got killed? Something like it happen at Mississippi State, too. Anyhow, they never did press charges against the National Guardsmen that did it. Dismissed it, or some mess, cuz of a lack of evidence. Well, we been thinking about that. We don't like the way that officers and police is allowed to treat us whenever they feel like it. We planning to organize a protest at U.K. sometime soon." Albert don't look at none of us when he say this. He look at his chicken and at his hands.

Mama clear her throat. She clear her throat when she about to say something her children don't want to hear. "Naw, naw! No protests. I done seen enough and done heard enough to know that it ain't no use in to protest. End up dead, like those four children in Ohio. Lord have mercy! Naw, Albert. You need to rethink this one." She shake her head and drink some punch.

Me and Ruthanne get quiet. Timmie finish his string beans and pour him some more punch.

"I done made up my mind, Mama. Malcolm say we the only ones with the chance for a bloodless revolution. Martin say we can be peaceful *and* be disobedient. I say, we don't want no blood shed, but it shed already, and it always ours what's shed. I gotta go do this, Mama. Maybe it help. And anyhow, it don't always end up bad, you know." He look her in the eye now, like he mean what he say.

"Where Malcolm at? Dead! Where Martin at—bless his soul? Dead! Left a mountain of beaten-down Negroes and books and philosophies between 'em, and for what? For what? So's we can eat and pee together? Have mercy! White folks don't want to be bothered with us. Folks' hearts got to change first, Albert. Can't no change come in the world until folks' hearts change, and that take time. No protest in the world gonna soften a racist heart, you hear? What you planning to do, anyhow?" I can tell she argue now more for her point than to keep him from going. Much as she talk like that about Martin, deep down she hope that what he say will work one day, even down here in Kentucky.

"A bunch of us is going down to the Student Affairs building and sit in. We making signs and stuff. Police brutality, Ma. These county cops are notorious for it. They find any reason they can to bash our heads in. You heard about Virg, right? Got picked up again downtown, say he was disturbing the peace. Next thing you know, when his uncle pick him up, he got a broken jaw and a dislocated shoulder. Ma, Virg ain't the only one, neither. I got a list a mile long I could tell you of folks got beat up by the ones what sposed to be protecting us. It ain't right. It just ain't right."

"Virgyl from East End? William Taylor's boy? Lord have mercy! When was all this?" Mama know Virg daddy from school; they grow up together. He left Virg mama years ago, and he run around on her, too.

"Two nights ago. He got his mouth wire shut and wear a brace. We can't change what they do to Virg, but we may be able to change what they do next time, if we can call attention to it. So, we wanna organize this thing soon, and see what we can do."

"*We*? What is all this *we*? Who you talkin' bout, anyhow?" Mama start to clear off the table. She always start to clear the table before we even all the way done. She don't like a mess.

"The CFPSC. Citizens For Positive Social Change. Meet around to the old church some evenings. We almost fifty folks strong, now, and still growing."

Now I see. He been going to those meetings Ev tell me about. He go on about this with Mama, and she say she don't mind if he go, but he better mind that he be careful. Don't sass nobody, and let well enough alone if the police come. No sense in him to end up like Virg, she say. Won't do nobody no good.

Kita start to fuss, then throw her muffin on the floor and scream to get out the highchair. Timmie say he wanna see a Western about to come on. Ruthanne ask me if I keep Nakita for a while so she can go round to Beverly house. They making they dresses together for the dance next week. I say I will, but she better not be out too late, cuz I bought this book I'm reading call *Love Story*. I sure can't read while I'm watching Kita. She don't let you do nothing that take attention away from her too long.

I ask Mama do she want help in the kitchen, but she say she don't. She shoo me out and say take Kita with me. Albert, me, and Kita go out to the living room. But Timmie in there with the TV on, so we decide to go out on the porch. Me and Nakita in the swing, and Albert sit on the step and smoke. Since when do he smoke?

"Albert, you a mess! Since when do you smoke? You act so grown!" I ask him, but I ain't really too surprise. All his friends been smoking since last summer.

"Yea. Bad habit. I don't do it too much." He flick the ashes out into the grass.

This news about Virg concern me, and about Albert and the CFPSC. I decide, real quick, I wanna tell Albert about me and Ev. "Say, Albert. I'm sorry to hear about Virg. This happen after that mess over on Limestone? How do he disturb the peace this time?"

Albert shake his head. "Girl, I don't know. He say he was hitching home cuz his ride left him, and they pick him up. They remember him as the one cause some trouble before, and they beat him up. They don't take him downtown at all this time, just beat him up. A shame. What's to stop them from doing the same thing to me, or to anybody around here?" Albert voice get deep and low when he mad, like if you add a drop of acid to it, it would blow you up.

"Mmm. Been wanting to tell you something. You know I been working round to the Madarenes', right? Well, they got a son name Evian, and umm. Well, we getting to be good friends." I leave it at that for now, see what his reaction will be.

He whip around to see my face, see if I'm for real. "*Friends?* Believe me, Sister. That white boy ain't none of your *friend.* He probably act nice to you cuz you clean up his shit and cook his food, but everybody who act nice to your face ain't your friend, Sister. Believe that."

"Maybe, but you may be wrong about Evian. He really do like me. For real. Matter fact, he ask me to go with him to that meeting you talk about to Mama. I know you meet at the church, and I know you have a meeting tomorrow night. Me and Ev coming to the meeting, too..." I feel contrary now that he talk mean about Evian. He don't know Evian the way I do.

"What?! What he coming to our meeting for? Last thing we need is some white boy wannabe liberal infiltrating at our meetings. You can just tell him he ain't welcome. Now, if *you* down with the cause, it's a different story. But your white buddy ain't welcome." Albert stand up and stamp out his cigarette. He put the butt inside the pack, put the pack in his pocket.

"Ev say sometime white folks come to these meetings, too. And *he* the one down with the your cause. I wouldn't even of known about it cept for him. How you gonna keep him from coming when other white people come?" His anger strike me strange and make me mad, too.

"Guess I can't. I don't trust the white ones who come round there, either, and if it were up to me, they wouldn't be welcome at the meetings. But brothers is split about this issue. They say some white faces may lend some credibility to our protests. They say they know more about U.K., too, since they run that school. Alls we do is play ball over there. All I know is no sister of mine is showing up to this meeting with a white dude. You make your choice. If you coming in there with, what you say his name is? Ed? Then you don't know me! Don't even try talking to me while you there, cuz I be ig'in you big time. You make a choice, Sister. Will you see me there or not?"

"Yes, Albert, I will see *you* there. Question is, will *you* see *me*? Because I am coming with Evian. We down with this cause, too." Listen at me saying "we." I guess Ev was right. We is an "us" after all.

CHAPTER TWENTY-THREE

I'm putting Nakita in the bed when the phone ring. I turn out her light and run and get the phone. Probably Pam, got something she forgot to tell me when I talk to her before. I remember when we was in high school, we use to talk on the phone non-stop. Soon as we get home. Soon as she leave my house, and soon as I leave hers. And don't let something happen on TV or with one of our friends at school! We likely to be on the phone all night, then.

But, when I get to the phone, it ain't Pam. "Say, Sugar. You sleep yet?" Ev. What he doing calling me on the phone?

"No, not yet. Just finish dinner and put my niece to bed." I don't say who it is out loud, cuz I don't want Mama to know. Even though she already in her room. I close the kitchen door so Timmie can't hear me talk, sit at the kitchen table. Still wet from where Mama wipe it down after dinner. I dry a space off with a napkin and put my elbow on the table.

"Where are you? I'm in my bedroom on my bed. Can you see me?" Evian talk sweet and slow. Make me tingle somewhere down low.

"No. I can see your room from me and Mama room. But not from here. I'm in the kitchen. What you doing?"

"Thinking of you, mostly. I miss you. What did you have for supper?"

I tell him about the chicken and all. He say he had some delicious croquettes somebody made up for him special. I say this someone must be mighty kind to cook him croquettes special. He say they just like he like them—crisp on the outside and soft on the inside. We talk about this show he seen where the girl get hit in the nose with a baseball and it swell up to twice it size. I tell him I bought a book at the drugstore I'm fixing to read. He say he come over and read it with me. I tell him he crazy. He ask me what the name of the book is, and when I tell him, he say he got that book, too. I think he joking, but then he tell me to hold on. Next thing you know, he reading me the first page over the phone.

Timmie come in and say he going to take his bath and go to bed, and I'm still at the table on the phone. Next thing, I run upstairs and get my book. Then I pull the phone in the living room and sit on the floor. We take turns reading to each other from *Love Story*. It about this couple live in the city. They in love, but after while she get sick, and he don't know what to do about it. Sometime they fight about the simplest things, but you could tell they really do like each other. When Ruthanne come in and see me on the phone with a book, she start to laugh. She say she must not have come home early enough, cuz I can't wait to read my book. She check on Nakita, and I stay on the phone, listen to Ev voice tell me the story of this couple live in a city I can't quite picture. But I can picture how much they must love each other. Because maybe they love each other like me and Ev.

"Sister, you still there? It's your turn to read." Evian speak in a whisper, almost, right in my ear. Sometime ago I stop hearing the words and just hear the soft sound tickle in my ear, like his tongue that first time we...You know.

"Oh. I got caught up in your voice, I guess. Sound so sweet to me. Evian, do you remember when we, umm, spent some time together last week?" I don't know what words to use for what we do that won't sound like I'm nasty to think of it.

"Honey, please! I think about it all the time. Really. All of the time. Is that what you were thinking about just now?"

"Well. Sort of. Mainly how you hold me and stuff after. I like that part."

"So you like to be in my arms, huh? I thought you were one of those cuddly types. It feels right, doesn't it?" You could barely hear Ev because he talk so soft.

"Yes. Very much. You smell like soap. And donuts. Warm donuts." I giggle.

"Donuts?! What did I do to smell like that? And here I thought I smell rugged and outdoorsy, and all the time I just smell like donuts? You're nuts! What kind?" He laughing, too.

"Honey glaze. My favorite kind."

"Mmm. Mine, too." Then somebody pick up the phone at Ev house. They listen for a minute, then hang up. Ev say, "I guess Mama wants to use the phone. I better hang up." Just as Ev say he love me, someone pick up the phone again. It Cordial.

"Ev-yun, who are you talking to at this hour? I thought I heard your voice." She sound suspicious. Ev say he talking with a friend and he about to hang up. I keep my mouth shut.

"So, I guess I'll talk to you tomorrow. Goodnite." Evian hang up the phone.

Oh, Lord. Wonder if she hear him say he love me? Wonder if she know who he talking to? But I don't want to think about that. I wanna think about how Ev read to me from this book, and how his voice sound low and raspy, like he whispering this story he thought up just for me. And how he got the same book as I do, and how he wanna read it with me over the phone. And how he like to hold me as much as I like to be held. And how he think about what we do all the time. All the time, he say. Me, too, Ev. Me, too.

CHAPTER TWENTY-FOUR

Next day, round to Ev house, Miss come in the library whiles I'm dusting. She sit down on the couch and act like she fitting to read this magazine. *Ladies Home Journal.* My mama read that sometime, too. Use to take it every month, back when Timmie youth group sell magazines to make money for they uniforms. They have a softball team, but they don't play so good. But Miss just thumb through the pages, never really stop to look at none of them. I speak to her when she come in, but I keep working, act like she not there. But she there, and she make me feel uneasy.

"Sister, did I ever tell you about Ev-yun's illness? We don't like to talk on it much, but you been with us a while. You might as well know. Ev-yun has cancer." She pause for a minute, like she drop me with this news. Like he don't already tell me about it his self weeks ago.

I stop in my tracks, act like I'm shock to hear. In a way, I am shock. I try not to think about Ev and how he get sick. "Lord, Miss. That seem serious." I face her, out of respect, but I don't look at her face none.

"Very serious. He is in what you call remission now. That means that the disease is no longer active in his body. Long about the time you first started here, Ev-yun had chemotherapy. Made him awful sick, but it seems to have worked. Now we just watch after him and pray that it doesn't come back. "

"Yes, Miss. I pray for him, too. Must be a terrible thing to have your son get sick."

"Sister, you just don't know! I thank you for your prayers, too. I know that they work. But Ev-yun, he's a special child. Been sick on and off since he was 6 years old. Then, you know he lost his daddy. And, well, it hasn't been easy for him. He's had a time of it—we all have. I hate to see him get hurt..." Lord have mercy, where she going with this? I take a respectful stance and stare at the floor, make sure she know I'm listening, but I still don't look at her.

"Bless your heart, Miss, I bet you have had a time..." I don't say nothing about how she don't want Ev to hurt.

"Ev-yun doesn't know a lot of young folks here, and I expect he gets lonely. You and my son about the same age, too. I suppose that's why he is so fond of you, talking with you all the time. I'm quite sure he doesn't mean anything by it. Quite sure..." She look at me funny, now, like she want me to agree. I don't say nothing.

"Yes, so, you are very valuable to us here, Sissy. I am glad that Ev-yun took a liking to you. May do him some good. He doesn't have a lot of, what you call, outside contact. Very naïve, my son is. Ev-yun may never get to have a...well...normal life, so to speak. How awkward! Thank you for taking a special interest in my son, Sister. At least until he can find some real friends his own...well, you know. Thank you kindly." Miss say this like she not really all that glad I got what she call a "special interest" in Ev. And what do she mean when she say "real friends?"

"Yes, I like Evian, and I am glad to be his real friend, too. I think he be all right, Miss. I really do." I turn and start to straighten the magazines on the bookshelf. I don't know what else to say.

"Of course. I suppose I should call Willie-Mae. She will want to know what became of me and Mr. Howard yesterday. I'll just get out of your way." Miss leave the magazine she thumb through on the couch and leave the den.

I pretend like I drop something near the door and close it "by accident." Really I don't want Miss to see me cry. What she mean, she don't want Ev to get hurt? Do she think I intend to hurt Ev? And what about how she claim I ain't his real friend? Like he only like me cuz he don't know nobody else. But, maybe she right. He *don't* know nobody else—he say so hisself other day when he ask for Edward to come and do the yard. Really, I ain't upset by what Miss say. I just ain't particular for what she *don't* say. She don't talk like she glad me and Ev is friends. She talk like she think Ev too sick or too stupid to take up with somebody better than me. Should have known Miss wouldn't be glad that me and Ev is friends.

But I get sick to death of crying. Cry over Blister and how he hate me. Cry over Miss and how she don't *sanction* for me and Ev, like she sanction for him to smoke corn when he sick. Well, then she don't have to know what we do. I sure ain't planning to tell her no way soon.

I'm about to turn on the vacuum when I hear the phone ring. Miss talk in a high-pitch voice, like she just hear the very best news. Then she say, "Well, that'll be just fine. Thursday, unless something special needs to be done. Fabulous!" And I hear her hang the phone up. Next thing I know, she knock on the den door and come in.

"Sister! That was your friend, Edward. He says you recommended him for doing yard work! How thoughtful of you to remember! I've arranged for him to come by on Thursdays to mow the lawn and whatever else. Isn't this nice? Now you'll have one of your own...another friend here to talk to some days!" (So you don't have to mess with my son?!)

"Glad you can use his help, Miss. I guess I see him around here tomorrow." I plug in the sweeper, so if she say something else, I don't hear. I keep a wide grin on my face, though, so she know I don't mean her disrespect.

When I get done in the den, Miss take Norman out to the doctor. Norman funny when he go with Miss. He make a production of it, like he going to see the queen, or something. For one thing, he don't never wear his jeans or coveralls, like he usually do. He get dress in a suit and a tie. He shine his shoes before he go, too, and wear aftershave. Sometime Miss take him visiting after they get done. Evian say he don't have many friends left. Most of them dead. But he got a lady friend name Hester he like to stop in and see. And another man name Jud Tate who known him since "the old days." Whenever that was. He always seem so happy to go—never seen somebody so dress just to see the doctor and an old friend. Miss take her crochet needles and yarn with her, so I know they be gone a while.

I got the vacuum drag behind me and about to do the hallway when I hear Ev call from his room. When I open his door, he stretch out on the foot of the bed with his feet on the headboard. I sit down next to him.

"Hey, Sister. I thought you were ignoring me. You been here two hours and haven't been in here yet." He rub my back with slow, circle strokes, while he talk to me.

"Your mama say that you got cancer and act naïve. She say she be glad when you make some real friends and don't have to bother with me." I almost start to cry when I say this to him, like everything she say in the den all rush back and come down in my eyes. I don't know what make me act so simple, but I can't help it.

"What?! Sister, what are you saying? Did my mama ask you about us, or something? What happened?" He on his knees next to me, and he put his arms around my shoulder.

I explain how she say he been sick and been through it, how she say he don't have no real friends and all. How it don't seem like she want me to mess with him. But I make sure he know I don't tell her nothing about... whatever we been doing.

"Oh, Sugar, is that all? That's nothing to get upset about! I told you, Mama is kind of backwards in her ways, but she doesn't mean anything by it. In her own way, she is probably really glad that you and I are such good friends. Really."

"Then, how come she say I ain't your real friend? And why she so glad to have Edward come on Thursdays?" I wanna believe what he say true, but I can't.

Evian put his hands on either side of my face, pull it close to his. "Listen. Mama has some things to learn, I'm sure. But she will get used to the idea of you and me. She hasn't got a choice. Sister, I can't promise you that we won't get any hassle for being together, but I can promise you that it will be worth it. You're gonna have to toughen up that sensitive skin of yours." He kiss my nose, my forehead, and both my cheeks. Then he put his hands inside mine. "We're in this thing together, okay? It's gonna be all right."

By the time Evian hop off the bed, I feel a little better. He rush over to the closet and ask me what should he wear to the meeting tonight. I say just wear some jeans and a T-shirt, and when he look in his drawer for socks, he start to cough. He cough for a long time, real deep, like it come from deep inside his stomach. I don't say nothing until he stop. "You getting a cold, Evian?" But it don't sound like no cold to me.

"You know me! I'm allergic to everything in the world. I probably just rubbed against something at the lake that I shouldn't have. Nothing to worry about."

All he rub against at the lake is me. So I don't worry. I tell him about how Albert go to these meetings, too, and Pammie brother, Edward. I tell him that I probably won't get a chance to talk to Albert since he be so busy planning for the protest and all. That way he don't think it strange when Albert don't talk to me. He say he anxious to meet my brother and Edward, especially since he coming and work in the yard. Then, I feel like I gotta say something about what Albert say to me before. "Know what, Ev? My brother crazy. He say he ain't for sure that you and me should...you know...be coming to this meeting together. He say he don't know you that well. But I tell him you and me is real close, and he say maybe he don't want to talk to me if...if I...if I show up with you." I don't want to hurt Evian. I know he thinking that we can all be friends, but, Albert, he see it another way. I gotta tell him.

"So, what did you say to him?" He look at me like he testing me for the right answer.

"What you think? I tell him we coming anyway, and if he don't like it, too bad!"

"Well," Evian say, "I guess I'll just have to win Albert over with my charm!" He slide to the side like James Brown. "And while I'm at it, I'll teach him some of my moves." He dance around me.

CHAPTER TWENTY-FIVE

Lucky for me, Mama take Timmie to get new sneakers, so she ain't home when I leave to meet Ev. Just before 7, I go out the back door and wait. He come walking up casual, and he got on jeans and a T-shirt say *Kentucky is for Thorobreds.* To me, he look cute. His hair growing long, and he brush it back off his face. Ev got real nice eyes, and he smile with his eyes when he look at me.

He take my hand when we walk across that field. We stroll together, real slow. Ain't no hurry. Ev say folks don't really start to come until 8 or so. I guess I should be nervous, going out for the first time with Ev, but something say don't. Seem like what this group do, I got enough to worry about if I get involved.

Really, we got a lot to worry about living round here. Virg and his jaw and his shoulder. Albert call it Police Brutality. Funny how he always give titles to stuff we never really put a name to before. Always been a fact around here that if you black, you got to be careful not to offend the cops. Grannie say just smile and play dumb. She say they wanna believe we dumb, so if we do something wrong, if we don't act smart, then they believe we don't know we do something wrong. In some ways she right. But, I know Virg. Use to sit behind me in algebra. Don't never do no work. Miss Simms always call him up to the board and make him work the problems up there. Then he cut up and act stupid, make us all laugh. He don't know no math, but he funny.

Seem to me that cops take Virg the wrong way. He just want attention. I know boys like him from school. They don't care what kind of attention. Like, even if they be in trouble, they like it, because it mean the teacher gotta pay them some mind. What they want is somebody to pay them some attention. Like Virg, he ain't never gonna get no attention for the work he do. He don't know no algebra, can't write and stuff. Nobody gonna single him out for that. So, for him, best thing he can do is make somebody laugh or act up. Then, sure enough, everybody look at him. Even the teacher. So, I feel bad for Virg. I ain't saying that the stuff he do, the way he act, is right, but don't seem like he should have to get beat for it, neither.

In the car, I tell Ev what I know about the CFPSC. About how they try to organize something around to U.K. About how Virg got beat up, and how Mama knew his daddy from before. I even tell him how Mama say ain't no sense in to protest since when you do somebody bound to get hurt. He listen close for a long time.

"I didn't know you had a vested interest in this group, Sister. But I'm glad you told me. You remember my cousin, Franklin? I hate to call his name, after...anyhow, his daddy was with the police force for years. He is a crazy son-of-a bitch. Tom Chasinger. I can remember staying out to their house a long time ago, before Daddy died. Blister was so proud of his daddy, like the sun just rose and set on that fool. He would come in wearing his uniform, all the shiny gold badges and the black shoes and the hat. Seemed real important. Blister always begged to go out with him, so's he could ride in the car and play with the radio and all."

"You ever go out with your uncle, Evian?"

Evian say he and Blister ride out with Tom Chasinger one night, and they get to sit in the front seat. He tell me how they go on a call out to Old Stream Farm where's a lady had her baby took from her. He say Tom Chasinger yell at the woman like she an animal, and all the time she crying cuz her baby got took. Then Mr. Chasinger shot the lady dog, since he yelping and whining, scared from all the confusion. He say, ever since then, he don't like to go round to Blister house, and he don't like Tom Chasinger. He say folks gets a badge sometime and think they God, and it ain't right.

"Yes. We got a problem down here, sure enough. May be that your mama is right. May be that we can't change a damn thing. But, like Pap says, if nothing changes, then nothing changes. Simple as that. You gotta start somewhere." Evian look out the window when he talk. I wish he take my hand, like he usually do, but he don't.

They ain't got no air conditioner at the old church. At my house, we got a unit in the window in the living room. We don't spose to turn it on lest it get really, really hot. Truth, most the time it don't work. Mama got a friend what put it in two summers past, and I don't think he charge her much to do it. Good thing, cuz it don't half work. But when it do work, and when Mama let us put it on, it really do help. I wish they had a window unit around to First Baptist. I like to burn up in there.

They got one fan to move the air around, but they so many of us in there that you can't barely feel it lest you sit right in front of it. They got two long tables up at the front, a few tall stacks of papers, a cup of pens, and a pad where you sposed to sign it. At the corner of one table, they got two pitchers of water and some yellow Dixie cups. I count fourteen cups, and I count twenty-six people. Look like somebody ain't gonna get a drink. But they got a water fountain in the hallway, if it still work. I plan to go get me some from there if the cups run out.

I recognize some of the faces when we walk in. Bishop Wheeler. His father the Pastor at the new sanctuary. He up front with a short, light girl got her hair in a flip. She use to live around my way. Think her name Bernadine. Wonder how she get her hair to stay up like that. I say she use hairspray, but Pammie swear she use fake hair. She say that the only way it could stay up like that. She say the Supremes do it, too, because she read it in *Jet*. She say she read where they got a special plane that carry all they wigs and dresses. Bishop Wheeler talking soft to the man up there next to him—I don't know his name, but seen him before, I think. Dark brown with a natural. Elisabeth Bradshaw up there, too. She use to take piano from Miss Minnie. Boy name Britches, use to play on the football team. Another boy, can't remember his name, use to go to my church. And Albert. Albert don't look at me at all, act like I ain't there.

They got folding chairs set up in rows, with a walkway through the middle. People file in and talk to each other, but mainly they look real serious. Go up to the front, write down they name, have a seat. When me and Ev walk in, nobody say nothing to us, one way or another. Not even Albert. We go up to the front and put our names on the list. Then we find a seat in the second to last row.

After while, Bishop Wheeler stand in front of the tables and speak. He say, since some of us ain't been here before, he explain who we are. He tell us how they the ones that do fundraising and have speakers to come out sometime. They the ones held a rally at the State college last year to make sure they integrate the lunch counter near the capital. They seen some positive things happen in the past few months, and they hopeful. They trying to start a free breakfast program like the one they have in Paducah. Some of them writing a grant to show they deserve federal funding for this program, and if somebody got special skills they can lend, to let him know. He say they take donations and welcome support from everybody, all races, sexes, and colors that want to see the world change for the better. When he say that, I look at Ev and smile. I notice Albert roll his eyes. Bishop say we got a lot to do, so we should get started. He say, put your hands together for tonight's speaker.

Then an older woman come in from the hall. She look around the room real fast, like she wanna make sure she see everybody there before she speak. She heavy-set, got a big bust that end somewhere around her waist. Colored beads at her neck, and a big flower dress look like a house coat. She got on white shoes look like what a nurse would wear. She wear thick glasses and got some papers in her hand.

"I'm Alice Mace. Live here all of my life, born over near the hospital. My people been here, all of us, for almost sixty years. I work in the Geriatric Center at the hospital, and I know how to take care of folks." She stand with her feet spread out under her, and I bet it take a team of mules to move her if she decide she wanna stay. She explain how folks come to her when they need some medical advice, and sometime she can tell them what to do, and sometime she can't. She do the best she can to help. But when William

Taylor come around to her place, said his boy look like wild horses done step down on his top half and drag him by the bottom, she can't think of one remedy that would help.

"I help bring Virg Taylor into this world. Born with a head full a deep brown curls, and a mouth the size of a full-grown man. And I told his mama that this child was born to talk, born with something important to say. I know this child have some disrespectful ways, and I done told his daddy about that. But he got a sweet spirit, too. Look like the world want to break this child spirit and shut him up. Now Virgyl got messed up to where you can't hardly recognize him. Gotta take his meals through a straw, and ain't said a word in more than a few days. They made it so he gonna be quiet for a long time."

Alice Mace say there come a time when somebody got to stand up and say something. When you done said all you can say, and the world has done all it can to shut you up, somebody, somewhere, got to stand up and say something for you.

"I seen them disappear and show up down to the lake, swole where you can't identify them. I seen them swing from trees and left for dead behind the bushes. I seen them locked up for what they did do and beaten for what they couldn't do. And I done seen enough. Winds of change, young people. Winds of change is blowing. Virg ain't got no wind left. And maybe I ain't got a lot of wind left. But I still got a little more left in me. Let us blow, real hard, together. Maybe we stir something up. Maybe we make a change down here. Maybe we speak for Virgyl Taylor and everybody else what got the voice beaten out of them." Alice Mace nod her head at us. She walk over to the table and get her some water in a Dixie cup, leave thirteen on the table. Then she sit down next to Bishop Wheeler.

Next, the light-skin girl with Bishop stand up. She say she figure we break into groups and work on special committees. Some folks is gonna make fliers and pass them out; some others gonna make signs and banners we hold up at the demonstration. They took to calling it a demonstration soon as Bishop friend, Bernadine, finish talking. Some others gonna work with some friends the group know around to the college, make sure they know we coming, what time, and where. They think somebody may write about us in the school newspaper. Albert and some others wanna "solicit support" from some more people—maybe mothers of other victims and other "credible people." And still some others gonna arrange transportation. Me and Ev talk for a minute, then we decide to work on the transportation committee.

Before, when all us sit in the chairs and listen to folks up at the table, I don't worry about how I come in with Ev. Then, when we break up into groups, and I know I got to get to know these people, and they gotta get to know me and Evian, I ain't for sure. I scan the room and start to count. Twenty-eight people now: twelve girls, and sixteen boys. Most of them young like me, but some of them, like Alice Mace, seem older. And three white people—two girls, and Ev. One of the girls name Nancy, and she ask to be on the transportation committee, too. She from Ohio and go to U.K. She say she major in Sociology. This her second semester. Nancy real tall and got long, straight brown hair, swing when she walk, almost touch her butt. Got on tan color shorts, a tie-dye shirt, and leather thong sandals. I almost hate her right away.

She say she been involve in social protest since she 16. She been to rallies, sit-ins, and everything. She say she think she can help us organize. First thing she say let's do is get us a pad and pen, then we poll the group to see who got cars and how many people they think they seat. She say she got a friend got a VW we might could use, too. Evian face light up when she talk with all her bright ideas, and when it do, something in my side crack and break. But, I don't show this to Ev. Instead, I get me a pen and paper, too, and off I go to Britches, see what he drive and how many people he think he could fit. And maybe see if he could fit me, since Ev so busy with this Nancy.

I done talk to Britches and find he got a car, but he tell me that the passenger door broke, so you gotta climb in on the driver side. He say he could fit three people, and I could ride shot since he known me from before. He say I grown up a little since he knew me, and I'm looking good, too. On another day, if he didn't have a crack tooth in front, and if I didn't know Evian, maybe, then I take what he say as a compliment. But I smile at him just the same. I talk to three more people, but only one of them got a car, but he say he could fit five or six people, depending on how big they are. Four of us on the transportation committee. Besides me and Evian and Nancy, a boy I don't know name Roger Elliott. He went to technical school. He wanna save up some money and go to the State college. He say he would do engineering, cuz ain't enough black men in science and math careers. He say he probably could have got a scholarship if he play sports, but he got two left feet. Two big left feet! Roger look like he about six-foot-five and big as I don't know what.

After we all go round the room and "poll" everybody, as Nancy say, we sit down in the back and compare notes. Bishop say we hope to have at least fifty people commit to go with us. He say we plan to do it in the first week of August, when fall registration start. That way, plenty people be on campus, and we get plenty attention. Plus, it the last week of classes for the summer session, so people still around the dorms and all. After we poll the folks at the meeting, we see that we got car space for about thirty-five people. That ain't enough. So, then Evian say we could plan bus routes and print them on the back of fliers, tell people where to get off and where to meet us on the yard. That way, everybody who ain't leave with us can still meet us there and be part of the effort.

Bernadine stand in front, and she waving her hands to get our attention. She say we take a five-minute break, and then one person from each committee share what they come up with. After that, we plan an agenda for the next meeting, figure out what we gotta do next. Brainstorm session, she say.

During the break, people head outside, try to get to some cool air. Some people go up and get a drink. Me and Ev, we go out to the hallway and see if that water fountain work. I'm thirsty. Ev put his hand on the small of my back when we walk, sort of push me through the door and into the hallway. Usually when he do that, I like it, but today it make me feel...funny.

"So, what do you think? Looks like these folks are really on the ball, Sister. I am impressed." Evian stand behind me while I drink. I stand up and catch my breath, then I bend down and drink some more. Then I move over and let Ev drink some, too.

"Yes, me, too. Remind me of when we was in school, like when I was in the drama club. We work in special interest groups. Some of us do props, some do set, some do publicity, and all that. You could get a lot done that way." I talk cool to Ev, don't know why. Maybe cuz it feel like people look at us, and maybe cuz he seem so happy to hear everything that girl, Nancy, say.

"True. I just want to make sure that people don't get the wrong idea about us. I mean, sometimes when a lot of young people get together, the establishment gets nervous and acts crazy. Wonder if we could do something, you know, channel all of our energy, while we meet that day." Ev run his fingers through his hair while he talk, and he look over my head like he trying to picture his thoughts.

"What you mean? Like on the news, when they sing protest songs— *We Shall Overcome*, and all that? Seem kinda corny…" I seen how people link they arms and sing that song before. Truth, first time I seen them march in Alabama, and the ladies got the heels on and they matching hats and gloves, even though they walk for miles, it give me chills.

"Not that, exactly. But, I mean, think about it. Fifty people with a mission and an attitude in the hot August sun. If we aren't careful, you know? I don't know. I just think we need to make sure that we organize the rally itself. Make sure we got stuff going on, positive stuff that everybody can be involved in." By now, it been five minutes, and we start to go back into the meeting.

"Yea, I guess you right. Maybe you could say what you said to me in the brainstorm session. See what the rest of the group think."

When we go back inside, Nancy meet us at the door. She save us some seats in the back, and she smell like smoke. She smile at me and say, "So, which one of you wants to share our notes with the group? I can't do it, because crowds make me nervous, and Roger isn't up for it, either. Are either of you game?"

Me and Ev look at each other. I might would do it, but Ev volunteer right away. "I have no problem doing it. Let me look at what everybody's got real fast." Roger come in and sit next to Nancy. We all pass the lists we make to Evian. Then Bishop in the front again, got a cup of water in his hand, say we ready to start.

Britches on the flier committee. He say he can print the fliers around to his job. Next meeting, everybody in his group gonna come up with some catchy slogans and figure out the important information that should go on the fliers. He say he hope we make a definite date by then, so we can start spreading the word after the next meeting.

When it Ev time to speak, he put the papers down in his chair and stand up. When he introduce hisself, he speak in a loud, clear voice. Everybody turn around in they seat to see who talking. He put his hands in his pocket and turn sideways so's he can see the people in front of him and in back.

"I'm Evian Mandarene, and this is my friend and neighbor, Sister. We worked with Roger and Nancy to come up with some transportation ideas for the rally. Here's what we came up with..." Evian explain how we could meet around to the church on the morning of the rally. He tell them how we got room for about thirty-five people in the cars. He say we can pass sign-up sheets around the week before the meeting, so we know who going in which car. And, he say we can put the bus routes on the back of the fliers we pass out, make sure folks know they can come out and meet us there on they own.

CHAPTER TWENTY-SIX

When Evian speak, Albert look at him square, like he try to see through Ev. He don't smile, but I can tell he like the way Ev talk. The rest of the group seem to like it, too.

While the other groups present their information, I'm busy think about what Ev say about the rally. Grannie say that when it get hot, folks can get into trouble. Something about the heat make people tempers shorten up and flare. So, I think he right about keeping stuff going on while we gather on the yard.

I don't know if we sing like they do on the march on TV, but maybe we could do something like it. I remember Edward tell me about this festival he read about where a bunch of bands and singers and stuff got together and perform for thousands of people. And didn't nothing bad happen. There was people there from all over, all races and stuff, and they had a ball. Edward say it remind him of the festival they have in New Orleans he went to with his cousins last summer, except not as many people at the one he went to.

So, that make me think. When Bernadine say thank you to all the committee reps for sharing they notes and Bishop say we need to brainstorm an action list for the next meeting, I surprise myself and stand up. Albert lift his brow when he see me stand, and Evian turn around and grin at me full out.

"We been thinking. What we gonna do while we there? I mean, like Evian say, it gonna be hot and all, and, well, maybe we could plan some activities for the rally, you know? We don't want folks to think we come for trouble. We gotta show that we want peace and all, but we also want a change. Maybe we could plan some acts to perform, you know? I know some of us sing and stuff, and maybe we could have somebody to speak. I don't know. Just a thought..." I shrug my shoulders and sit down. I didn't plan to say nothing, really, so I don't have a real plan for action, like Bishop say, but I figure I throw this thing out there, since we brainstorming.

People start buzzing when I sit down, like they think I got a good idea. Evian speak up, then, but this time he don't stand up. "Exactly. I mean, Sister's got a voice that would blow you away, no joke. And I can play the guitar. I know a bunch of us write and stuff, and like, Miss Mace, she speaks so well. I bet we have a mess of talent right in this room. Enough to keep us entertained for a few hours. And if we have a program planned, it could serve a few purposes. First, it may attract attention from people on campus, and they may check us out. And, of course, it gives us another aspect to plan for. Showing we can work together and, I don't know, make things happen..."

After Evian speak, seem like a fire start in that church. Folks throwing out suggestions and saying what all they know how to do. I hear Nancy talk to Roger, and she say, "It could be so cool—like a minor Woodstock or something. Excellent."

Albert speak up for the first time. "Seem like we got a lot of really solid ideas. I know they got a platform next to the Student Union. Maybe, if we get with the right people, we can arrange to center the action there. Do anybody know who to talk to about that, at the college?"

The other white girl, she say her name fast but it sound like Sally, say you gotta schedule use of the stage through the special events manager. She say you got to submit a proposal and get it approved. Sally say she did it once last year, when the English Club had a poetry reading. She volunteer to work on this committee next time, if she can get somebody to work with her. She say we got to move fast, though, because all kinds of groups wanna use the stage, and you got to submit your request early to get a spot.

Bishop say he glad that she around to help with this, and he ask Sally to come up and write down her name and phone number for him. He say he and a few of the others wanna talk to her, make sure they got all they ducks in a row. Whatever that mean. Sally switch her fat tail up to the table. She short and plump, but she got a nice shape. Short, frizzy hair, glasses, and real big nose.

Next thing you know, close to 10, Bishop say we need to close. He ask everybody to bow they heads while he lead us in prayer. He say how thankful he is that everybody can come together to work for something positive. He ask the Lord to be present in our meetings and smile on our efforts. He ask the Lord to send everybody home safe and bring them back again next week. He bind out Satan and hope we work smooth and overcome any obstacles thrown in our way. And at the end everybody say amen.

When the meeting break up, a few people dig in they purse or in they pocket for paper, and some people exchange numbers. Roger stand up to leave, and he tell us, since we on the same committee, that maybe we should take down each other numbers, too. Nancy seem to like that idea. She pull a small pad of paper got peace signs on the front out her back and a purple ink pen. She write down each of our numbers, then she tear off a paper and write her number down three times. She give each of us a piece with her name and number on it. I decide that I will lose mine as soon as I get home.

Me and Ev on our way to the car when Bishop and Bernadine call to us to come up to the tables. Bishop got his hands in his pocket, and Bernadine don't look at Ev, she look right at me. "Sister. Glad to see you taking an interest in this thing we got going. Ain't seen you in a while. What you doing for yourself these days?" She got her arms cross in front of her, and she don't seem sincere. Like she spects me and Evian is up to no good, or something.

"Doing fine, Bernie. Just fine. Did you meet Evian? He and his family move close by few months past. We neighbors. Evian, this Bernadine. She use to live in our neighborhood."

"Say, Bernadine. Nice to meet you. You guys really keep things focused and organized here—I like that. Wish I'd known about you sooner. I'd have gotten involved a long time ago if I'd known." Ev move toward me, like he about to take my hand, but I shift over a little bit, lean on the table. No sense in to advertise anything yet.

"Yes, we try to run a tight ship. So many groups are well-meaning, but they spin their wheels, dig? We are on a mission. We got a list of items that we want to address in the next several months. Evian, I just want to say, uh, welcome. And to you, too, Sister. I can see you have a lot to share. I wanna make sure you know that, well, you are welcome here " All while Bishop talk, Bernadine got her arms in front of her chest, like the last thing she want to say to Ev is welcome. But she keep quiet.

"See you later, Sister. Now that we in this thing together, I'm sure we get to be real close. Nice to meet you, Evian." She say this last part over her shoulder while she collect her papers off the table. Ev put his hand on my back again, like he usually do, and we head out the door. This time, when I stand in front of him, I hope Bernadine see he got his hand on my back. Give her and Bishop something to talk about later.

CHAPTER TWENTY-SEVEN

When me and Ev get in the car, I see Albert come out the church. Look like he heading for the bus stop. Before I can say nothing, Evian honk the horn light at him, get his attention. When Albert look up and see who it is honk they horn, he stop in his tracks. Look like he think hard for a minute, look over his shoulder, down the street toward the bus stop, then he walk slow over to the car. He come to the driver side and wait.

Ev got the window all the way down, and he got his most charming smile on, the one he use when he show me he could dance like James Brown. "Say, Albert. I didn't get a chance to meet you inside, we were so busy planning and all. My name's Evian. I guess you figured that. I live around the corner from you guys. I am giving Sissy a ride home, and, uh, no sense in your taking a bus when we're going that way. Can I give you a lift?"

Albert roll his eyes. Funny thing about Albert, he ain't usually disrespectful. At least not to somebody face. I can see him struggle with this, like he wish he didn't even have to talk to Evian. "Believe it or not, me and my people been riding buses for years. Good news is, now we can sit in the front. I don't think I wanna miss out on that." Albert turn like he gonna walk away.

"Oh, so your thing is that you want to sit in the front. I can arrange that. Sister, will you mind sitting in the back tonight, and let your brother grab shot?" I'm so uncomfortable with this whole thing, I just open the door and get in the back seat. I leave the door open, so's Albert can get in.

Albert don't look at Evian at all. Now he just look at me. I look straight at his eyes. I try to make them say let it go and trust me. I guess he hear me, because next thing I know he in the front seat and Evian driving away.

"So. Blah blah blah, yatata yatata yatata. What is there to say? I'm no good at pulling punches. I love your Sister, Albert. She feels like home to me. You for us or against us? What say ye?" Evian blurt this out, no hesitation, and I can't believe it. I turn toward the window, put my head on the glass, and shut my eyes. Oh, Lord.

Albert don't say a word. Me neither. I hear Ev drum his fingers on the steering wheel.

After a few more minutes of silence, Ev say, "Well, you know, silence implies consent. So, I take it you're in our corner. Cool." Ev stick his hand out at Albert, like he wanna shake on it.

Albert just look at Evian like he nuts. Then, all of a sudden, he burst out laughing and shake Ev hand. "Sister, where you find this crazy cracker, I don't know, but I know one thing: Either he mean what he say about you, or he a damn fool."

"Probably a little bit of both. At any rate, I'm behind the wheel. You're in my car. You made a decision to trust me, and I really think you made the right choice. Really."

We ride along in silence for a while. I notice Ev take the long way; stead of cutting behind the church, he drive through downtown. No music on, no talking going on, and all you can hear is everybody breathing. It ain't exactly what you call comfortable. I still got my head on the cold glass, got my eyes close. I can feel the steam rising off the window from my breath. Then, all of a sudden, Evian swerve and call out.

"Jesus! Get out of the way!" Ev slam on the breaks and pull over to the side of the road. Then I see a small cat, got a brown stripe down his back, and he standing in the middle of the road, right on the yellow line, like he don't know just what to do.

Evian pull the car into park and get out of the car. He run into the middle of the road and pick up the cat. He bring the cat over to the side of the road and sit on the car, with the cat in his arms. Both of them look scared to death. The cat got his arch up, and the fur standing on edge. Evian stroke the cat steady, and talk to it. "Oh, my goodness. What a scare, huh? It's okay. Where were you going anyway, huh? Walking in the street like that. It's okay..."

Albert turn around in the seat and look at me. He got all kind of questions in his eyes, like, is this guy for real? And, what if we kill that cat? And, Sister, who is this Evian, anyway? I can't answer, cuz I got the same questions he got, and a few more besides. But when Evian get back in the car, and he still holding the cat, I can see Albert got at least one answer that he must have like.

"Give him here. I hold him while you drive. You need both hands to steer." Albert take the cat in his lap and hold him firm, so he can't move. But that cat cross his front paws and settle down real fast. Albert stroke his back, and I swear I hear that cat purr.

Albert always did love pets. We use to have a dog when he was five, but he got run over by a car. Albert took it hard. Mama, too. We ain't had another pet since then. Less you count Timmie goldfish. But Ruthanne never like to have pets, anyhow. She say they stink.

We get close to my house, and everybody still quiet. I lean up a little to look at Albert. That yellow cat asleep in his lap. He still pet it, though, and look out the window. When we pull up in front of the house, I open the door and wait. How Evian gonna drive home with this cat? What he planning to do with this cat, anyway?

"Home again, home again, jiggity jog..." Evian put the car in park again, but he don't shut off the engine. I get out and walk around to Evian window. But Albert still stay in his seat, got the cat in his lap.

I stand there for a minute, and Evian open the door. He take my hand for a minute. "What an eventful evening, huh? In one night, I acquired a new cause and a new cat. Wonder what's in store for me tomorrow?" He squeeze my hand a little, and it make me feel warm.

"What Miss Cordial gonna say when you walk in with that cat, Evian? You thought about that?"

"I'll just play it by ear, Sister. That's half the fun in this life—making it up as you go along." Then, seem like Ev remember Albert in the passenger seat. He give my hand another short squeeze and let it go. "I guess this is your stop, too, huh?" He close the driver door and smile at Albert.

Albert shrug and don't look up. "You live across the field, right? I just ride with you to your house, so you don't have to worry about the cat. Walk on home...No sense in waking him up. Look like he had a rough night." I see him smile a little, but he still don't look up.

"Hey, sounds like a plan. All right, Sister. I guess I'll see you tomorrow. Put your thinking cap on tonight. Looks like we've got plenty planning to do!" He back out of the driveway and go. I stand there for a minute and watch him drive away until I can't see his car no more.

CHAPTER TWENTY-EIGHT

Soon as I get in the house, I sit down at the kitchen table with my head in my hands. On one hand, I'm excited about this organization, you know? Seem like everybody really interested in doing something positive to change how life go for us Blacks. And I'm glad they listen when I talk, and glad they don't seem too concern about me and Ev. On the other hand, this thing with Albert and Evian? I mean, Albert seem like, after he see Evian in the car, like maybe he don't hate him so much. But I didn't expect him to go with him to hold that cat, neither. What do he have on his mind? Maybe he fixing to say something mean to Evian, he don't want me to hear. I hope there ain't no trouble. Besides, what Evian gonna do with that cat, anyhow? Wonder if Miss gonna be mad that he brung it home without asking first. I wish I would come walking up in this house with a cat from somewhere downtown. Mama would have a fit. Maybe, if I talk to her first and explain how important it is, then she let me keep it, but I never would just bring it home without to say something to her first. Guess Miss Cordial and my Mama different. Or me and Ev different, one.

So, I sit at the table and think. That girl Nancy—I don't care for her. I think about how she always so excited and how she look at Ev when he give the notes at the meeting. How he look at her. Wonder do he like her? Do he think she pretty? I guess she pretty, kind of. I mean, I like her hair and all. And her face ain't bad. She real tall, too, and sometime people like it when a girl is real tall. Oh well. Nothing I can do about Nancy. She have a right to be in this CFPSC, too. But I wish she wasn't in the transportation group. And I ain't never gonna call her; she can forget that. And neither is Ev, if I can help it. I don't know what he think of Nancy, but ain't so sense in him to call her and find out.

House sound quiet. I wonder where everybody at. I peek in Nakita room, and she sound asleep. Come to think of it, it after 10, so Mama probably gone to bed. I get me some punch and sit back at the table, wait for Albert. While I'm waiting, the phone ring.

"So, girl, what happen? They give you a fit for showing up with that boy?" Pammie on the other end, sounding out of breath, as usual.

"Not really. They surprise me. You know, Albert the main one I was worry about. He act like if I bring Evian I do something personal against him. But, you sitting down? Cuz you ain't gonna believe this one!" I act like Pammie do, draw the news out and make her wait.

"Well, they got it set up so you sit in these chairs, you know, that fold out, and they got tables up at the front where's all the, I don't know, important people sit. And Albert was right up there with them, too. And Bishop Taylor, you remember him? He go with that girl use to live around here, Bernadine—real light, got nice hair? She was up there, too. Running thangs..." I take my time, cuz I know I got her attention; she want to know what all went on over there.

"Really? Don't seem like she would be his type. She seem fast, you know? And he grew up in the church. What she got on?" Pammie love to hear what people wear and how they got they hair.

"She had her hair in a perfect flip. It look good, I hate to say, because I ain't too particular for her. Had on a sleeveless green dress and sandals that strap up her legs. Not too bad, but she ain't as cute as she make out." I tell her how she introduce herself to me and Ev, and how she act like she don't really trust Evian. I tell her how Evian got his hands on my back, and how I wanna make sure she see, give her something to think about.

"You say Albert was around to the front? Do he, like, run the meeting, too? What he do up there?" Would know she be all concern about what he do. I tell her that he don't do much but sit up there like he overseeing what everybody else do. I tell her about how me and Ev wanna have a program, you know, music acts and readings and stuff like that, and she sound like she interested.

"Really? Maybe I need to show up at one of these meetings, huh? Sound like y'all got it going on, girl!" Pammie always perk up if she think she got a chance to perform. She like to sing, but mainly she like to have a lot of people watch her so she could dress up and show off.

"Yeah! We can use all the help we can get. Anyway, guess who rode home with us? You won't believe..." I take a swig of juice.

"Who, girl?"

"Albert, your main man! And he still out with Evian right now!" I sit back for a minute and let Pam Elisabeth wait, like she always doing to me.

"Girl, please! Are you for real? What he doing with Evian? They get into it or something at the meeting? What happen?" She sound like she ready to have a attack or something, so I go ahead and tell her. I ain't great with building suspense like she is, much as I try.

"Well, when we get in the car, we see Albert head for the bus stop, and so Evian honk the horn at him..." I explain how Albert get in, even though he don't seem like he want to. How he sit in the front, and how Evian ask him if he with us or against us. How he nearly kill a cat, and how Albert hold it on the way home. When I tell her that, how the cat seem so comfortable in Albert lap, Pammie sigh.

"Girl, he so sweet, you know? Like, gentle. I love that about him. So, where is he at now?" Pammie try to keep tabs on my baby brother. Please.

"I told you, he round to Evian house. When he go to drop us off, I get out, but Albert stay in the car. He say he ride round there with him, so he can hold the cat. He say he walk home. Matter fact, he should be walking in any minute now." I rinse my glass out and put it back in the cabinet. Mama hate to see even one dish in the sink when she get up in the morning if she leave it clean that night.

Pammie say she bored. She ask me what I plan to do now, since it ain't that late and she don't have to get up in the morning. I say I ain't tired neither. Then, Albert walk in, and he still got that strange grin on his face. When I ask him what take him so long, he ask me who I'm talking to. When he find out it Pam, he grab the phone from me, which get on my nerves. But when he hang up, he say let's walk around to Pam house and get her. She don't wanna stay in the house, but he don't want her walking round here alone. Which sound crazy, cuz Pammie been walking round here alone since I don't know when, but now that they go together, he gotta go get her. Oh, well, I say I walk around there with him, but I gotta go to the bathroom first. Today my stomach been acting strange. Like a sour feeling, but a tight feeling, too. I hope I ain't getting sick.

At the last minute, I run and get me a sweater to put on. Seem crazy, but I feel kind of chilly, for some reason. Inside, sort of, like when you eat ice cream too fast, and your body have to work to melt it down.

"Name is Shadow." Albert pull a cigarette out his back pocket and light it. He got it rip open from the bottom, like those workmen do, when they work with grease or cement or something else messy. They do that so they don't get nothing filthy on the tip. Pammie told me that. She hear it from this dude name Philip she use to hang with.

"Who? You? You changing your name?"

"Naw, girl! The cat. We decide to name him Shadow, since he slip up on us in the middle of the street, nearly getting hisself kilt." When Albert exhale, the smoke bubble up over our heads, and the smell from it almost make me sick. I fan it away with both hands.

"Man, I wish you quit with this smoking already, making me sick! But Shadow is a cute name. Kind of corny, though. What you and Evian talk about? You go inside the house, or no?"

I picture Miss Cordial coming round to the kitchen door to see who with Evian, and how she try to be hospitable to him, maybe offer him something to drink, even though it 10:00 at night.

Albert turn and look square at me while we walk back through the field, through that small stretch of woods, and out to Pam house. He smile a little, like he think it funny how I wanna know what go on with him and Ev. "Mighty concern for this cracker, ain't you? Seem like he concern for you, too. Don't know what to make of that. Anyhow, we ain't say much. I ask him what type of music he be playing on the guitar, and he say all kinds. He say this group seem like it do some good, and he got some more ideas about this rally. I say me, too. Tell him we should name the cat Shadow, and he say he think we should, too. Then, I get out the car and hand him the cat, walk on home. He say he see me later. About it..." Albert get done with his cigarette and smash it into the ground with one step and keep walking.

"So?" I look at Albert square, like he just look at me.

"So, what? Nothing else to tell, Sister. Don't take that long to drive around the corner and drop off a cat, dig? What you expect?"

"So, you like him? I mean, he real nice to me, Albert, and...I mean. I don't know. I guess I wish you sanction for Evian is all. So somebody could be on our side." I look at him with tender eyes, hope he understand. I use the word Ev teach me down to the lake. Like the way that word sound—sanction.

"Sister, you know, this thing is complicated. I know he seem like a nice guy, but who knows? I mean, y'all is up for who knows what, dig? People around here just ain't up for a lot of oaky-doke with race mixing and all that."

I don't say nothing for a while. I get so sick to hear people say this stuff all the time. They act like I don't know that, like I ain't live here all my life and don't know this stuff already. "Right, Albert. Get past all that. Do you like Evian? I mean, from what you seen tonight, do you think you like him?" We almost at Pammie house, and I don't really want to take this conversation inside, so I stop walking for a minute, cross my arms in front of my chest, and wait for an answer.

"What do it matter what I think, Sister? You hell bent to do this thing, right? So what do it matter what I say? Anyhow, from what I seen, he do seem...all right. I see how he look at you when he drop you off, like he wish he never have to let you go. I look at Pam Elisabeth like that sometime. Y'all rush and push and hurry. Give a nigger some time, Sister. I'm sure I come around." Albert shake his head now, like he don't want to talk no more, and he start walking again. Next thing I know, we in front of Pammie door, and I see Edward on the phone and Pammie at the sink washing her hands. Albert let hisself in with me right behind him.

"Don't come creepin' in here like you own the place! I would kill you for less than that, man." Edward box with Albert for a minute, throw fake punches at his stomach.

"Stop, man! You play too much!" Albert fan away Edward hand and sit down at the table. Look at Pammie with soulful eyes and wink. He still got his habits on from the conversation we just finish about me and Evian. I wonder why he act like this all the time when I mention Evian name. I mean, he met him now, and he got a little more to go on than just a name with a blank white face. Seem like he would get use to it better now that he meet Evian. But I guess he right—I do rush and hurry. I'm like that. Always have been. Once I make my mind up, or figure something out in my head, I just go with it. No time to warm up or adjust. I just go on and do it. But everybody ain't that way, especially not Albert.

By time I get round to the other side of the table, say hi to Pam, Edward shut down the phone, gulp the rest of the Coke he holding, crush it with his fist, burp real loud, and toss it in the trash. He snap his fingers and point to the door. "Let's roll. We gotta do dis. Like Bru-tis." He hold the kitchen door open and usher me and Pammie out. He ball up his fist and slap Albert fist, first on top, then underneath. Then he yell into the house, "We gone, Ma." Close the screen door. Somehow, even though he the last one out the door, Edward manage to be in front of us once we start walking.

But Eddie don't walk. He dance when he move along. Right, pop, down. Left, pop, down. Dip with the wrist, swivel with the hip, and a whole lot of trouble in the middle. Lots of time he pull at the center of his clothes, you know, like he wanna make sure his shirt is hanging just right, or his jacket hits just on top of his knees when he move. He like a firecracker, leave a lot of smoke behind him when he gone. Albert up next to him, breathing all this foolishness in. They always been like that. Eddie come up with these crazy schemes, and Albert think about them and make plans to them. This time, Eddie talking about this car he seen for sale downtown. Eddie got a mess of tickets he ain't paid for, and only just got a job to even think about paying for them, and now he bent on how he gonna get this car he seen for a couple hundred dollars.

"This junk was tight!! Leather seats. Four doors. Stripe down the side. Sound system inside—for real! I needs this ride." He swat at Albert from the side when he talk, cuz he know if he can get Albert excited about this car, he maybe help him think of a plan to really get it. They like that. Eddie have great ideas, you know, but he ain't much for sitting down and thinking them through. Albert the other way around.

We get close to my house, and Edward decide he don't wanna be inside. He got another idea. He say lets us sit out in the field, you know, bring out a blanket and the radio and just kick back under the stars for a while. It real warm out, even though it don't quite feel that way to me, and the sky a deep, dark blue. This time of year, you could smell the wild flowers and honeysuckle when you out in that field, and it smell so good. Make you breathe in real full and hold it a long time, like maybe you could fill your heart up with that smell and live with it inside if you don't breathe out.

So, that seem like a good idea to all of us. Albert say he gonna go in and get an old quilt to sit on and Ruthanne radio, and of course Pammie say she go with him. These days, seem like everything Albert do, Pammie wanna do it, too. While they inside (and something tell me they may take a while...), me and Eddie sit on the front porch. I start to sit on the swing, but something about seeing it move back and forth that way don't appeal to me, so I decide to sit on the top step instead. Eddie sit on the bottom step, and he turn and look up at me.

I got my legs cross and my hands folded over my chest, still a little cold. I look out over Eddie head, toward where Ev stay, but you can't see his place from the front yard. Wonder what he doing, and his new cat, Shadow. But Eddie interrupt my thoughts with his babble about that car he seen. An Impala, I think he say. Silver with a dark gray stripe and leather seats. Not even 70,000 miles on it, he say, and in mint condition. Like I care. I guess I ain't being a good audience for Eddie, because all of a sudden I feel him jiggle at my legs with his hand. He poke me in the knee and jerk hisself to his feet. He got his hands on his hips now, and he mad.

"Sister? Sister! Wake up! You ain't even listening to me—damn! You could at least show a brother some *respect*, at least *act* like you care what I got to say." When Eddie look at me, he got a pout in his eyes, like it really hurt his feelings that I didn't pay attention to his description of this car. Then he start to mess with me, try to get me to uncross my arms from in front of me, boogling me. But I feel irritable and don't feel like to have him mess with me. I sorta swat his hands away and then cross my arms in front of me again.

"Quit! You forever playing, Eddie, and I ain't feeling it tonight, so just quit!" I roll my eyes at him. For some reason, he bug me tonight.

Eddie jump down the step to the ground and spin around so his back to me. He lift his arms up to the sky, like he pleading to God Hisself. "Why you *curse* me, Lord? Huh? Why you send me all these evil women; don't care if a brother have a ride or not? Why Lord? Why me?? I mean, what do she want me to *do*, walk? Answer, Lord, don't just leave me hanging..." Eddie pacing around with his arms in the air, like he so confused and upset that he got to argue with God. He so silly.

Even though I don't feel like it, I start to laugh. He look so foolish, talking to the sky, like I ain't even there behind him on the steps. "Eddie, you so simple! Sit your crazy self down, hear? You got my attention now. My attention, the Lord attention, you got everybody attention now. Tell me all about this car. I gotta know! Do it have a transmission and all? What kinda gas you think it take? Can it run fast? How long it take to go from 0 to, I don't know, 70 miles a hour? Tell me all about it! Fast!" I giggle, knowing he will be glad that I will listen, even if I ain't really all that interested. Eddie is like that. He just need plenty of attention, don't care how he get it.

He hop up on the top step next to me, but he swivel his body in the wrong direction, so his back is to me. "Naw. I don't guess I will tell you, now I think about it. This car is too *special*, Sister. It's private." He cross his legs, too, and put his arms up in front of his chest, imitating me. "Nope. This here's a top secret car deal, see. I can't be giving every single woman that come down the road all the intimate details about it. Look like you done missed out, Sister." He sit with his back to me for another minute or two, for dramatic effect, then he look at me over his shoulder and start to laugh.

"This car is *serious*, though. For real. I mean, if I had this car, you know, I could, like, *do* stuff. Maybe even take you for a ride sometime, if you nice to me." Eddie look me in the eye when he say that, and I see a little bit of sun in there for a minute, just a flash, and then he look away.

We sit out in the field, about halfway between my house and Ev house. Eddie roll up four fat ones, and each of us got our own. I'm on the edge of the quilt, got my legs under me, Indian style, and Pammie and Albert on the other end, Pammie between Albert stretch out legs, all lean up against him. Eddie sit down for a minute, get up, walk around some, try out a dance for a minute: popcorn, washing machine, hand dance alone. Then he sit down for a hot minute. By this time, it late, and all of us got the munchies. Albert remember that we got half a watermelon in the fridge, and he head inside to get it. He love watermelon. This time Eddie go with him. Pammie tell them to bring out the salt, too. She like salt on hers. Not me. The thought of it make my stomach flip over inside. I feel like I'm gonna be sick.

I pick up the magazine Pammie got with her and start to fan my face real fast, lay back on the quilt prop up on my elbows. I must look bad, cuz Pammie get scared.

"Girl, what in the world is wrong with you?! You don't look so good. You all right?" She standing over me now, with her hands on her hips, squinting down into my face.

I close my eyes and take some deep breaths. Keep fanning and create a breeze. I take that sweater off real fast and fling it on the grass. Feel like the grass spin under me like a record. Then, fast as it came, it go away and I feel better.

"Mmm. I don't know. Must have ate something that don't agree with me today. Stomach been acting crazy. But I feel better now. I hope Albert bring me some grape soda! That's what I need, some grape soda right about now!" Either I must have look real bad and it really scare Pam, or we both really bent, because when I say I need grape soda, both of us start to laugh real loud.

"Girl, you so crazy! Look! Here they come now..." When Eddie and Albert come, they hands full. Albert got the watermelon, some salt, and a bag a chips. Eddie got the whole bottle a grape soda, no cups, some napkins, and two packs a Twinkies. Both of them look like they ready to throw down. As soon as they get close and we see what they got, me and Pam start to laugh even more.

First thing, I grab the soda and start to chug straight from the bottle. It feel so cold going down, and I am so glad that he brought it out here! This make Pam laugh all the more. She say I act like I'm on some desert somewhere, like I ain't had nothing to drink in weeks. I say forget you and keep chugging the grape soda.

Eddie excited about these Twinkies he found, but he having trouble with the plastic. He hold the plastic in his teeth and try to tear at it with his hand, but when he do, one of them fly out the package and sail into the field somewhere. Albert drop the watermelon and catch the Twinkie with both hands. Sure enough, the melon fall on the ground and split straight down the middle in two.

I'm in the middle of a big gulp when it happen. But I see this Twinkie fly out of the pack, Albert surprise catch, like he in the middle of a football playoff, and start to laugh, mid gulp. Whatever you do, don't fix to laugh when you also took a drink! Next thing I know, purple soda is squeezing out my mouth, out my nose, all over the place, and it burn, which for some reason make me laugh more. That was all she wrote. Next thing you know, all of us roll around in the grass cracking up. Except Albert. He forgot to bring a knife to cut the watermelon, so he glad he don't have to break it with his hands. He sit down in front of it like he sitting down to Sunday dinner. "Necessity brings ingenuity!" He slurp into the watermelon.

We look a sight! Some of us rolling around, can't stop laughing, and Albert with a big hunk of watermelon in his hands and the juice all over his face.

"Where you learn that? Enginuity, or whatever?" I ask Albert.

"Read it somewhere. Thoreau, I think. But really he just a throw back to Gandhi and Aquinas, and all a them. Whoever, whatever, it seem true. When you really need something, you find a way to get it, even if it ain't been invented yet."

Something Eddie say get Albert started.

"Wish the CFPSC could see us now! They be like, they ain't change! One hundred years later, and these niggers is still in the fields, acting silly and eating watermelon. So much for progress..." Eddie shake his head at us and sit down. He got the other pack a Twinkies in his lap, and he got a napkin underneath the plastic. He open it carefully, slowly take it out the pack, and then he smile. "Ahhh...Now I got you!" He say this to the Twinkie, before he break it open and eat all the cream out the center.

But Albert say we shouldn't have to be careful about having a good time. He say we have traditions, dig, that do come from our past. He say our history, good and bad, a part of us. Even though he my little brother, Albert surprise me when he talk. He have this way of expressing hisself, and he can take what you thinking, what everybody thinking, and put it in words that you could understand. In a way that you never thought of.

"Straight, straight. But, you have to admit that they do be looking at us, man, like they *wanna* see us slip up and say something crazy or act stupid or prove that we like, I don't know, don't have no *sense* or something. I mean, whenever I do be around them, I'm like, *different.* I mean, I watch what I say. It's like, when I be around them, I feel like I am not just me. I'm everybody, you know?...Us..." Eddie finish his cakes and start on the chips. They barbecue, so his fingers is red on the tips, and he keep rubbing them on the napkin, leave red prints all over the paper.

"Well, I don't be around them much, really. I don't be around nobody too much, except y'all and people at church and in the neighborhood and all. So, I don't know if I act different or not." Pammie got Albert feeding her chunks of watermelon. He break out a piece, sprinkle it with salt, hand it to her. She flick off the seeds and pop in the chunks while she talk. Pammie always would roll her ankles when she eat, but now when she do it, and got Albert in on it to feed her the chunks, it bug me a little.

Then I think about Evian and the Mandarenes—Miss Cordial and Norman. Do I act different when I be around them? Sort of. Mainly Miss Cordial. Specially after she say that stuff about Ev and how he have such a hard time. She make me sort of uncomfortable. But not Evian. In some ways I feel more comfortable with him than I do with, say, Pammie. In some ways. Like the way I don't have to say nothing and feel like he know what I'm thinking. But really, I do tell Pammie more than I would tell Evian. Different, is all. The way I feel about Pammie and Ev is just different, but I don't guess my thing with Evian any better than what I have with Pam.

CHAPTER TWENTY-NINE

It was that night, when we all sit out in that field and eat watermelon and barbecue potato chips and smoke corn, I find out we could sing. I mean, we all knew we could sing, but didn't none of us know how much we could really sing together until that night.

It happen by accident. Pammie look up at the sky and get sentimental, right? I tell you, she a softie. Moonlight, flowers, poems, love songs—she into all that stuff. And, to top it off, she real religious. It don't make sense, because if you could see Pam Elisabeth, you wouldn't think it. She come off kinda fast and coarse. Talk fast. Switch hard. Boy crazy. Least she was til she got with Albert. She been wearing makeup and stuff since we was 12. Heels, too. She love her some shoes. She say a high heel make your leg line look better, or some mess. Say it make the calf seem slimmer and make you look taller and thinner. She read it in one of her beauty magazines. But she never convince me, because I hate heels. And any kind of shoes, really, except sandals or white sneakers.

But maybe we had smoke too much or been out there too long, because real late, way after midnight, the sky turn this full-blown shade of purple-red-blue. With spots of gray-black. And up out a that, the stars was bright and crystal clear, look like black angel babies laid out on pillows, winking up at God. And, if you lay flat on your back and look up, it push the house across the field and the Mandarenes and Mama house and the street beyond way out to the side and make you breathe out. Pammie say that how come she know about God.

We all laid out on the quilt, out in that field under the stars, and Albert sit up and look down at Pam Elisabeth. And that when everything start to change.

Pam love gospel music. All she will play on the piano, and most the time on the record player or the radio, is church music. When Albert lean over her, looking down, and he start to rub one finger across her eyebrow, that when she start to sing. "Oh Lord, my God, when I, in awesome wonder, consider all the worlds thy hands have made..." Pammie sing high, but she got a thickness in her voice that shake so much, she could barely keep on pitch. Her voice jump all over in the middle, but at the end, she always smoothe it out and clean up the pitch. Before you know it, I add an alto part, close up under her melody, and Albert take a counter melody, almost seem like he sing in another key, right under me. Edward voice sound like gravel, almost, like if you was to throw little stones on the ground in just the right spot so they vibrate in tune, heavy, to keep the other parts in place. And it sound so good, so natural, we sing the song through twice, all four verses.

When we get done, none of us look at each other. We each in our own little world, but next to each other, and ain't nothing we can really say except we all know it sound special when we sing and it make us all feel God, and it make us all stay quiet. And that was how I found out we could sing.

Also, it was when I found out I was pregnant.

PART II

CHAPTER THIRTY

Mama started giving me the blues as soon as she hired Pam Elisabeth's brother, Edward. Or maybe it was when I joined the CFPSC; I can't really tell which. But she began to act differently whenever Sister was around. It was subtle, but I could detect it. One day, I found this cat and brought him home. He was so cute. I always wanted a cat, but Mama would always claim that it might interfere with my wellness. She would say that whenever she didn't want me to do something—claim it would interfere with my wellness. And she put it that way, because she read this book when I was 12 about positive thinking. So, she wouldn't refer to my cancer or say that something would make me sicker. She would turn it around backwards to say that it would impede my wellness. Didn't much matter how she put it. What she really meant was that she didn't approve. She didn't approve of the cat, and at some point it became clear that she didn't approve of Sissy, either.

She tried to cover up her feelings about Sissy, but she was real obvious about the cat, Shadow. She would not touch him, and you could see how disturbed she would get when he came into the room. Her whole countenance would change. And if Shadow ever came up to her and, say, wound himself around her legs, she would visibly stiffen. It was so weird. Then, she was hell bent to hire someone to take care of the yard. We got a lot of grass and foliage and stuff back there, and it can start to look craggy if you don't tend to it. And she wasn't about to do it herself, and she wouldn't have me doing it either. Not that I was all that pressed to do it. I am not one of those physical types. Truthfully, I am kind of lazy. So, that's when Sister told us about her friend's brother.

I'd like to say I never had a problem with Edward. I mean, he was cool and everything. He knew an awful lot about issues and stuff. He and Sissy's brother, Albert, were closet nerds. They'd sit around and swap theories that they'd read about—Thoreau, King, Malcolm X, W.E.B. Du Bois. All kinds of shit. Used to bore me to death. No offense, but I don't want to sit around and contemplate everybody's views on everything. I'm more of a *do it* type. Don't write about it, don't sit and think about it. Just go do it and shut up already. But I could never say that at all to those cats, because they would put me in the same category as they put every other white person. They'd wink at each other and be thinking of me as "THE MAN." But, really, it didn't matter who the philosopher was, black or white, I didn't want to hear about it really.

One day when they were over at Sister's house, when their mama was at the convention in Tennessee, I came over to be with Sissy. By then they were hip to us, and they clearly knew that we were fucking around and everything, but we were still low key about it. We didn't go waving it in their faces. But it was cool for me to come around them sometimes and hang. One thing I can do is hang. I mean, I can find some kind of neutral ground with people and dance with them on it. It's like a gift or something. I remember this one day, a Saturday afternoon, and I had gone to this record store in town the night before. That's another thing—I love music, all kinds of music. I mean, I have listened to blues, rock, country, gospel, everything, since I was little bitty. I would like listen to the songs over and over and imitate what I heard. That's how I learned to play the guitar. I would sing, too, but I was way better on the guitar.

But I had bought a few new albums that night, and I had already listened to most of them, but one of them I bought especially to listen to with Eddie and Albert. It was by this group called The Last Poets. I'd read about them before in one of my music magazines, and they sounded interesting to me. They, like, take their words, this really decent poetry, and they speak over music. This album was brand-new, and nobody around here was even talking about it. But, where I go, this man named Otis owns this little shack where he has like a gazillion different crates of music. He even imports some of his shit from overseas. I don't think he puts any money into fixing up the place—that place is a dump. It even smells in there sometimes. He's quirky like that. But he keeps a fantastic assortment of really killer tunes. And, sure enough, he had this Last Poets album, so I bought it.

I go over to Sissy's house, and we're supposed to just chill for a while since her mama is gone out, and Eddie and Albert are over there, too, so I thought I'd bring this record I had bought. When I got there, those two were already lit up from home-grown. Around here, especially in the summer, there's not a whole lot to do. Kentucky is not exactly the swing state or anything. So, after work, folks get a bottle or they roll up some home-grown, and they do whatever comes natural. Natural for Eddie and Albert is to argue over stuff. Anything. One of them takes a side, and the other defends the opposite side with venom. That day, Albert was talking about Martin Luther King's thing about non-violence, and, of course, Eddie was countering with Malcolm X and how you can only be non-violent with people who are non-violent with you. So, here I come, the white boy with cancer, with a record under my arm by The Last Poets.

Well, I knew that the album was controversial and all, but I guess I didn't realize it would be so Black Power oriented. They had this one song about Blacks being afraid of revolution. By the time it came on, I had smoked a little with them, you know, to come from their same space or whatever, and I was feeling comfortable. We were in the living room with Sissy's record player on the coffee table. They have an air conditioner in there, but, for some reason, they didn't have it turned on, so the front door was propped open, the fan was going, but it was still hot in there. So, Sissy brings me a cold glass of iced tea, and she sits down next to me. It was a big tumbler, and we started drinking out of the same glass. We weren't touching or anything. We were still really subtle back in those days, but I guess something in the intimacy of it made Edward uncomfortable, and he started to trip. He didn't say anything about it directly, but I saw him glance at Sissy when she drank from my cup, the sweet, gliding way she has of showing a closeness without saying a word, and he cringed or something.

So, he starts in on me. It seems like Edward would grill me sometimes, to hear what I had to say, waiting for me to say something wrong and prove that I am the white devil his philosophy books claim I am. And at these times, Albert and him would get into this good cop-bad cop scene, where Edward would fire off these questions, and Albert would sit back with this smug look on his face and listen. Sometimes he would come to my defense, you know, same as when he is debating with Edward, offering the other side of the argument or whatever, but it always seemed like he was quietly pulling for Edward. Hoping he'd slip me up somehow. But truthfully, at the end of these grilling sessions, Albert would look at me with renewed respect, like he knew I had it in me to stand up to even Edward. He never really said it, but it felt that way. The whole deal made me uncomfortable.

Now, when Edward asked me what I thought about it, if I thought it was true that Blacks are afraid of revolution, I felt cornered. Maybe it was because I saw how he looked at me, how he looked so disappointed and angry with Sissy, when he saw her drink from my glass. Or, maybe it was the language that they used in that song, the fact that they used the "N" word that made me nervous. I don't know exactly. But, I took a drag from this johnson, and then I said what I thought was true, in the smoothest way I could.

"Absolutely! And why wouldn't they be? I mean, I think everybody in their right mind is afraid of it, in a way. Because a revolution, by definition, means a drastic change. Even if change is for the better, it can be weird." I said most of this with a mouth full of smoke, and when I finished, I exhaled long and hard, waiting for the inevitable counter attack from Edward.

He pulled his lips together in a thick, straight line and forced his eyebrows down next to his pupils to glare at me. "Figure you come out with some pussy shit like that! Niggers ain't afraid of *nothing*, man. What we got to fear by now? What else could they take from us or do to us by now? Now all that's left is to take it back. Nothing scary about that!" He got his own johnson in his teeth, but he changes his mind and squelches it out in the ashtray.

I could feel Sissy hold her breath next to me. She is funny that way. She so wants me to be accepted by her brother. Seems like she takes it personally if he or Albert confronts me, but then she remembers they are family, and she is caught in the middle, so she holds her breath and stays quiet.

"True. True. I believe that. I mean, once somebody has been through a lot of crap, they get angry, and I guess anger can override fear. But, like Malcolm says (and I saw that Edward lifted his brow when I mentioned Malcolm X), revolutions have been historically bloody. I mean, people die and shit. I don't think anybody looks at the possibility of death without a certain amount of fear."

I guess Edward felt like I was stepping on his holy land when I started referencing Malcolm X. I could see he didn't appreciate it. Sissy saw it, too, and she took the glass of iced tea and went in the kitchen. Albert just sat there. He was leaning against the reclining chair, sitting on the floor with his knees pulled up to his chest, like he was watching a chess match or something.

"Yea, well dig this, Evian. Some things ain't never gonna change, hear? They ain't gonna change unless we put a foot in its ass and make the shit change. And if that's what it takes, I think brothers are up to the task. If you sit around and think about it, yea, you might get scared, but in the heat of a moment? Bump that! It's on!"

But when he said this stuff, it didn't exactly seem like he was talking about a theory of revolution anymore. Seemed like more than that. It seemed like a challenge, or something. And I didn't appreciate the tone in his voice, either. I mean, I didn't know what all he was getting at, but all I know is I don't back down when somebody comes off at me, regardless.

"Whatever. I guess we'll have to wait and see when the time comes, won't we?" I found myself leaning to the side a little when I said it, standing my ground.

"You got that right. We shall see what we shall see..."

The song stopped, and Albert got up to turn it off. The vibe had changed somehow, and he knew it. When Sissy came back, she didn't sit down on the floor next to me. Instead, she sat on the couch behind me. I could hear her clink the ice in the glass she went and refilled, but this time she didn't offer me any.

And we sat like that for a few minutes, with this thickness growing in the living room, festered in the summer heat, and for whatever reason, I was fuming. Edward suddenly got real interested in this cowry shell necklace he had on his neck, looking out the window, and Albert clicked on the television. Some soap opera. And that's when Sissy started talking.

"Revolution is funny. Maybe don't nobody notice it happen, but you look up and it done happen. Quiet. I mean, y'all talk like a war or something the only way something can change, but it ain't always like that. People don't work like that. They get busy and don't pay attention, and one day they look up and ain't nothing the same as it was. That's what revolution seem like to me. But don't nobody ask me, so let me be quiet." She went on drinking her tea and swinging her foot while she sat up on the couch, behind me but away from me.

That's what I love about Sissy. She seems quiet and, I don't know, meek or something. And she never makes a big fuss about stuff, and sometimes she won't say anything at all. But she is always thinking. Then, out of the blue, she will come out with something like that, something simple and brilliant. Just throws it out there, and you have to stop for a minute and think about what she said, and if you don't know her, you wonder if she even knows how deep she sounds. Gives me a woody, to be quite honest. She's smooth, and that is so sexy to me.

But, maybe I am being egotistical because I bone her, but I don't even think Edward got the implication of what she was saying. I honestly think it went right over his head. I looked around for a second, took it in. There I was, in Sissy's living room, arguing about the Last Poets with two Black guys on a Saturday afternoon, with my Black girlfriend behind me. I didn't plan it. None of us had planned it, but somewhere down the line, just like Sissy said, everything had changed.

Anyhow, much as I'd like to say I did, I didn't exactly like Edward. In some ways he was such an asshole to me. I mean, he wouldn't back off or lighten up for a stretch of time with me. He found every opportunity he could to challenge me or argue with me. I could understand some of it, because in a way that's just how us guys act around each other. But after a little more time I realized that it went beyond that, even. Part of it was race—sure. But part of it was Sister. Not only did he not want her being with me. He really wanted Sister for himself. And that pissed me off. Because it didn't seem like he was all that particularly interested in her until he got hip to how she was with me.

And at this time, Mama started to trip, also. It wasn't just Shadow, and it wasn't just Sissy, either. She became more neurotic than ever. Maybe because of that guy she was seeing. Even though he lived in Louisville, he came out to see her all the time. Normally I would have been glad that she had the company, because that way she could lay off of me. But it didn't work that way. In fact, it was opposite. She started obsessing over me more than ever. Now that I think about it, she must have been worried about appearances. Mama is strange like that. She claims to be this big liberal and everything, but really she's not. She just wants to appear that way. She's old South if I've ever seen it. She is one of the few people left who still says "courting." And at first I didn't even know where she was coming from on it, but then I realized that she meant dating.

She'd come back from one of her lame courting sessions, or one of those damn teas with Miss Willie Mae, and she'd lay it on me. Why don't you ever call that nice girl from the organization you belong to, and, now that you're on an upswing, why don't you enroll at U.K., and you seem to spend a lot of time planning this event at the college; don't you have time for anything else? And when Mr. Howard would "come to call" (she'd actually say that!), please! She would lose her damn mind. She'd want Sissy to clean the house up special, but she would make sure that Sissy left out way before this dude arrived. She didn't want him to see me fraternizing with the help, I guess, which the idea of pisses me off, to be quite honest. Sissy is my help, all right. She saved my life, but never mind that. Just make sure she's gone before this phony dude shows up with his howdy-doos and small talk and a heap of other fake shit.

I don't know whether he started banging her, and that idea makes me really sick, frankly, or if she fell in love with him, or if she just realized that she was losing me and maybe Norman soon enough and wanted a gig of her own, but she started to talk about marrying this idiot. And around that time, right after we hired Edward, everything got really sketchy.

CHAPTER THIRTY-ONE

I think Pap was the first one to recognize that Sister was pregnant. More than that, I think he also realized that it wasn't my kid. I have a cool relationship with my grandfather, when I think about it, but nobody wants to talk about really heavy shit with someone as old and peculiar as Pap. So, that day when he came back to my bedroom, I knew I had a reason to worry.

Mama went on this weight loss kick when she started dealing with Mr. Howard. She and Willie Mae started going to Weight Watchers on Thursday nights. Then, she got Sister involved in it by asking her to make those weird recipes she got at her meetings. I wouldn't have anything to do with that crap. She had her make this stew once that was just plain ridiculous. It had tomatoes and cabbage and onions and garlic or some foolishness, and the thing about it was, it was supposed to take more calories to digest than it contained or something. So it was like, the more you eat of it, the more weight you lose. Never mind the fact that the mess was completely inedible. And it smelled bad, too. I mean, it was just unnatural. Anything that takes calories to even digest has got to be questionable. But she wanted to drop two dress sizes, and she didn't care if she had to eat a weird stew to do it. I thought she looked fine just the way she was, but she never believed it. She thought she had a big behind. And she does. But what she doesn't get is that guys like big behinds, and as much as I hate to think of it, I'm sure old Griffin Howard does, too. But she was hell bent to lose the quality that probably attracted Griffin to her in the first place.

So, she'd go to these meetings, and sometimes she'd hang out with her gentleman friend afterwards, which was cool, because it meant that I had some time to myself when I didn't have to worry about her nagging me around. So, I'm back in my room blasting Santana, because I went heavy into a phase with them during that time, and I hear Pap knocking on the door. At first I thought he was going to ask me to turn the music down, which he would do sometimes. But, when I said, "Come in," he pulled up the desk chair and got this ponderous look on his face. Uh-oh.

But I didn't panic. I just went blank through the face. Whatever it was he wanted to talk to me about, I wasn't going to react to it right away. You had to do that with Pap, because he can come from left field sometimes. You never knew. He could want to talk about my health, or about Mama and this new guy, or he could want to talk to me about my relationship with Rebecca. He started calling Sister Rebecca after she'd been around for a few months. He asked what her real name was, and when he found out, he started to call her that right away. He's the only one who did that. But, not knowing which direction he was going to come from, I thought it best to just lay back and listen.

"So, who is it this time? Another one of those California bands? You ever listen to jazz anymore, Ev-yun? What happened to those records, or did you lose interest in them already?" He picked up the album cover and glanced over the back, like he was looking for something notable to explain why I was playing the thing so loud.

I chuckled. Pap could be pretty hip when he wanted to be. He even seemed to like some of the stuff I would play. But he was turning his nose up at this one. "Santana. This guy Carlos is completely major. I mean, I can learn so much about form just from listening to him." I sat up on the bed and leaned against the backboard.

"Yes. I see. Sounds foreign to me, Spanish or something. Not that I have anything against the Spaniards, of course. Err, Evian, Rebecca...Uhh. Have you stopped to consider Cor-jul in this thing? Not that I'd have you to, ahh, mold your actions around your mama. But just the same, you may want to at least consider her, ahh, as you plan for the future..." For the first time I could remember, Pap struggled with his words. And I didn't make it easy on him, either. I kept that same vapid expression while he talked to me, waiting to hear what angle he was going to take. Not that I was especially worried. Pap had always been cool about this thing with "Rebecca." For some reason. And I never questioned why—I was just glad. I mean, we had potential for so much flack that I was glad Pap wouldn't be another source of it.

"Now, with your mama taken up with this Mr. Griffin, you see, you might want to step back and take a look at things. She's entitled to her happiness, too, we have to remember. She's been through enough. Of course, we want to, err, make this transition easy as possible for her. And uh, I reckon you, ahh..." Pap stopped mid sentence and began stroking the fine, gray hair at the back of his neck. He'd let his hair grow out that summer, and it was climbing down his neck and onto the tops of his shoulders. He was beginning to look like Moses. I kept blank and let him continue. "And you'll want to consider her in this and, uhh, make it tolerable."

"Now, ahh, what precautions are you young people taking these days—any? In my day, you were at a loss for protection really. Except that counting business, and I can tell you that unless she's regular as a clock it isn't gonna work, and they never are. Haven't met a woman yet who was regular. Of course, in certain instances, I, uhh, I don't suppose you can truly be cautious anyway. Sometimes it's out of your hands, and before you know it the dirty deed is done, good or bad. What's your plan for this, son? How'll you account for it?" Pap scrunched his lips and leaned forward, as if anything he said to me had made a lick of sense, and now he wanted a response.

"Okay...I don't really know what you mean..." And I really didn't at the time. Which is amazing to me now that I look back at it.

Pap looked disappointed and resigned, which I couldn't figure out. But, when he thinks he's said his peace, he won't elaborate or anything. He just nods his head like, there, I've said it, and then he moves on.

"Well, in any case, you'll want to think about it, what's already done and what is not done and what it's not possible to do. You young folk just jolt forward, thrust ahead, and never once think about what will happen as a result. And I don't aim to have history repeat itself in this house. Not anymore. No. We can't take back what unfolds when we're not around to stop it. But when it does occur, well then we can take hold, son. Take hold." He trailed off again and started rubbing his knees with both hands.

I had no clues at what he was getting at, and he was beginning to scare me to death. I mean, he was old, and I know that people can start to lose their minds when they get old, and the way he was talking I was wondering if *he* even knew what the hell he was talking about. I wondered if he was having an episode, like where they forget what's going on and all. But, then he changed the subject and asked me what I thought of Mr. Howard, and did I think that he and Mama'd get hitched, and did I think Rebecca was gaining weight, and do I like those meatless spaghetti dishes Mama had Sister make. And when he talked about that stuff, I felt a lot better, because I knew that he knew what was going on, that he was still grounded.

But before he left, he got at it again. He stood up and pulled a cigarette from behind his left ear, and he fiddled for matches in his pocket, so I knew he was going to walk around outside and smoke. I wouldn't mind getting back to Santana, but I was going around to Sissy's soon because we had a meeting that night. I flipped my legs onto the floor and scanned the room for my shoes.

"Son, you got to take a hold to what's yours, even if the world says it isn't yours at all. Because it is a matter of respectability. Every now and again in this life you get the chance to turn something ugly, something wretched, into a beautiful thing. God willing, if the Lord blesses me to stick around that long, I'll hold your hand through it and help you make it stick, make it shine. It's the right thing. You remember that, Evian." Then Pap winked at me and shuffled out the door.

Shortly after that, later that night, I think, Sissy got on her kick with cornbread. Good Lord, women can be weird with that shit! Always so concerned with what they'll eat and what they won't eat, claiming they do it to please us, when actually the whole process is a pain in the ass for us. I mean, you can tell where a woman's at from what she's eating. If it's carrots and cottage cheese and that crap, you know she's one of those neurotic, insecure chicks who dreams that everything she eats goes to her hips.

Those are the ones who look into your eyes and only see a reflection of themselves, and the reflection looks fat. Or they're the ones who walk everywhere and take the steps rather than the elevator. But if you can get one who isn't all that concerned with it, one who'll barbecue up some ribs and make a mess of bacon for you in the morning, halleluia! You can bet her head's on straight.

But you gotta be careful when they start eating one certain thing, because you can bank on a mood change to go with it. If they only want ice cream, or keep baking brownies, or whatever, they're working through something, and they can only eat a certain thing while they do it. I know, because my mama is the same way. She gets on kicks, too, when she's working through something in her head. With Sissy, it was cornbread. Middle of the summer, hot as hell outside, her mama won't turn on the air conditioner, and she's up in the kitchen making cornbread, as if that makes any damn sense. And, she would make it in this one special pan, too. It was shallow and square, and she actually would bring it with her in her bag when she came around to our house. So strange. But, if that isn't bad enough, she would eat the cornbread out of a bowl. Great big hunks of it, and she would mash it up in a bowl with butter, and sometimes she'd pour honey all over it, and eat it with a spoon.

By this time, I would go around to Sissy's sometimes, mainly when her mama wasn't around, but I would pick her up for meetings once a week, until later when we started meeting practically every night for one reason or another. That night I had walked over early to pick her up, and we were going to walk down and take the bus to the church. Not that I don't have a car, but Sissy'd decided that she wasn't getting enough exercise since she was getting a little thick in the middle. I wasn't too worried about this supposed thickness, but I said we'd take the bus anyway because it was easier than having an argument, which we'd started having lately. And when I knocked on the back door, the one that leads into the kitchen, she was at the table with a magazine and a big bowl of cornbread. And she was going at the bowl with a gusto, too, and it made me laugh. I mean, Sissy is cute. She's got all these ringlets of curls all over her head, and when the sun hits them, they get shiny orange almost. And, around her temples, she starts to sweat a little bit, and her hair curls up tight and makes a frame around her face. And she's always got this one long curl that hangs just off center down her back. And for some reason it knocks me out. She pins it up sometimes, just scoops it all up and pins it on top of her head, and while she's working, the curls fight loose and fall down in periodic spurts. She knocks me out, I swear.

So, I walk into the kitchen, and there she is with her bowl of cornbread, shoveling it in with a spoon, and I sit down at the table with her. She starts complaining about how she can't button her jeans and it's craziness that's got to stop, and she's so glad we're taking the bus so we can have a little walk, and maybe we'll walk all the way home, which is almost four miles if you take the back ways and all. So, I just agree with her and say, yes, we really should walk.

But all of a sudden she freaks out on me and says that I'm saying she's fat and maybe I should just go walk with that girl, Nancy, since she's probably still thin enough for me. *(???!!)* And at first, honest to God, I don't know what or who she is talking about. And my instinct is to get mad because I don't have patience for foolishness. But when she starts to cry, what am I supposed to do? So, I'm all putting my hand over hers and telling her she's beautiful and we can walk or drive, her call. And that's when she jumps up from the table and runs into the bathroom. And I thought, oh Lord! She has really lost her damn mind, and the weird thing is I got this sinking feeling way deep, like down in my shoes or something, because I was like, what if she dumps me over this, and I don't even know what I did wrong?

So, I sat there and clinched my fists and tried to regulate my breath. When in doubt, I just regulate my breath is all. Don't think of anything, just breathe and try not to take action. I have found that it is better to think, really think, and breathe before taking any action.

And I'm at the table breathing and not acting when it becomes clear that she's in there being sick. I know all the signs since I've been down that road a few times. Water's running, fan's going, etc, etc. And I'm like, did I really make her so mad that it made her sick? But at the time I didn't get the connection. And neither did she. Not until a little while later.

On and on with the cornbread and everything you can think of that calls for cream: coffee, strawberries or bananas, oatmeal. Got to be where she'd meet the milkman at the door. She was ready for him, all ready, had the coffee or the oatmeal waiting in the kitchen while she cooked one of those meatless soybean scrambles my mama forced her into, or while she soaked the pots and pans or cleaned the fridge. And she was erratic as hell, too. One afternoon, as soon as Mama was out the door, she came back in my room and attacked me. Literally pushed me back on the bed, straddled me, and rode me like a bike. That was fun, actually. She had this fevered look in her eyes when she did it, and I never heard her cry out like that before. But, when a girl pushes you back and straddles you, you don't question it or complain. You just go with it. Who knows where that came from, but God love her for it! And not to be crass, but her tits tightened up in a way that day, I noticed. Like, around the nipple, you know, that dark place, got smooth and tight in a way, and it stuck in my mind. And I remember thinking, hmm, wonder what that's about.

So, one minute she's rocking on my lap and squealing like I'm the best thing to happen since toilet paper, and the next minute she won't speak to me because I didn't read the article to her in a sweet tone, or I didn't feel like singing with her, or I didn't grab her hand like I usually do on the way home from church. But, the thing I remember is, Sissy gets this little rash on the edge of her forehead every few weeks, and that's how I know she's on. And the way she'd been going at me, wanting it at this furious pace every day, she was wearing me out, but I would never have said it in a million years. But quietly I was looking for that little rash, because I sort of wanted a break. Not that it wasn't good—it was fantastic. But it was kind of too good. Like, I can't explain it, but sometimes when we fucked, I felt like I could feel her heart, actually feel her heart or some shit, dancing over mine. And it felt awesome. But it also felt scary as all hell.

But the rash never came. And when I coupled that with the cornbread and the sickness and the mood swings...actually I still didn't pick it up. But when she came and said we had to talk, and we went down to the lake that day and she told me her friend was late, it didn't take a rocket scientist to know that she wasn't talking about Pam.

CHAPTER THIRTY-TWO

This one day Sissy comes over to work, same as usual, and she makes this pot of oatmeal for breakfast. I'm not big on oatmeal, but she also made bacon and toast, and she can perk the hell out of some coffee, so I didn't mind breakfast that day. I ate at the kitchen table with Pap and Mama, but Sissy never joins us, even though we tell her she is welcome. At least Pap and I do. Mama never really says anything about it one way or the other, but I get the feeling she doesn't really want Sissy sitting down with us to eat. And anyhow, she stopped looking Sister in the eye soon after I brought home Shadow. She'd, like, focus on this point at the top of Sissy's head and never really look straight at her.

On the other hand, Mama relied more and more on Sister once she started seeing Mr. Howard. She'd want Sissy to do the grocery shopping and pick up flowers for the living room and dining room, and she'd order special cuts from the butcher or want fresh fish from the fish man. It was good when the fish guy came, because he was a trip to talk to, and when we bought fish from him, Sissy would fry it up crisp and serve it with coleslaw or hushpuppies. That's my favorite thing almost that she cooks. And Mama didn't mind if I drove Sissy to the store even though she would nag at me later for spending too much time with Sissy. Because there was this girl named Nancy who worked on the transportation committee with me at the CFPSC, and she would call me sometimes. Just to figure out stuff or to plan or to give me information—no big deal. But Mama would always ask me why I don't go out with her or something. But I never even thought about Nancy that way. She was such a ditzy girl.

So this one day Mama had a bunch of errands that she wanted Sissy to do, which really meant that I had to drive her. It would have taken her all day if she had to do all this stuff on the bus, and later she wanted her to make a special dinner because she was having Mr. Howard over to eat. She was working on this painting, too, and it was kind of cool, actually. My mom is rather talented that way. This one was all of these bleeding pastel colors, but in the middle, there were all of these fish swimming upstream. She said she'd been dreaming of fish lately.

Well, on the way back from the butcher (Sissy was making porterhouse steaks and asparagus for dinner, and she was gonna try out this white sauce, too), Sissy said she wanted to talk to me privately. Keep in mind that she'd been acting really crazy the last few weeks, and I really wanted to keep a positive vibe going with her. So, I suggested we go out to the lake for a little while, and that way we could talk. Sissy loves the place where I take her down there. I do, too, because it is so green and peaceful. I figured it'd be hard for her to get crazy in such a beautiful place.

So, we hike down to the spot I like so well, down near the water, and she seems so nervous and anxious. I put my arms around her and give her a warm hug, and I hope that she doesn't get too hot and bothered from it, because if we start to screw down there, the way she'd been acting lately, we'd never get home in time for her to cook dinner. She takes a bunch of deep breaths, and then she tells me.

"Lately seem like I ain't been feeling myself, Ev. Don't know when it started—few weeks past, I guess. But I been sick at the stomach sometimes and can't help but cry over the strangest stuff."

I don't want to break her train of thought since she seems so nervous about whatever this thing is. So I just hold her hands and keep quiet.

"But, umm, what you think if we start to use some of them, umm, you know, Trojans and all, when we get to be close? I mean, if it don't turn out to be true."

Sissy kept looking at me, like she wanted help with what to say and what to think, but, at the time, I was really clueless. "What do you mean—if what isn't true?"

"Well. Maybe you might have notice, but I ain't had my friend to come in a while. And, now I think about it, I do be sick a lot these days. And that thing of not being able to get into my jeans and all. So, I guess what I'm saying is, maybe we pregnant. But if we ain't, then next time maybe we could use something, you know, so's it don't happen no ways soon. That is if it ain't already too late."

Boom. It felt like she had dropped a bomb on me. My mind started flashing back over the past several days, and I began to panic. Really. It felt like I couldn't breathe for a minute. I dropped Sister's hands without even meaning to, and, even though there was a breeze blowing off the water, I started to sweat profusely. I just kept thinking, *pregnant?! Pregnant?!*

Than I started praying silently. *God, please don't let this be true. Please. I will be more careful—I promise, just don't let this be true. Because I am not ready for a kid. And what about Mama and Pap and...and...Sissy's family, and what about me? How am I gonna get better at the guitar and plan the rally and...I don't know, be part of the revolution if she's, if we're pregnant, as she says?*

And I must have looked mighty strange, and she must have started to sense that I wasn't thrilled, and she must have gotten a little angry, which is just what I didn't want. I saw her eyes narrow, and in her spirit, she moved away from me and glared down like "how dare you!" And then I felt bad, because, for those few minutes, I was only thinking about me and my fears, and I wasn't even thinking about her. And the weird thing is, when I finally did look at her, I felt her eyes pierce into mine, and it felt like magnets pulling me back to her. It made me take a sharp breath. Because in that instant, I just sort of knew that she, that *we* were pregnant. I could feel this new entity coming between us and blending us together. It was heavy.

That's when I started to melt over inside. I just felt like I couldn't contain it, how much I felt for her, how much I, I don't know, dug her. I mean, there she is, and she's got her hair pinned all over her head and falling down in little coils all around her face, and her skin has gotten smooth and creamy and brown in the sun, and I can see where her tits are tight like the other day in my room, and it wasn't just that exactly. I mean, why should she have to feel anxious or at a loss for words? Ever? Much less for something that we did, that we might have created, out of love for each other? That wouldn't make sense.

So, I just pulled her next to me, and she buried her face in my shirt. We were sitting in the grass, and she was facing me with her legs stretched out around mine, with her hands in my hair and her face deep in my tee shirt. And when she does that shit, it's crazy, because I can actually hear what she's saying to me, only she's not using any words. But somehow she's saying she's proud of this thing we created and she wants to please me and I make her happy and I need you and a whole lot of other stuff. And without words of my own, I said the same things back to her.

And that's how I found out that we were pregnant.

Nothing really seemed so different at first. She wanted to go to the doctor, and she didn't want to have me go with her. At least not officially. She had Pammie go in with her, but I drove them both. They have this clinic on campus, and all you have to do to go there and get tested is call and make an appointment. Sissy said they had all kinds of information there, too. About support programs where if you're single you can maybe find housing or get public assistance for medical care or food for the baby or whatever. They could put you in touch with the state adoption agency if you wanted to go that route, and they had classes so's you could learn how to handle the pregnancy or whatever, but one thing they lectured you about was not having an abortion. They were really against that sort of thing. They would say that women are given a gift when they give birth, and you shouldn't go screwing around with that.

It was uncomfortable when I drove them to the doctor. Pammie was there, and I guess that just changed the dynamic between us, because usually we spend time alone. I'm not jealous or anything, but I did notice the difference. A lot of times, not all the time but a lot of times, Sissy is more quiet with me. Conversation comes and goes in spurts, but with Pammie she just kept talking away. It was rapid fire with them. One would say something, and the other would finish the sentence and start another, and then the other would finish, and back and forth like that. And a lot of giggles, too. I never knew Sissy was so silly!

At first I tried joining in. Because, I mean, I know Sissy, too, and I am not unfamiliar with Pammie. I could finish Sissy's sentences if I wanted to. So, if one of them said something, I would chime in with what I thought was a relaxing or humorous comment. But it didn't really go over. Both of them would get silent. I'd notice Pam getting extremely interested in something out the window at those moments, and Sissy would start to hum whatever was on the radio. Then, a song would remind them of something, something girlish, I guess, and private, and they would be at it again. Oh well. So, I decided to keep quiet, let them have their thing.

When we got on the yard, I parked right in front of the Science Building where the clinic is. I stopped the car and looked at Sissy. Pammie got out and said she'd sign Sissy in and wait for her. I guess she wanted us to have a little time alone since I wouldn't be going inside. But, truly, even though it took me a while to get it, I already knew what was up. So, I folded her in my arms quietly and tried to give her some strength. I didn't want to upset her or make her cry. I just wanted her to feel...safe. She didn't say anything to me, either. She got out and walked into the clinic.

At first, while I sat in the car, I started to pray again. Not like before, though, because I wasn't praying that it wasn't true. I was just asking God to take care of Sister and my child, to bless them or something. I never know quite what to say to God. It's weird. So, I just let my thoughts flow, and I direct them toward God, and when I am done, I think to myself, *Amen.* I thought about what it means to be a father, what my father was like before he died. About Sister's family and Edward and Pammie and the kids at church and all. What in the world are they gonna think when they know Sister is pregnant? And Mama?!

And when I thought of Mama and Pap, I started to get anxious again, so I stopped praying and started regulating my breath. When it started working and I felt more calm, I lit a cigarette. It would work itself out. It would have to.

More and more time passed, and I was getting bored sitting out in the car alone. I didn't want to keep playing the radio and wasting the battery, so I got out. I took my guitar out of the trunk and walked to the plot of trees on the left side of the Social Sciences Wing. You can still see the Science Building from there, but it is sunny and comfortable, and the trees create the illusion of coolness. I took my cigarettes and my guitar, and headed over there.

So, I'm sitting there strumming a little Dylan, not singing, just strumming and stuff, working the kinks out, when who should come out of the Social Science Wing but Nancy. And she's with another girl that I don't know, short and big-hipped with big red hair. Neither of them is wearing shoes. Truthfully, I don't feel like dealing with them, but they're right there, and there's no way that they're not gonna see me. So, I just keep strumming and await the inevitable.

"Hey, Now! How's it going, Evian! Look, Amy, it's Evian, the one I told you about, from the CFPSC?" She makes a beeline for me with Amy close behind her. Both of them plop down on the grass, and Amy sticks her backpack under her knees and smiles like she knows me.

"Hello, ladies. What brings you to campus today?" I try to sound casual and polite, but really I am kinda annoyed. I mean, I didn't exactly ask them to join me or whatever.

"Oh, we are taking this class on Human Sexuality—really interesting. You know, people seem to think that sex is so natural that it doesn't bear study. Not true! There's all kinds of useful stuff to learn. Wouldn't you say, Amy? Oh, sorry! I am such a clod. Amy, this is Evian. Evian…Amy."

"Hi, Evian. I have heard a lot about you from Nancy. Nice to finally meet you."

Now I am puzzled. *Finally meet me? Why would Nancy be talking to her about me?* "Good to know you, Amy." I nodded at her, and then I went back to fingering the guitar, though I stopped actually playing. I didn't want to give them too much attention, because I didn't want them to stick around for long.

"As I was saying, this class is too interesting! I mean, positions, suggestions, interpretations about sex. Crucial!" Nancy's the type who talks in exclamation points. It could get on your nerves if you weren't careful.

Amy giggled.

"So, Evian. What are you doing up here? Did you finally decide to enroll in our grand institution?" She turned to Amy. "I keep telling Evian that he should go to U.K., but he won't budge! He is so stubborn!"

Amy giggled.

"Nah. Just gave some friends a ride is all. Thought I'd wait for them rather than haul it all the way home and back again. Just enjoying some sunshine and waiting." I stopped fingering the guitar since they didn't seem to be getting the hint.

"Groovy! Evian plays some killer strings, Amy. He is gonna play for us at the rally, huh, Evian? I keep asking him to show off for me, play a tune or something, but he never wants to. Maybe he'll do it if you ask, Amy!" She poked Amy in the side. Amy giggled.

But, since she asked me, and since I didn't feel like making any more giggly small talk with Nancy and her carrot-headed friend, I said I'd play when Amy asked. I felt like Hendrix that day, so right away I went into "Little Wing." I only hummed along, no words. But I thought that would satisfy the two and help them on their way. But there's this part in the middle that is kinda hard to finger, and I was busy concentrating, so I didn't notice when Pammie walked up with her hands on her hips. Cold moment. I stopped playing immediately.

Amy got this look on her face like a deer caught in the headlights, and Nancy just looked at me for some kind of answer. I wasn't really up for giving any. I just scooped up my guitar and thrust my cigarettes in my pocket. "Oh, Pam. I didn't realize you were done. Y'all ready to roll?"

Pam had daggers in her teeth when she said, "Yes, Evian. *We* are ready to go. All of us." Then she flipped her hair back and started for the car. I could see that Sister was already there, but she had her head back on the seat with her eyes closed.

Nancy looked at Amy and shrugged and said, "Okay…I guess I'll see you later!"

I nodded and said, "Nice to meet you to, Amy." I walked to the car without looking back. Not that I owe any of them, Amy or Nancy or Pam any explanation, but it was a little weird.

By the time I got to the car and put the guitar back in the trunk, Pammie was in the back seat, and Sister was back there, too. Pam had her arm around Sister's shoulder, and Sister still had her eyes closed. She didn't look upset, exactly, but she wasn't saying anything. I got behind the wheel and looked at Pammie. She just nodded her head like to say yes, it is true. I nodded back, smiled, and gave a thumbs up. Then I drove them back to Sister's house.

CHAPTER THIRTY-THREE

But deep inside me I had a slow and sinful panic. I mean, it didn't seem right for someone who loved God to be housing this kinda fear. But, I felt like, on the other hand, who am I to feel panic? There's Sissy, in the back seat with her eyes closed and just as calm as you please. She's the one who's pregnant. She's the one who'll go through the sickness and the labor and whatever else. I mean, I can stick beside her, but I know it won't be the same for me. Then I thought, *who's to say she doesn't feel a panic, too?* Turned out that she didn't, because when we got alone and it seemed okay to ask, she told me she had a sort of peace about the whole thing. But at the time I didn't know, so the thing that kept me from driving off the road was this noble thing, where I was gonna be strong for Sissy, and for our baby.

OUR BABY! OUR BABY!

Yeah, so it struck me with urgency first off. And I kept picturing this time when we went to Cape Cod when I was 10, and I was so intrigued with the ocean. The way it kept coming and going, flipping and turning, powerful as shit. I kept thinking, *how can I get involved in that?* It was way too much for me, especially as a little kid, so I kept standing there staring out at the water like an idiot. I wanted to be a part of it, just float out there and feel its strength or whatever, but I was a chicken shit. Then, Pap caught me glaring at the water, and he scooped me up and took me out there. And somewhere between his arms and the moody sky and my own desire, I started to float. I got the same feeling at first when I thought about Sissy, about the baby and all. I didn't know what to do to float with it. Then, just like at the Cape, I decided I'd do the same thing. I'd go home and talk to Pap. I wasn't exactly sure what I would say to him, but I was sort of comforted by the concept of telling him what was going on. Seemed like I'd be able to trust him, maybe even lean on him. He's good that way.

But, strangely, my mind was occupied with this concept of flow, and it helped me stay calm in the car. I kept thinking of how you can look up and see forever when you're on your back in the ocean on a clear day with a moody sky overhead. Plus, I had turned to a classical station, and they were playing Bach. The whole vibe of flowing and ocean and Bach really saw me through that car trip, that seemed like it took forever. Because nobody was saying anything. I mean, I felt like a hired driver, practically, since Pam and Sissy were in the back, one with the arm around the other, and neither of them paying a bit of attention to me. But I decided I'd talk to Pap, and I would do whatever to make this thing work.

Since nobody said anything, I just drove back to Sister's house. I wasn't thinking that maybe Pam wanted a ride home. I wasn't thinking about anything, really. So, when we pulled up in front of the house, everybody just sat there. I could hear Pam and Sissy whispering in the back. I was almost afraid to turn around, because it was like, if Sissy was crying, or if she was emotional in anyway, it would have really thrown me off kilter. So I just sat there like an idiot. Then, I felt Sister's warm hand on my shoulder, and she gave a gentle squeeze. Pammie got out and climbed in the front seat. When I turned to look at Sister, she motioned to me to get out of the car, and when I did, she put her arms full around my waist. She never does that. She always hugs me at the top, with her arms around my neck, but this time she caught me at the middle with a full-bodied hug. She felt closer than sex. She rubbed her face in my chest, which knocks me out, and then she whispered in my ear, "I got a little something for you, but you gonna have to wait a few months to get it. You think you could wait?" She had a little grin at the left corner of her mouth when she said it, and after she laid her head on my chest and breathed easy.

I whispered back, "I guess I would maybe wait forever for what you got to give me. I waited this long. What's a few more months, between friends?" And it was different, because we almost never show that kind of affection for each other in public, especially near both of our houses. Soon, I guess we came to our senses, because Sissy broke out of my arms and took some steps back. She put her hands on her hips and shook her hand. For some reason, it made me blush.

Sissy told me to call at 10:00, and she would pick up the phone. She mouthed *I love you*, and she waved to Pam as she went in the house.

When I dropped Pammie off, I didn't go straight home. I drove down to the lake instead. I guess I wanted some time to be alone and just blank out or think, which ever felt better. When life alters, sometimes it takes me some time to regroup. So, I had my ditty bag and my sketch pad, and I just hiked down to my spot. Changed my head some, and worked on this picture I'd been drawing. I thought, in that setting, with the sky and the grass and the water, that maybe I would be able to find a stance, you know, like, decide how I was going to handle this next phase of my life. As a father. As a... husband? I mean, shit, I don't know. But, as it turned out, I just worked on my picture, and that's it. I didn't really think about anything. It felt good.

When I got home, the phone was ringing, and it was Nancy. Great. Mama had picked up the phone in the kitchen, and she looked thrilled to find out who it was. She had all this sun and honey in her voice when she told Nancy I'd just come in and she'd call me to the phone. I told Mama I'd take it in my bedroom, and she must have liked that answer, figuring I would want privacy to talk to this nice, *white* girl from around to the college. If only she knew...

"Yea, this is Evian." I must have sounded a little annoyed, but I couldn't help it, under the circumstances. She just bugged me, that's all, especially since Mama was always after me to "fraternize" with her, as she calls it.

Nancy was masking her usual bubble over with a blanket of warm concern. Right! "Hey, Evian. You okay? I mean, earlier, you rushed off so quickly, and your, uh, friend seemed upset. Is everything okay?"

Maybe she was sincere, and maybe she just wanted to express concern as a friend, but it seemed more likely to me that Nancy wanted to be nosey. Like she wanted to know what was up with Pammie. And I guess she might have seen Sister in the car, also. "Sweet of you to ask, Nancy, but it's cool. We were just anxious to get back home is all. No big deal, really."

Nancy paused for a minute, and I could hear how she was struggling to say something that she found difficult or whatever. So she goes, "Evian, I'm not sure how to say this, so I guess I'll just blurt it out. Is Sister in trouble? I mean, like, you know...ahh, in a family way? Because, if she is, I think I can help..." She waited for an answer.

Seriously, I was blown away. I mean, this one really had come from left field, and it caught me by surprise. I had to sit down on the bed and breathe, which I've been doing a lot lately. "Umm." I laughed nervously. "Why do you ask that?" I didn't want to respond one way or another.

"I feel like such a sneak, but I really didn't do it on purpose! I swear. It's just that Amy's roommate works in the clinic, and she told Amy that Sister had an appointment there today, and it was a long one, and that's like, code or something, because really girls only come there for testing on certain days, and when it's negative, well...let's just say it isn't a long visit. So...then I thought, maybe that's why you all left in such a hurry...I hope I'm not overstepping my...I don't know. It's just that, Sister is such a bright girl, and...I think I could help." I guess Nancy is like a lot of those girls that ramble on when they get nervous. When she finally stopped talking, there was dead silence on the phone.

I didn't know what to say. Nancy was like totally on target with this one, and she seemed to have an inside source, and I didn't know whether to confirm or deny her information. So, I go, "You're putting me in a really awkward situation here, Nancy. I don't really know what to say except that...I don't know. Sister and I are good friends, okay? What she tells me, she tells me in confidence. I wouldn't want to, uh, break that confidence...but I appreciate your concern." I was stuttering all over the place. I was coming off like a complete idiot, but what was I supposed to do?

"Oh, God! Of course! How stupid of me, Evian. Can you forgive me? I...don't know. I just felt like I was in a position to help, or whatever. I mean, I have seen Sister at the meetings and all, and I figured...I mean, I don't know who she's involved with, but I know that we're all young. Let me just say this—I was in the same situation last summer, and I went to that same clinic. Okay? They are like, really old-fashioned, and they had me thinking that I had no choice but to drop out of school and raise a kid. It scared me. But, then I went to another place downtown, and I got some other information, so I just thought...I don't know. Maybe Sister might want someone to talk to..."

The whole conversation was making me want to vomit for a lot of reasons. Over the past week or so, I'd started getting that slow burning in my stomach, where it feels like waste is traveling up to my chest like a train of thick smoke that makes me cough and wheeze. So, maybe it was partially that thing again. But, mainly I wanted to vomit because I had just heard the news about Sissy myself, and I hadn't even had the chance to get straight with it. Now, I've got this perfect stranger telling me she knows my business and wants to help. So, I just got off the phone as quick as I could and didn't even try not to be rude. I mean, overstepping? That's what happens when you're dancing with someone you love, and an idiot comes over and cuts in. This thing of saying you can help when you find out a near stranger is pregnant is something else again.

But, I promptly ignored it, the burn in my stomach that itched me in the chest. I knew the pollen was still really bad, even though it was late in the season, so I thought it might be allergies. Plus, Sister had been so volatile in the recent weeks, so I thought it might be a reaction to that, too. Bottom line, I had too many other things going on to worry about traveling waste in my stomach. The rally was coming up in two weeks, for one thing. And I was on the program committee. We had three speakers scheduled, and one was notorious for being a radical. I had to meet with him to hear what he was planning to say and make sure he understood that we wanted a peaceful assembly. There were people from the group who would be doing some short readings, and Sissy and I were doing two numbers. And all of a sudden, under my nose, Edward, Albert, Sissy, and Pammie had formed some kind of a singing group where people just fell all over themselves to hear them harmonize a capella. And, truthfully, I couldn't blame them, because their blend was incredible. But, they had problems keeping organized and making decisions, because they're not used to working together. Fought over everything—what key they'd sing in, which numbers would be best to perform, who would stand where, what outfits they'd pick. And I sometimes had to act as a mediator when they practiced, just to make sure they got anything accomplished.

I had a heap on my plate. And truthfully, the normal regulation of my breathing was not always so quick to work after that to calm me down. Maybe it was the idea of Nancy knowing about Sister that had me on edge, or maybe it was the pregnancy or the rally, but all this stuff together was beginning to wear on me. For the first time in a long time, I got on my knees, right there next to my bed, and laid my head down and prayed. Real prayer, too. Not just me directing my thoughts toward God. Because something inside me knew that all of this stuff going on was out of my control, even if I wanted to play like it wasn't. And I knew that more than anything else, I was going to need strength, or something. I don't know.

And when I got done, I felt hollowed out. Not empty, exactly, because then it would seem like I was wanting for something, but truthfully I felt hollow, and the hollow feeling made me happy. I waited until Mama had gone out, and then I headed back to Pap's room. No sense in letting this Sissy issue get any bigger before I got a handle on it. I guess I would rather have sat on the information a little longer, but with Nancy calling and saying she's wise to us, I felt like I needed to work it out in my head right away.

Now, Pap is funny. He practically met me at the door, like he already knew what was coming. And when I told him, in my roundabout way, that I had gotten Sissy in trouble, he didn't flinch or start. He just looked at me flatly and made room for me on the bed. He told me that he thinks the world of Rebecca. That she's decent and giving and comes from a sound family. He said he couldn't see how having a baby would be called trouble, since youngins are a blessing from God. He actually says stuff like youngins. But the rest of what he said filled up the happy hollow I'd come in with.

"Err, the matter of paternity, Ev-yun. Now, there's the contention." Pap leaned forward with his arms on his knees and rubbed at his bony thighs.

Always the idiot, I didn't get it. "Contention? What do you mean, Pap?"

"Call it a contention or an impossibility, but be straight about it."

Then, I guess the whole gig started to wear on me, and I got irritated. "Always with this riddle talk! I don't know what you mean, so could you just do me a favor and speak in plain English?! I mean, God! I just need some advice or something, that's all."

Pap cleared his throat and looked in my eyes. "It isn't your trouble, Ev-yun. And I don't know whose it is, exactly, but I do know whose it isn't. I knew, from the first time that you got sick, that your, err, fathering would be impossible. Some of that treatment left you less than what you might have been, but, praise Him, it left you alive. Small price, I felt. I knew that since you were 13. Well, Cor-jul doesn't like to talk about what doesn't come easily. So, I never discussed it with her. My job to talk to doctors when she needed, my job to keep a secret if I needed. And until now there has never been a reason to say anything. But now, with Rebecca in her family way, seems best that you should know."

I looked at Pap in dawning horror. What was he trying to tell me? He had to be wrong, because Sissy...I mean. There must've been a mistake.

"Pap! You said you liked Sissy! Like you want to make it seem like this kid isn't mine! Why would you make something like this up?! I mean, God! Do you think I believe that Sissy has been with someone else? Because I can assure you, that isn't the case. And the test is positive, so...You need to get your facts straight!" I was feeling that burning pull, rising from my stomach to my chest, and I was trying my best to regulate the breathing, but the effort was for shit. I was practically hyperventilating. For some reason, the idea of being sterile or whatever didn't bother me as much as the idea of Sissy being with someone else. I just knew that couldn't be true.

Pap brushed through his long white hair and looked at me directly, with calmness and penetration. He's like that. He'll look at you, through you, and he'll will you to be calm and reasonable. It's weird, because, when he gets mad, he can get as irrational as the next guy. But when I'm upset, well he just looks at me and waits.

"Ev-yun. This thing of bringing forth a new soul, it is a miracle and a mystery, Son. We can do a lot of things as gentlemen, but that's one thing we can't do. And we gotta respect that. Leave your Self, put Self away for a time, and think of young Rebecca. And if you love her, then what belongs to her also in part belongs to you. Even with your, err, impossibility. There is no shame in that."

And off he went again with the riddles and the wisdom that I couldn't half grasp. All I knew was he was supposed to be making me feel better, telling me what to do. Instead he tells me that I'm sterile and that my girlfriend sleeps around. Not what I had in mind for this conversation. I just kept shaking my head and giving empty gestures. I could barely listen to what he was saying about making a plan and considering the women, about Ma and her fragility. Finally, I stood up to go. Pap rose with me and caught me around the shoulder with his arm. He clinched for a moment in a half hug. Then, he squeezed my shoulder and told me to think and pray and act. He said he'd back me up, whatever I decided.

But I had no idea what to decide. I wasn't even clear anymore on what I was deciding about. And, really, I felt like crying. Like, sobbing like some idiot. Because if I didn't father Sissy's kid, than someone else did, and the possibility of it made me half sick, half crazy.

So, I left Pap's room and headed out to the field. I needed a head change, and I didn't feel like driving or walking anywhere. And I'm off on the side of the house, in the direction of Pammie's house, under a tree, in a clump of tall grass. I lit up a johnson, and I inhaled deep. It felt like wind running through that sour burning I felt in my stomach and chest. It made me cough, but it made me feel better, too. I sucked deep and hard until half the thing was gone. I dragged twice more before I snuffed it out and put the roach in my pocket.

Everything was whirling around inside of me. I wanted to go to sleep or cry or run, but I didn't really feel up to any of that, so I just sat there. I had to organize my thoughts and come up with a plan or something. So, I unfolded the events from the past few hours. The baby. Nancy. All that shit Pap said. None of it made sense. But, somewhere in the center of me, I knew that Pap was telling the truth. I sort of remember sterility being an issue when I was a kid, before I started treatment, but it never really made a difference at the time, and I never had to think about it since. Until now.

So, I went back in my head, in my heart. That way that Sissy pulled me in at the middle and breathed on my chest. In broad daylight, right there next to Pammie and the rest of the world. That felt real. And, underneath of the panic, I was excited, too. I mean, at least I was a few hours ago. Because I love Sissy. And I love this baby, too. And I remembered how I'd felt a few days ago when she got mad at me because she thought I said she was fat. I remembered how I felt when she was puking her guts up in the bathroom, and how I was afraid that I'd lose her and never really understand why. And I remembered that way she pins her hair up, and how her tits got tight, and how she sings when it's just the two of us. And I loved her so much.

That's when I started to bug. Now, Pap says that I can't be the father. Who is? Who is?? And I don't know if it was the corn or the stress or what, but I started thinking about Edward, Pammie's brother. How he hates me so much for being with Sissy. How, all of a sudden, the four of them are this singing sensation, rehearsing all the time without me. And how he clearly wants Sissy. Badly. How he openly flirts with her when I'm around. And Lord knows what he does when I'm not around! I started thinking about every time that I have left Sister alone and gone home. Times when she goes around to Pammie's house to bake or talk or practice or whatever. And I start to wonder if she and Edward…I don't know.

So, at 10, when I'm supposed to call Sissy, I close my door and call in a soft whisper, because I don't want anyone here to hear what I'm saying. Hell, *I* don't want to hear what I'm saying! But, I tell her all about Nancy and how her roommate knows the clinic and how Nancy knows she's pregnant, and about how I didn't confirm it one way or another. And I throw in that part about Nancy saying she has other options besides having the baby, and maybe that's how we should handle this thing. And that's when I heard that stony silence from Sissy, and I guess that's where it went wrong.

CHAPTER THIRTY-FOUR

Right after I go to the clinic, find out about me and Ev baby, seem like Evian change. Like to break my heart, too, because I don't expect it. But that night he call me and tell me he talk to that Nancy from the CFPSC, and she say she know I'm pregnant. And Ev say Nancy say I don't have to have this baby if I don't want to. And it seem like maybe he don't want me to have this baby. And that make me mad, because, to my mind, it ain't no other way. And anyways, I want this baby because it something that me and Ev make, and that seem beautiful to me. But he say that Nancy say she know some places downtown whereas you can go and do something else. So, I got mad.

But, next thing I know, he asking me if he be the first one I was with. Felt like he slap me in the face, for real. How he could fix his mouth to ask me that, I don't know. But when he do, I don't say nothing. I mean, truth, it make me cry. I cry easy these days. But I don't want him to know that, so I just stay quiet. First he tell me maybe we should not have this baby, since he talk to Nancy, and then he ask me if he the only one I been with. I'm so mad and sad at the same time I can't say nothing.

Ev keep pressing me, got this mean, serious tone in his voice, and I don't want to let on that what he say make me sad and make me cry. Because if he don't love me, and if he don't want to believe this baby we make his, then forget him! So, I make like me and Edward getting to be real close. Which ain't exactly true but ain't all that much of a lie, neither. See, Edward been knowing me as long as I known Pam, and it do seem like he want me for hisself sometime. Specially since he know I be with Ev. He a flirt, sure enough, and he like to see me blush. I got this sick feeling inside my heart when Ev ask me do I be with anybody else, and it hurt. So, I figure if I gotta hurt over him, then let me see can I make him hurt over me some, too.

I tell Ev it ain't his business to know who all I be with when I ain't with him. I tell him how I know what he do when he leave me at home, way cross the field somewhere, when he ain't with me. And I add how I seen how Nancy look at him sometime, and how it ain't no surprise to me that she be the one to say go get rid of this child, like she think I'm the type to kill children. And I say, he don't have to worry what me and mine do, if he don't feel like it, because ain't nothing to have a baby. Ruthanne done it, and I don't see her making like she in such a bad way.

Then it Ev turn to be silent. It sound like he been running around or something, cuz his breath don't sound even. And he talk real low, like a machine humming, when he finally say something.

"A part of me thinks you're just jerking my chain to get my reaction. But the other part of me is not sure. I mean. I think you're lying about Edward. I hope you're lying about Edward. And if you're trying to hurt me, then…I guess you're succeeding." Ev stop between each word, like what he say he got to think about careful before he say it.

Any other time, I would cry full out and tell Evian how he hurt me when he accuse me of being with somebody else when he know he the only one I want. I would tell him how I don't want him to look at Nancy, how I want us to have this baby, and how happy he make me. But seem like a part of myself gone crazy or something, and I can't do it. Because I feel so…I don't know. Like if I tell him all that, then I have to admit that he can hurt me, that he got what it take to make me cry. And, right then, I couldn't make myself admit that to him.

"Well, Ev. I done tell you the truth. And you could see for yourself. If you don't want me, and if you don't want this baby, then I think I know someone who do. For real. I ain't press for you or nobody!" And I slam down the phone. Put my head down on the kitchen table and cry so hard, feel like every organ I got in me gonna fly out and land somewhere in the kitchen sink. I just keep thinking, why? Why he do me like that? Why he try to make like I be playing out on him? Why he tell me to do what Nancy say and not have my baby? How Imma do something like that? But, then I remember what Grannie use to say. How she say you can't trust white folks, cuz they crazy. And how Ruthanne tell me I better be careful sure enough. And how Pammie try to say that maybe I don't realize how much I'm into if I be with Ev. And that bigger part of me, the part that *know*, the part that come out when me and Ev be together and talk or be quiet and just feel, that part slip under this other part that say Ev a crazy white fool who say I sleep around and tell me to kill my child. And for a while I'm so hurt and confuse, I don't know what all I might do.

Bunch of days pass. I go to work, same as before, but Evian ain't never there. Miss say he down to the church, or he meet with the speaker for the rally, or he at the site, which is what they call the piece of land outside the student union where they got a platform and all, where the speakers and entertainment set up for the program. And she got me doing all this busy work, like sort through the winter clothes she store, and organize the library where she got all these papers and pictures and stuff. A lot of the time, I don't say much to Miss. Just do what she say and stay out her way. Sometime, when she in the other end of the house, I may start to cry. Outta the blue, tears start to roll down my cheek. I feel so lonesome around to Ev house now, because he ain't never around. And, for all I know, he round to Nancy house, planning how they get me to go downtown and "do something else" with this child I just found out I have so they could be together for real.

In those days, Norman gone to stay with Clive Manderene, the only relative he got left that he still friendly with. Cousin Clives, as Miss call him, they cousin live down in Lexington, and he come get Norman few days past, have Norman to stay for the whole week plus the weekend. Norman ain't due back til two days before our rally. Bless his heart, he say he don't want to miss that. Norman was real sweet to me when he left out, too. Took time to ask me how I was and do I think I be okay with him down in Lex. And I ain't talk to Ev since we fight on the phone the other night, so I ain't for sure, but it seem like Norman know, or something, that I am, you know. In a family way. But I don't say nothing to him like that. I just tell him he sweet to ask me, and I guess we all make out best we can without him, and have a good time.

So, I'm in the library toward the end of the week, got a box full of statements from everything Miss pay for from the last five years. And she want me to categorize them according to the company she pay to, and then put the envelopes in order, from most recent to least recent. Then she want me to bind them up and place them just so back in the box. And she up at the front of the house, sitting on her lounger, with a two-piece on. She sunning herself, cuz now she say she ain't got no color in her face. Why white people spend so much time trying to change they color, make it dark like ours, I don't know. But she on her stomach, last time I seen her, so's the sun can get to her back. Even though she want to get tan, she don't want nobody to see her. She tell me when Edward come to mow the lawn, tell him he don't have to do the front side today. He can do that part tomorrow. That way she don't have to worry about him coming round there and see her in her two-piece. Like Edward care one way or another. But Miss, she modest like that.

Since I know Miss asleep on her lounger and getting sun in her face, I got the radio up loud in the library. I'm singing along while I sort through Miss bills. And Aretha come on with "Bridge Over Troubled Water." And the bridge I been using to hold everything up inside me collapse. The bridge that hold what I feel for Ev and pretend I don't feel no more. That hold how he ain't been here all week when I come and ain't talk to him since we fight. The bridge I make to keep Ev from knowing he hurt me when he accuse me of being with other people break, and I start to cry. I mean really cry, sobbing, the kind where your chest pump up and down and you can't hardly catch your breath. And I'm wailing out loud to Aretha, and I see Edward out the window, cutting the grass, and he see me, too. He give me this pitiful look, like, girl, why you crying, and Sister, don't cry all at the same time. I feel like I been holding all this stuff in for so long, and now I gotta let it go. So, I get up and walk round to the back sliding door, where

Miss usually stare off and paint, and I rush up to Edward. He cut off the machine when he see me coming, and I fall straight in his arms.

"Eddie, what I'm spose to do, anyway? I can't let him know he hurt me and all, and I don't want him to know I don't want him look at Nancy, and I wanna keep this baby, and now what I'm spose to do?" I blurt out this stuff, and none of it make sense to him, but he put his arms around me and tell me hush, hush, sound like Miss Minnie when he try to comfort me. And I slow up a little, but I keep pulling at the air with my mouth, can't hardly breathe.

"Sister, you talking crazy! What chou mean, keep this *baby?!* I know you ain't saying what I think you saying! Watch what you saying so loud, now, Miss right around the corner! Come on, now..." He take my hand in one hand and drag the lawn mower with the other, and we head further around the house, back in front of the library window, where he seen me cry to Aretha. Miss got a dogwood there that done lost most of it blossom, and the pink petals is all over the trunk of the tree and on the ground right next to it. I don't care. I flop down under the tree and hitch my knees up to my chest, put my head down on my knees.

For a minute, Edward just stare at me, like he don't know what to make of all this. Then it seem like he get mad or something. He and Albert both act like that. When somebody get real upset, they get upset, too, but can't show it. So, instead they get mad or something. "All right, I don't know what in the world is wrong with you, Sister, but you must want to talk. So, stop this foolishness and tell me what the hell is going on, now." He move up close to me, sit right in front of my knees, so he can hear whatever I got to say.

I breathe a few times deep, and then I tell him. About how me and Ev and Pammie go to the clinic, and how I'm in a family way. How at first it seem like Ev glad about it, but then he ask me do I be with other people. About how Nancy say I should "do something else" besides have the baby. Mainly how I am confuse and don't know what to do since Evian ain't never here no more, like he put me down or something. I leave out the part about how I tell Ev me and Eddie is close. I don't want him to know I use him to make Ev jealous, specially since it seem like it backfire and Ev don't care no way.

Edward shake his head, like he done heard it all now. He talk real soft. "Sister, when you say you in a family way, ahh. What you think you gonna do? I mean, damn...Your moms ain't gonna be, like, oh, congratulations, baby! You done slept with the white folks! It's like...I don't know. Damn..." He look like he at a loss for words.

"I know. I done thought about it every since I knew about it. But, what can she do? It the truth. I know she ain't gonna be thrilled and all, but, oh well. And, I wanna have this baby. What else I'm gonna do?" I'm so confuse, I don't have no more words to say, and so tired I don't have no more tears neither. I just sit there, with my chin on my knees, which ain't that comfortable, cuz now my belly starting to get bloated and bigger.

Edward skooch his butt up a notch closer to me, and he rest his chin on my knee, too. He give me this silly, puppy dog look, and I laugh. He take both my hands off my knee, and he lean in close to kiss me soft on the forehead. He tell me, whatever happen, he know everything gonna be all right. He say, we work this out. All of us. We figure something out. He keep my hands an extra minute after he kiss my head, and he give me a little squeeze.

That when I notice Evian look at us from the window in the library. I pull my hands out from Edward, and back away some, but it too late. Evian look at me like I shoot him in the stomach, then he slam out the library where I can't see him no more.

Edward notice how my body change from a minute ago, and when he turn around, he see Evian slam out the library, too. He look at me again, and for a minute I see fire in his eyes, like he mad that I would pull my hands away just cuz I seen Evian.

"Sister, I don't understand you! What do it take for you to know that you can't trust these crackers?! What he gotta do, tell you to your face that he don't want you and your half-breed baby? I mean, shit!" He move away from me, like if he don't he might hit me or something.

"No. I mean, I don't know for sure what he want. Always use to seem like I could trust him, but, now I don't know..." I don't want to make Edward mad, but I don't want him to call Ev a cracker can't nobody trust neither.

Edward breathe deep and try to keep cool. "Look. I been knowing you a long time, and I know you a nice girl. Any man should be tickled to know you carrying they child. I know if it were me, I would want to stand by you, not question if the kid is mine or tell you to kill it. If it were me, I would have your back. I wouldn't put you through that. That's all I know. But what you decide to do, that's up to you." He talk soft, like every word he say a diamond he giving me to treasure and hold onto. But I ain't for sure that I want these jewels from him.

"I hear you, Edward. You probably right. I don't know what I do, but whatever I do, I'm glad I got you to talk to, if I need to. You ain't gonna tell nobody what I say, is you?"

"Nah. I guess I could keep a secret. Do Albert know?"

"Uh-uh. Just Pammie and Ev, and now you. Unless you count Nancy."

"Oh, Lord. You got a bag a shit do deal with, don't you?" He sound like he really feel sorry for me.

"Yes, I do. But I make it through. Let me get back inside, though. Thanks for hearing me..."

I head around to the sliding-glass door, and Edward go back to mowing the lawn. Inside, I stand in the library for a minute, think about what just happen and what all Ev saw and what he must think. And I feel like Imma be sick. I know I tell him I be close to Edward, but really I ain't. And, to tell the truth, I don't like this thing of not seeing Ev and not talk to him. I feel like I want to clear stuff up with him, tell him he the only one, ask him do he still love me and all. I mean, he look upset when he seen me with Edward, so maybe he do still care for me some.

I head on down the hall to the end and knock on Ev door. He got The Beatles on loud, and I know he play that when he ready to go out somewhere. I wonder where he going, but I knock anyway. He don't answer at first.

"Yeah?" He sound like he change his clothes or something, cuz his voice is cover up and don't sound clear.

"It's me, Sissy. Can I come in?" I try to sound casual. I got my hand on the knob, though, ready to come in and talk this stuff out, so what he say surprise me.

He turn down the music for a minute and he say, "Umm. I'm kinda in a hurry. Heading out in a few minutes. Can we do this another time?"

What he say take the wind out of me, and I can't hardly answer. So, I clear my throat, cough away the tears I feel coming on, and I say, "Oh. I understand. Never mind." I walk down the hall real fast like ghosts chasing me. I get up to the powder room next to the library, close the door and turn on the fan. I start to sweat. Because I feel like everything has turn upside-down and backwards. And I feel like I got myself to blame. Because if I didn't lie to Ev about Edward, then maybe I never have to cry to Edward about what happen, and maybe Ev never see me and him close and Edward kiss my head, and maybe Ev still love me and want to hear what I got to say. But now. Now, I don't know.

CHAPTER THIRTY-FIVE

Completely blew me away. I mean, I was upset and all when we were on the phone the other night, and that stuff she implied about Edward made me mad. But part of me really believed that it was some craziness she fabricated, you know, to make me angry. I mean, I guess I came off at her the wrong way that night, partly due to being stoned, and partly due to being stressed. I mean, give me a break! This stuff about being a father and not being a father was fucking with my head, and I was on overload. But, I knew Sissy had been acting strange ever since she got pregnant, or whatever, so I guess I should have handled that whole conversation differently. I just thought she would tell me of course not, that she could never be with anyone else, that I had nothing to worry about. Then, I would tell her we should keep our baby. But, the whole Edward dynamic really threw me.

So, I just backed way the hell off. I do that when I feel like I'm drowning or getting overwhelmed. Just back off and keep to myself. I just couldn't take anymore. Seriously. I mean, if what she was telling me about her and Edward was true, then I had totally misread our whole relationship. And if it wasn't true, then I had totally misread her personality. And if what Pap said was true, then I had totally misinterpreted my whole role in this whole thing. No matter how I looked at it, I couldn't win. So, I backed the hell off.

Then, I come home, and finally I am ready to talk to her, to tell her how much I love her and how I, I don't know, would even forgive her if she had been with Edward. And there she is, with him! Son of a bitch! Right in my own back yard, cuddling with that arrogant bastard, just as sweet as you please, under some tree and shit! I couldn't handle it. I felt like killing him. I felt like killing her. I felt like shaking her and screaming, "How dare you!" But, instead, what do you know, I backed the hell off. Because, what could I say to her? And what could she say to me? I mean, obviously she'd played me like an instrument! She'd probably been fucking him the whole time, and it took me asking her for her to finally tell me. Or, maybe she just started fucking him. Who knows? Who cares? Fact is, I couldn't deal with it. I didn't know if I could forgive her if she was with him, and I knew I didn't want to hear her tell me that she was sleeping with Edward. I just wasn't ready to deal with that kind of pain. So, true to form, I backed the hell off.

Norman was down in Lex, at Cousin Clives' for a visit, so I didn't have him to talk to. And I couldn't exactly talk to Mama about this shit. Pammie and I have a sort of friendship, because of Sister, but she's really Sister's friend, so I couldn't talk to her. But, I felt like I might go nuts if I stayed in my room, stewing over all of this shit. So, I called Nancy. What else was I gonna do? She said to meet her on the yard at school, since she lives on campus, and we could find some place to talk.

I didn't know what all I would say to her, and I didn't know for sure that I could trust her, but at least she knew me, sort of, and at least she already knew what was going on with Sissy. So, I met Nancy down at the student grill, and we had some coffee and talked. For some reason, the smell of grease and hamburgers and fresh strawberries were mixed together, and the smell was making me choke. I sat there and swigged coffee and chain-smoked. Which I don't usually do, but these days, I had taken up smoking, because it was something I could do with my mouth and my hands besides pulling my hair out or screaming at the top of my lungs.

She really is a soc major, too, because she is nothing if not tolerant, as they say. She listened to me with this wide-eyed, accepting stare, nodding at the right times, and leaning in to show how much she was listening. Actually, I hate that type. It comes off so insincere. But I wasn't in a position to complain, because I really needed to knock some ideas around, or whatever. I ranted on about how I couldn't believe that I misread Sister like that, how I couldn't believe she could be with Edward, how he didn't seem like her type. And the weird thing is, I kept stopping to cough and choke. I must have seemed like a lunatic. I actually hacked up a loog at one point, and had to use the empty coffee cup to get rid of it. But Nancy just kept staring, wide-eyed, and nodding, and listening. I left out the part about me being sterile, or whatever, because, even though it's not my fault really, and even though I can't regret it, seeing as how the treatment saved my life, something about not being able to father a kid made me feel...inadequate. So I skipped it.

After she'd listened to me rant, and watched me cough and spit, and nodded her concern to me, she goes, "Well, do you really love her, Evian? I mean, really love her?" She looked at the table, like she might not want to hear the answer.

I didn't have to think about that. At all. I quickly blurted out, "Hell yes. More than I want to admit." Now, it was my turn to look at the table. Because love is so, I don't know, tender or something, you don't want to admit it as quickly as I just did, even to a sympathetic head-nodder like Nancy.

"Then, act like it! This stuff is silly, Evian, if you don't mind my saying so. It seems like both of you care deeply for one another, and both of you are afraid of getting hurt. But in the process, you're hurting each other, and yourselves..."

She sounded like a textbook to me, and part of me resented it. I mean, she was right. But I didn't like hearing it from her, for some reason. So I got casual all of a sudden. And I started coughing again. Nancy said she'd get me a glass of water, and when she got back, I smiled at her. "Guess you're right. I am acting silly. But, it seems so out of hand now." I took the glass of water, sipped it, and reached for another cigarette.

"You know, you really should look into that cough, Evian. Sounds like it might be serious. You may need an antibiotic, or something."

"Yeah, I got an appointment next week. So, we'll see. But, ahh, when you say I'm acting silly, what is it you think I should do, exactly?" I really wanted to know. Because, if Sister were sleeping with Edward, I mean, shit!

I didn't know if I could hear her say that to me. I didn't know that I could handle it.

"Talk to her, Evian. Talk to her. And if she really loves you, she'll tell you the truth. And if it's worth it to you guys, you'll work it out, whatever the truth is. You know, a baby is...a big deal. Don't make her go through this thing alone." Nancy sipped her own Coke and looked me in the eye. And for that moment, it felt like she was being sincere.

I took a moment to look around the grill. There were posters and fliers up all over the walls, some of them about our rally next week, and a whole lot of other stuff. That's when I noticed the white banner on the back wall with the Confederate flag. It had block letters sprawled across the center in purple ink that said: "White Power." At the bottom, it said, "Have you had enough? Bring your concerns to the table. Weds from 6-7 pm. Room 217, Humes Hall. Stand up and be counted." I was transfixed looking at it for a minute. College campuses are such queer places! I mean, everybody, all these kids from all over the place, in one place. And everybody's got a different view, and everybody wants to be heard. What in the world do they mean by "white power," I wondered. People can have such wild ideas.

Nancy and I talked for a while longer about the protest. She told me she'd been talking it up on campus, and she expected a big turnout. She told me how she'd gotten the equipment all arranged through a girl who lives in her dorm. How she couldn't wait to hear me sing. How, if things went well, the press might show up, and we might actually end up on TV, which would be really good publicity for our cause. But, what she said about being silly, about talking to Sissy, was weighing on my mind, and I was only half listening. I knew she was right, but I was still really antsy about hearing what Sissy had to say. Believe it or not, the worst part of all this was imagining that she had been with Edward. I just didn't know what to do with that information.

I was about out of cigarettes, and my throat was beginning to bother me. Felt like I had used up all my spit or something, and it hurt when I swallowed. So, I told Nancy how much I appreciated the ear, how I'd consider what she said. And I told her I'd see her at the next meeting, the night before our big rally.

The weekend passed, and I'd managed to stew a little further. I offered to drive down to Lex to pick up Pap, so old Clives wouldn't have to make the trip. Of course, Mama didn't want me to do it. She's always afraid I'll drive off and die, so, to shut her up, I told her I'd drive in the morning, stay out there that day and sleep over, then me and Pap would make it back the next day. She bought it. I was glad, because I needed some time away. I knew I was not gonna be able to avoid Sister forever, but I wasn't ready to talk to her yet, either. Love is weird.

The way I planned it, I would come back the day before the rally. I'd made this appointment with my doctor, because I'd been having this cough and this burning in my middle and all. I figured Pap could come with me to the appointment, and then we'd head back home. I had this thing in my head where I sort of thought that Pap was wrong about the sterility angle. I mean, the first time I got sick, that was a long time ago. Shit had changed. How should they know if I am sterile or not? I figured, well, before they count me out of the game, old Dr. Lawrence could just check and see. You know, make sure. Because maybe this baby *is* mine. And if it is, then this whole thing about Edward is out the window. And I really wanted to believe that the Edward thing was out the window.

So, I'd go down to Cousin Clives'. I had arranged to stop at the lab that morning on the way to Lexington, so they could draw blood. Seems like they always want to take blood for one reason or another, when you go to the doctor's. Crash at Cousin Clives'. Pick up Pap, stop past the doctors on the way home, find out his take on this sterile thing and get an antibiotic for this cough. And by that time, I'd have my head straight. That night I'd go to the meeting, square away the details for the next day. Then, I'd pull Sister aside, and we'd talk. I'd tell her I loved her. I'd take this time in Lex to stiffen my heart so it wouldn't kill me if she said she'd been with Edward. I'd convince her that what we have is special, you know, worth keeping. And I'd tell her how much I want her and her baby. *Our* baby. I was finally getting it straight in my head.

But, Dr. Lawrence's office called me at Uncle Clives' later that night. I guess I should have expected it, when the nurse asked me for a number where I could be reached after taking my blood. She said my white blood cell count was off. She told me not to worry, but she took down the number just in case. And she called just before 5 to say that Dr. Lawrence needed to see me in his office right away. And I got that feeling I get, like the blood is running out of my veins and into a hole somewhere. Like there's ice chips under my skin. Like I better look up at the sky and remember in case I never see it again. I was scared.

I never even felt bad at first. When Mama met me at the hospital. When Dr. Lawrence explained how the cancer was back and spreading. When he told me we'd try this chemo but he didn't know if it'd work. When he said how aggressive it seems this time, how he wish'd we'd seen it sooner, I didn't feel bad. I didn't feel anything. I felt like a kid again, with Mama and Norman buzzing around me and taking care of everything. I didn't have room to feel, and I didn't have time to think. If what they were saying was true, then, I might not have time for anything. Ever again.

CHAPTER THIRTY-SIX

Ev don't never come to the meeting. We wait and wait, and finally they ask me do I know where he at. I say I don't. Somebody volunteer to run the program, so we can make sure everything smooth tomorrow. Bishop give his opening remarks, about how we concern for our young people. How we lost too many of them to violence. How the police spose to protect us. He talk about those students over in Ohio last year, and how we don't want to see nothing like that happen again. Next on the program spose to be that speaker from downtown. He ain't come to the rehearsal, and don't nobody but Ev know exactly what he gonna say. But Ev wrote down that his speech take ten minutes. Couple of us have readings we plan to say, and we run through those. Everybody excited cuz we work so hard to put this thing together. And everybody sound so good when they go up front to do they act.

Ev and me spose to sing a song together, but he ain't there. So I say I think we be okay, since we practice it so much and know it by heart. And last, me, Pammie, Edward, and Albert spose to do two songs. We had start to sing together that night in the field, and it sound so special. So, one day we out back of my house singing, and Ev come walking from our house. He say we sound unbelievable. First we think he partial, since he know us, but since then we done sung for a bunch of people, and everybody say the same thing. For all our family. And twice at church. Folks shout and carry on when we sing. So, that when Ev convince us to sing at the rally.

Albert say we could arrange a song that everybody know, you know, one that make sense with the theme we putting out about non-violence and stuff. But Pammie, she say she can't sing that stuff. She say she can only sing gospel. We fight about that, cuz both of them is strong-minded. But finally we decide we sing one gospel and one spiritual.

That night, I'm concern for Ev. Because he work hard at this rally, and he the one put together this program. Don't seem like him to miss this meeting. We sing the gospel song first. We got the tempo wrong, cuz I'm nervous about Ev, and I rush through it. When we get through, everybody clap and carry on, except Pam. She look at me like, girl, calm down. She nod her head to lead the next song, "We've Come This Far By Faith." We stand in a "U" shape, so all of us could hear each other. She keep her eyes on me the whole time. In the middle, we each take two lines to sing by ourself. And then at the end, we go back to harmony. For real, we do sound tight. And when we get through, everybody lose they mind. Clap and congratulate us and all. Make me feel good. But in a way, I am still worry about Ev.

Bishop and his friend Bernie give some closing notes. Roger stand up and tell the drivers what time they spose to be at the church. Nancy tell us how she arrange a cooler for us, since it be so hot, and she say don't forget your lunches, cuz we be out there all day. No Ev. I keep looking at the door, wonder if he come in and stay quiet and I just ain't notice. But, end of the meeting come, and he still ain't there. Nancy tell everybody she call his Mama, make sure he all right. She say she sure he be there tomorrow. Even though I know she try to help, in my mind I think, what do she gotta call Ev mama for??

Bishop give his closing prayer, and since Eddie got his mama car, the four of us head outside to go home. Don't take Eddie long to make the money for his tickets every since he work around there with Miss.

Some of us on the committees volunteer to come to church early next day. Pack up any materials we need in the back of Bishop and Bernie van. Answer the phone if somebody call and have a question. Tell folks where to meet us, which car they could ride in, which bus they could take. You know, whatever come up, cuz he say can't nobody know for sure what all to expect on a day like this. So, since we spose to be there early, Edward say we should head on home and get on to sleep. Most of the committees is packing they-self picnic lunches since we be round there all day. Pammie packing the lunch for all four of us. She say she need to go square it away before she go to bed, so Albert say he go on home rather than to go round to her house for a while like he usually do. Everybody excited that we finally ready to have this rally we been working on for so long. Me, I'm quiet cuz I don't know what happen to Ev.

Pammie notice how I'm quiet. She know how hard it been since that day I found out, you know, about the baby. She the one I cry to first when Ev say I been with other people and all. Then, when Ev ain't around for a few days, I cry to Edward. Seem like everybody in the car know what's up with me and Ev cept Albert, which don't seem right, but I ain't ready to say nothing to him yet. But, Pammie try to make me feel better. She know it strange Ev ain't show up for the meeting. She say, "Well, I bet Evian gone downtown to meet with Marvin Haggle, see what he got to say for hisself tomorrow. Haggle can be so crazy with what he say sometime. I mean, I don't mind Black Power and all that, but the way he talk, he make it sound like everybody in the world done the Black man wrong, and only way we could fix it is to blow they butts up. He probably wanna make sure Haggle know we ain't about violence and all that. Bet that's why he wasn't around tonight. Probably met with Haggle and lost track of time. He show up tomorrow, though, if I know Ev."

"I don't wanna see any trouble. None of us do. But Haggle may be part right about blowing up white folks. I mean, they can be so messed up when you think about it. Part of me understand where he coming from." Albert in the front seat with Edward, but he don't look at nobody when he say this stuff. More like he talk to hisself.

"For real. But, let Sissy tell it, and ain't all white folks as bad as all that. Sister love her some white folks!" Edward try to sound like he joking, but I could see he was part serious. Cuz when he talk about Evian, he always got a little bit of a mean tone. I just don't say nothing.

Edward one of the drivers tomorrow. I'm really spose to ride with Ev, but we don't know where he at. So, Edward tell me he drive me if I need him to. Just let him know. I say I probably don't need him to, cuz Ev probably home from Haggle church by now, and he could bring me. I say goodbye to everybody and go on in the house. I sit at the kitchen table, got my hands palm up on the counter, and I notice they full of sweat. I start to pray silent. Then I just sit there and do nothing. I ain't see no light on round to Ev house. I know Norman in Lexington around to Cousin Clives. But where Miss at? And where Ev? I try to convince myself that he get home before us, and decide to go right to bed so he be ready bright and early in the morning. But it don't make sense in my head.

Nancy call me a hour or so later, say she call round to Ev house and ain't get no answer. She say she starting to worry. I thank her for finding out for me. She say, "What you think we should do?" I say, "I guess he be round there tomorrow, but if he ain't we go on with out him. What else can we do?" I don't tell her I'm glad she don't know where Ev, cuz then she ain't so close to him as I might of think. Course, I don't know where Ev neither. I don't tell her that now I'm scared sure enough. Because Ev might be mad and don't be home when I'm at work, and he might say he ain't got time to talk to me when I knock at his door, but don't seem right that he would not come to the meeting. Something wrong. I could feel it in my heart.

I go in the bathroom and run the water for a long soak. I try to remember what Ev say that night when I'm round to his house for ribs. He tell me to sing a special song when I feel like I can't hold up no more. I remember how we sing "Amazing Grace" together, him with that moody harmony he got up close underneath me. How later I take that stick and stab the ground. Ev say kill anything that try to take you from yourself. And then we make love in that field.

I'm busy remember what he say and what we do when the phone ring. It almost 11:30. Don't nobody call here that late unless some of us arrange to answer so's Mama don't hear. I jolt out the tub, quick wrap a towel around me, and run dripping wet to the phone.

CHAPTER THIRTY-SEVEN

When Dr. Lawrence told us about the operation, somewhere down the line I stopped listening. I had other things on my mind. I didn't feel sick. Except for this burning at my middle and the coughing, I didn't feel any different. The way he talked, there was not much of a chance that this operation was going to work anyway. He made it sound like I might not even make it through the surgery. Kept talking about my white blood cells and who knows what all else. And Ma and Pap wouldn't let me alone, either. I felt like I had stuff to figure out in my head, like I wanna go home, in my own bed and sleep. But when I said that, they practically laughed at me. Finally, at the doctor's suggestion, the two of them went down to the cafeteria to get some dinner. It was the first time I had been alone since yesterday when this whole thing came up. As soon as they left, I buzzed for the doctor. I knew that he would be stopping his rounds soon, and I wanted one more word with him.

I'll never forget the look on his face when I asked him about the sterility issue. A mixture of amusement and pathos and professional consternation. It spooked me. He told me that under the circumstances, becoming a father should be the last thing on my mind. I pressed him to see if it were ever possible, even before this most recent episode. He just looked me in the eye and shook his head no.

Sometime after 10, once the doctor left, sentencing me to surgery death, it started to sink in. And I felt like my whole middle section was on fire.

They had me hooked to an IV, one with antibiotics and one with a morphine drip, like they expected that I'd be in excruciating pain. And I was. But most of it was psychological. I have a high tolerance for physical pain anyway. I've had so much of it. I can train myself to ignore it. So, once I knew that Ma and Pap were somewhere in the waiting room arranging a hotel room so that they wouldn't have to commute back and forth to the hospital, I turned off the light and closed my eyes.

I could feel tears sizzle on my cheeks like acid. I always knew that there was a possibility of something like this happening, but I guess I never wanted to believe it would. At least not so soon. I cried for everything I had ever known. That spot at the lake. My daddy. How my mama doubled over in two when she heard the news about him, and how it took her three years to stand up straight again. I thought of my house, my room, my records, my guitar. The space that is bound to be empty for somebody, somewhere, because I'm not there.

I guess it's true what they say about your life flashing before your eyes before you die. I mean, I wasn't at death's door yet, but they were saying I was close. And I wanted to breathe and feel and remember. But all I could think about was Sissy. Sipping iced tea from the same glass when her mama was in Tennessee. That first time when I heard her singing along with Tammi in the bathroom at home. How surprised she looked when I joined in, too. That way she gives me her whole self, quietly, when she lies next to me. How I can honestly hear the thoughts she is holding in her heart for me when she says, without words, that everything she has is mine. Mine. I felt a warm thing growing out of this thought, and it didn't seem relevant what Dr. Lawrence said about me being a father.

What was I thinking before? Sister would never be with someone else. She may have implied it with her mouth, but her mind, her spirit says something else when we're together. I love her. I love how strong she is. Like that night in the field, when I told her to fight Blister and kill him. Then my eyes flew open, and I sat up straight in the bed.

Blister.

Son of a bitch!

Son of a bitch—that was it. He is the only other one that Sister has been with. Holy shit.

And if I am not the one who fathered this child, then…Holy shit.

I buzzed for a nurse, but it was too late. I was already hurling in the wastebasket when she got there. She supported my back while I got sick, all of this green with flecks of orange, and when I got done she took the mess away. She came back to help me clean up. I kept my eyes closed the whole time. I couldn't focus anymore. I could hear Pap and my mom whispering outside the door with the nurse, both of them deciding that it would be best for me to sleep now. Then I heard quiet.

I kept my eyes closed, but I couldn't stop my brain from churning up memories. It didn't seem fair, this whole thing. And I was mad and angry and tired and hungry. I remembered the rally tomorrow. How Sissy tried to talk to me the other day and how I turned her away. And now this thing about Blister. What time was it anyway? When I looked at the clock and noticed how late it was, my chest contracted. I'd missed the meeting. I was supposed to run the program for the rally tomorrow. What must everybody be thinking? And my sweet Sissy. She must be frantic.

I didn't know where I got the idea to do it, but I'd made up my mind in the space of an instant. This was horse shit! I couldn't lie around in a hospital room and wait to die. Forget about it. I had things to do. I had a woman who loves me and a baby and a family and a rally to attend. And if death is around the corner, it's gonna have to come looking for me. I sat up and reached for the phone. Sweet Sissy. She would have to suffer one death when she found out about me. But, if I could help it, she'd never suffer two. Pap and Dr. Lawrence may know about me and my sterility, but Sissy doesn't have to. To think her baby came from that rat bastard, that would be another death. No. Sissy will have enough of death when I'm gone.

I knew it was late, and I knew it might raise some questions, but under the circumstances I didn't care. I dialed Sissy's number. And when I heard her answer, out of breath, I felt the fire in my belly subside for a minute.

"Do you miss me?" I whispered into her ear to catch her off guard. But all I heard was hiccups and tears.

"Listen, Sugar. I am sorry. I am such an idiot, I swear to God! I love you so much; that's all I know to say. I can't take back these last few days. I know how fucked up I've been. I just...I don't know. But I love you like crazy, and I love our baby, and I want to be at the rally tomorrow..."

She told me she loved me, too. She listened about the surgery, the dim prospects. She said she'd been worried sick when I didn't come to the meeting, that she knew something was wrong. She said she would figure out a way to come get me.

CHAPTER THIRTY-EIGHT

It never dawn on me that I could call Pam and tell her about Ev. Because after he tell me, I'm half out my mind anyway. I went in the laundry room and find some jeans and a shirt. The jeans is tight around my middle, so I leave them unbutton. I got the shirt on outside the jeans, so it can cover up the part where they open. I grab my shoes without putting them on, and I head around the field, toward Pammie house.

Good thing I been going around her house every since I could remember, because this time I was blind. Water just pour out of my eyes non-stop, and I ain't got no tissue and no time to stop them. I just pull myself forward, toward Pammie house, and for the first time I don't think of bugs or snakes. Just Ev.

Why God? Why you wanna do this to him? To me? To his family? Then I think, well, that doctor don't know Ev. He don't know how strong he could be. He done make a mistake this time and don't know what he talking about. Ev ain't gonna die. He can't. Because I love him too much. So, this thought make me feel a little faster, and I move quick toward Pammie house.

The lights is off in the kitchen, but they still got the door open. Always have kept that door unlock, long as I can remember. I know they house so well, I can feel my way upstairs and straight to Pammie door. Her room down the hall from her mama, so I gotta be quiet when I knock. I can hear she got the radio on, and the light is still on. "Girl, I'm coming in. You sleep?"

Pammie sound shock when she answer, but by then I'm already in her room and at the foot of her bed. "Sister! What you...? Girl, you all right?"

But I don't never answer. She can see for herself I ain't all right. She slide over in the bed to put her arm around my shoulder. I ain't got no words. I can feel my whole body bending up and shrinking in. It take my breath from me. Pam Elizabeth rock a little bit, you know, like Grannie always would, and this help me to catch my breath and let up a little.

"Whatever this is, Rebecca, ain't too much for us to bear, you hear? Lord not gonna give us more than we can take. He promise us that. Tell me what it is, and we work it through. You and me."

I can't look at Pam face. I just look at the floor. Try to picture Jesus face. I do that sometime. If I could picture His face, you know, behold Him, then I could breathe. "It came back. The cancer, you know. And Ev in the hospital. They say he got to have some surgery, and maybe even that won't work. Either way, they say it spread all over his bones. Say he ain't gonna make it much longer...But they don't figure on how strong Ev is. They don't. And Ev wanna come to the rally we plan. So we gotta go get him. From the hospital." And I guess I don't have no more words, cuz I stop talking. Stop crying. Stop breathing. Cuz down in the carpet I could just make out the blonde hair and those deep eyes. Seem like they tell me to be still.

I can't look right at her, but from what I see Pam got tears in her eyes. She must don't see Jesus in the carpet yet. I hear her mutter a minute and pray. We sit like that for a minute, me being still and looking for Jesus, and Pam praying quiet. Then, she hop off the bed and go down to Edward room. I hear a mess of whispers and sound like pleading. Then I hear her say, "This ain't just for him, Ed. This for Sister."

Next thing I know, Edward at the door with the car keys in his hand. He say to come on downstairs and he take us to the hospital. He don't look at me at all when he say it, neither.

Wish you could see the way we slip into the hospital. Ev room on the first floor, but it around to the front. Pam go to the desk and say she work for Ev family, that he and some friends hear he sick and been asking after him. She busy with the nurse, try to find out all she can about his condition, but the nurse don't want to tell her too much since she ain't in the family. But she gotta keep trying so's we have time to break out Ev.

Meantime, me and Eddie slip through the window, which is easier for him these days, since I got this belly coming. Eddie throw Ev bag out the window. Then we gotta figure out how to get this tube out Evian arm. Ev say he done it before, last time he in the hospital, only that time they had it in his privates. They make me the lookout. We got the door crack so can't nobody see what we doing. Edward hold the back of Ev gown close and help ease him out the window. Next, I got to back my growing behind out the window, too. But I need a little help, so I lean against the bed table. As I'm pulling myself through the window, my leg hit the table, and it fall over.

Guess the nurse must have hear when the table fall over, so here she come looking in the room. By the time she get there, Pammie done run out the front door. Then me, Evian, and Eddie hightail to the car, slam the door, and take off. Me and Ev in the back, and Evian backside is naked on the seat since all he got on is a gown. He steady putting gauze on the place where his arm got poke from the tube, tape it on with fabric sticky tape he stole from the hospital. Eddie driving like a madman, taking curves too fast so all of us slam around the car at every turn. But the funny thing was the sound Ev butt make when it lose suction on the leather seat and slam him into me, to the other side of the car. Sound like somebody bust wind. We hear that, and I guess the heaviness we feel from having to bust Evian out the hospital catch up to us, and we bust out laughing.

But I'm so glad to see Ev, so glad to have him next to me, that my laughing is mix with tears, too. And when he put his arms around me, and it seem like I ain't felt him for a million years, the laugh fall away from the tears, and I bawl in his chest full out. I guess that spoil everybody else mood, because next thing you know everybody quiet in the car.

By now it really late, but Edward don't drive home. Instead he drive over to U.K. and park in the lot behind the student union. Even though they got concrete, it still pretty there, cuz you could see the trees and grass and all, and the plaques they got set up to celebrate old folks that went there and passed on.

Everybody turn and look at Ev, then they see what he got on, and they remember why we there, and look away. Nobody can think what to say.

✿✿✿

Evian still got his arm around me, and I'm as close to him as I could be without being in his lap. He put his nose deep in my hair and breath, but then he start to cough. We all stiffen up like we scared to death he gonna drop dead right there. Ev say, "Look, guys. What am I supposed to say? I mean, how weird is this? But, ah, I really appreciate y'all coming out to get me. I can't …change the verdict or anything. They can't give me anything that will change that. So, what's a few more days, a few more weeks if I have to spend them in there? If I had to do that, well then they might as well just kill me now. Let it be, you know?"

We hang on his every word. What we got important to add? We just listen to him talk. About how he love me, and how he love them, too. How we the first real friends he feel like he ever had. How he got a child coming who he hope he live to see. How he gonna make that rally if it the last thing he do.

And it was. The last thing he do, I mean. At least the last thing he do as himself, for himself. The rest he do for me. And for our baby. After that, we see a group of strange folk come out of Hume Hall. Most of them ain't got shirts on, but all of them hooting and yelling, slapping each other on the back and all. So, that's when we decide we better leave.

I never forget that night. The way Edward and Pam get out the car and walk a pace or two whiles Evian put on his clothes. The way we smoke corn all night and laugh and remember. When Ev say he hungry, after we seen those white boys from Hume Hall, we drive all the way back home to get Albert, so's he can direct us to that hamburger joint way on East End that open all night. And Pammie slip in his room, giggling, tore up, telling him to get his ass up cuz his sister bout to have a baby, and the father fitting to pass on. How we manage to laugh and sing even though. Even though. Even though.

Evian say he left a note to tell his mama where he at. Or where he ain't at. Because he know it only a matter of time before she find out he gone and come to find him. But he want to have some time before then, you know, to tie up loose ends, as he say.

Way late, just before the sun rise, when the birds up and lifting they wings to God, Edward drop me and Ev off around to the lake. He say he better get the car back before Mama wake up, so she don't think nothing is wrong. Say he pick us up in time to take us to the church for the rally.

We got our hands wound around each other waist and keep bumping into each other while we walk down to that spot he show me before. Seem like a long time ago, when I tell him I'm maybe pregnant, and he dance like James Brown.

And after we make love two times, and I cry and he cry. And after we both plead and curse God. And after both of us say we sorry to God and we try to understand, Evian tell me he love me and he love our baby. He say don't never let this child forget who his father. He say everything he got is mine. He tell me wait until he gone and talk to Norman. He make sure Norman provide for me and our baby. He make sure of that.

Later on we head to the church. Everything running smooth, too. We loading up the cars and directing. They all glad to see Evian, and he just say he had a family emergency he got to take care of, so's that how come he not around before. And they just glad everything okay.

We got a big turnout, just like Nancy say. Folks from in town and on campus stop to listen when me and Ev sing. They lean forward to hear every word the poetry group chant, and every time they say "peace is a verb," the kids go nuts, clapping and stamping they feet and cheer. But time tick on, and Marvin Haggle ain't nowhere to be found. So, we skip him, let everybody else go first. Alice Mace speak. Bishop read off the names of people who die or get hurt mysterious when they run in with the police. And hundreds of hot, young people from all over got silent when Bishop lead them in prayer.

But the heat was a thick sock over our face, shove down our throats to keep us from breath. And the drinks we brung in our coolers for lunch was long gone. The afternoon had worn us out, and folks was getting restless and ready to go. So, Bishop motion for me, Pam, Edward, and Albert to come up to sing, close the program out. Before we can get to the platform, we hear a voice rip through the air like when angry dogs bark in the wind. Haggle. He in the back of the crowd, and he got a mess a rhymes about how white folks got to put up or shut up. How cops think they slick cuz they got a billy stick. How our guns make sense when we doing self-defense, and some more mess.

I don't know what all happen next. When the White Power group show up, or who throw the first blow, but next thing you know everybody taking sides and yelling and fighting. But one of them jump on the platform and say the white folks there is nigger-loving pussies with no self-respect left. Edward take offense and say they the ones out here starting trouble. For you know it, seem like everybody on one side or the other. They throwing they empty bottles at each other and scream. I cover my ears for a minute, then I grab hold to Evian hand. But somebody from that other side seen us, and they charge. Knock me down on the ground and push Ev over where the White Power people stand.

It don't take long before Bishop try to rush us to our cars, and tell the CFPSC to keep they hands clean. And Albert say, let it be known that it ain't us to start the trouble. Because he the one pick me up when I fall, and he crack the nose of the bald white guy what done it. Let the record show that it wasn't none of us, he say. But the campus police drag him off anyways. And Edward and five others besides. Ev on the ground look like he don't know where he at for a minute. But, when I go over to him, he fast on his feet and follow the campus police.

They got my brother, and Pammie brother and some others from the CFPSC, and the bald guy from the White Power group cram inside the security office. And the bald guy say he got connections and he gonna call his friends, and he ain't gonna stand for no more shit. Bunch of kids who sat at the rally and listen to me and Ev sing is press outside the door of the security office. And me and Pam got our face press against the glass to see what they do. Then somebody call the police. And somebody call a lawyer. And somebody call a doctor, because when Ev see them take Edward and Albert, he say take me, too. He force his way in the office with them. But, I guess the noise and the confusion catch up to him. Before too long, I see Albert rush over to Evian, try to catch him before he fall out. That's when I punch my way through the crowd, with a sound like a pinch camel come from somewhere in my center, to take Ev hand and tell him everything all right. But it ain't all right.

Norman and Miss come. And they got Evian in the back of the ambulance. And Pammie got to hold me around the waist and twist my hands to keep me from getting in there, too. I try to forget the next few days. How Norman pay the fine for Edward and Albert so's they can go home instead of jail. How Miss don't let nobody come round to the hospital. How she appreciate my concern but she got it under control. How the operation they make Ev have don't take. How Norman call me four times a day, on the slip, to let me know Evian drink his juice, or how he ask after me, or how he ask to go home. But finally, when Ev got the strength to talk, he tell them he going home. And since he old enough, and since can't nobody stop him, they finally let him.

CHAPTER THIRTY-NINE

When they take Albert and Edward and some of the others downtown, the bald guy keep his promise and call some of his friends. Sure enough, who you think the bald White Power guy friends with? Blister. I known it was him as soon as Pammie describe him. She say he and his daddy come barking up a storm at the station, and before you know it, the bald guy is gone home. But not before he have some words with Albert and Edward and Bishop. Tell them they crazy if they think they gonna let them pollute our city and corrupt our women. And Blister say he get them back, and they nigger-loving friends besides.

Course, Albert and Edward got friends, too. Like Bishop. He manage to stay out the security office when this mess went down, so he at the station waiting for them when they get there. And later he got Pammie and Bernie with him. And he done call the press, too. Norman come around there, too, and pay the fines so's me and Pam brothers can go. And before you know it, all of them, Pam and our brothers and the bald guy, too, is gone home.

Mama and them say they seen Albert and Eddie on television. How they say don't nobody come to film us when we quiet, when we preaching non-violence, when we speaking the truth about police. But soon as the trouble start, and even though we ain't the ones start it, there go the press with the cameras to film the whole thing. And it ain't the bald guy they busy to film. It Albert and Eddie and Bishop and a mess of other black folk cuffed up and being hauled off. Albert say it just prove our point. He say he glad it end that way, cuz nobody hurt, and everybody can see who the real devil is. Right there on TV.

And Mama and Miss Minnie so proud they babies is on the TV, they forget the reason they on there. Mama on the phone to tell everybody she know to turn on ABC at 11 so's they could see her son, the next M.L. King. But, it ain't the last time she gonna look up on TV and see her son. And her daughter and grandbaby, too.

On the seventh day, after Norman tell me that Ev going home, I arrive at Miss house at 10, same as any other work day. I seen the cab pull up the night before, and I started to go round there right then. But Norman tell me on the phone to let it be one night. Give him a chance to talk to Miss and take care of Ev. He say he know what's best. And since he always good to me before, and since I know now that he know about me and Ev and the baby, I trust what he say and wait.

I know her son sick, and I know she got it taken care of, but she ain't told me not to come to work no more. And she ain't told me that she don't want me to see Ev, neither. And one day soon she gonna know all about us anyhow, if she don't already. We don't have time to be playing around because Miss worry about what everybody think. So when I come through the kitchen door, and seen Miss at the table with her eyes swole up like she took up boxing and lost, I try to say good morning. But she wave me on, say Ev in his room.

All day and late into the evening, we sit on his bed. Miss or Norman pop in now and again, see if he want soup or if he willing to drink. And he say he don't feel too bad, but he fall asleep sometimes. Me and him sit on his bed and look out over that field where seem like both of us live and meet and change. When he wake up, he want me to read to him from Job. About what God say when Job complain that he had enough and don't deserve it. He stop me in the middle and tell me he love me. He touch my belly and say I love you, too, to my navel. And I'm about to read where Job get his riches back seven times over when Ev fall asleep again.

Getting late. Sun just start to set. I figure I walk on home, back across that field, and head back first thing in the morning so's I could be there when he wake up.

Norman out back with his cigarette in one hand and what look like a cane in the other. I wave to him but don't come too close. Long day. Long week. I ain't got the breath to speak or explain or thank him for arranging to let me come. I think he understand.

Folks been running to the Mandarene house every since they find out Evian sick again. They been bringing Miss meals and coming round to pray all the time now. People who don't normally pay you no mind hearts' soften when they know you got your eyes swell up like you fight Ali cuz your son sick and your husband gone and your Daddy in law on his way to glory, too. So I don't turn around to see who coming to console Miss now. Could be anybody. I don't pay no attention when seem like somebody heading cross the field from the direction of Pam Elizabeth house. I don't pay no mind when I hear the car pull in the Mandarene driveway, neither. I got a mess of other stuff in my mind. By then I'm almost halfway cross the field, almost home, and I don't turn around to see who come around there so late.

But I do hear the swish and swallow on the ground like fast snakes. And I feel the hot sour breath on my back, and I know that cold fringe that come around my heart from before. When I whirl around, his shoulder blade smack my chin, and I see his face push out like old balloons left out in the sun. This time he got his shirt in his hand. He loop the armhole around my ear and twist it back around my neck. I can't take the breath to scream or there won't be enough to fight.

Blister crack at my knee to force me to the ground. On my way down, I shake one leg loose, and it catch him square in the nuts. I seen his lips twist and change before he gulp the air to holler. But I kept at him, my foot between his legs, crush at him and claw with my hands. I hear him squeal. I seen his spit stick in the hot summer air. But it don't make me stop. I spit at him. I rip whole chunks of hair from his sorry head. He done had enough of me. He try to take what Ev say I got to keep, what I *know* I got to keep. Maybe soon it won't be no Ev. Now, all I got is me, and what Ev give me, and what me make together. No room in here for Blister and his backwoods spit. So, if somebody got to die in this field tonight, it ain't gonna be us. I scrape and twist and pound on him til I feel dead weight and wetness.

I hear the gunshot break through the wind and through his pucker skin. And I smell milkweed, molasses, buckshot, and fresh blood.

I don't know if it his blood or my own I got all over me when I crawl out from under him.

I stumble to my feet. Alls I remember is his hair. Norman hair. Blown up to the sky like Moses. And the smoke from his cigarette and from his rifle, where he got it cocked and aimed with his one eye close, and how I know he a sure shot. And Evian behind him, too late to pull the gun away from Norman, who say I'm a friend to his family, with his hair blown up like a silver ribbon in the sky. I don't never notice Edward, how he watch between the deep weeds of that field where's ghosts play, where's Blister take me from myself, and where's Ev love me enough to give me back. Where's Norman say he never let the backwoods come into his land again. And to Edward mind it were Ev who got the rifle, Ev, who fit to die, that got the rifle to keep his cousin off his baby and his friend.

And they believe what Edward say. Because they believe what Evian say. They believe him when he say he hear me yell and seen Blister come after me and he shoot, half out his mind and fit to die. They don't know that Edward lied on Evian. That Evian protecting Norman. That Norman protecting me. That all of us protecting each other to keep the backwoods from messing up our lives for good. Police shake they heads, and they look at me with disgust, but they sorry for Norman and Ev, because they nigger-loving fools, and one of them about to die. So they see it as an accident and a tragedy. Don't much matter who it was pulled the trigger; there was a struggle, the gun went off, and best as the police could tell, it was a horrible mistake.

CHAPTER FORTY

Seem like I'm forever hear what Grannie say while she alive, even when she gone. Some of it I don't never understand. Some of it make sense now that I think of it.

She say death come in threes.

Nobody stop to see about Blister, with his peach-color back chunks fasten to the mud that got purple from his own blood when Norman kill him with two clean shots and Edward say it was Evian done it, and the police never bother to find out for sure one way or the other. Not even his own daddy. He don't want another scandal where the whole town know he and his family so trouble that some of them turn against each other to protect some color girl. Don't nobody cry for Blister.

Then, when Norman pass, look like of all of us, Edward take it the hardest. In the last weeks, whiles he round to the Mandarenes' to keep the lawn and all, Norman and Edward get to talking. Much as he don't admit it, it strike Edward that Norman kill his own blood for me. And make sure me and the baby got a trust. And pay to make sure he and Albert get out of jail. Why he do it? Don't none of us know for sure. Cept he and his brother ain't never get along too kindly. And Norman say he had enough of the backwoods to last him. He say that rat bastard Blister, as they calls him, have enough of his own to where he shouldn't feel like he got to take from me. But Norman must got a lot to say, cuz all while Edward mowing and clipping, Norman come round there, too, with a cigarette in his mouth, and a story to tell. I guess. I don't never listen. Too busy to listen. And too hungry. Look like in those last months, I eat like it going out a style. Eat and sit with Ev.

And, when Norman pass, when he got blue at the face and hold his chest, when it seem like his white hair what use to hang down like Moses go yellow at the root and he don't breathe, Edward the one who cry the most. Not me. Not Miss. Not even Evian, who say he spose he be back with Norman soon, but Edward. You think it might have been me. With all Norman done for me and for my baby. But of all of us, it was Edward carried on the most.

But, when Ev die, then it my turn to cry. I guess I cry for all of us then. For me, for Ev, for Norman, and for this baby who never know his daddy up close.

Miss decide she want to bury him down in Georgetown, round to the old church, where they from, where he baptize. She don't see no reason to have a bunch of his friends come down to see him home. She say she keep it private, just family. But I know it ain't about family. Only family he got turn against him when he make like he shoot Blister for me. What she don't want is me. Bout to bust with her dead son child. She don't want me. Mama say she trash anyway. Say she left here in the first place to make out like she better than what she was. Mama say she just trash what came into money. So, Miss want to hold a service private. Just her and her gentleman friend, Griffin Howard, who don't even much know Ev, at a funeral she hold private down in Georgetown.

When I lose Ev, it my time to cry. Soon as he slip his hand from me that night, I seen his mouth fall open. I see that sparkle come and go in his eye, and I know he seen Jesus. And I know the best of him gone on. Don't much matter where Miss take his body. The best of him already gone.

So me and Pammie and Edward, and Albert, and a mess of others from the CFPSC, and even some of Nancy and her friends from around to U.K., we have our own service right there in that field, same one that connect me and Ev in the first place. Edward call the press this time. Let them see what the CFPSC really about. Some of us read our poems and some of us pray.

Some of us play guitar and drums and dance. Some of us quiet. But none of us fight or throw bottles or move to one side. We all out there together to celebrate Ev.

I ain't shame to show my tears to the woman from ABC, when she say she take my picture for human interest on the news. When she look at my belly, how much I cry, and seem like she put two and two together. But I don't let my tears keep me from holding my part down, like a fort, when me and Pammie and Edward and Albert hold each other at the shoulder to sing "By and By." Straight through the sky. Straight through Blister blood and backwood spit. Straight through Miss private service, and straight into Ev ears. And I know he could hear. Because the best part of him gone, but the rest of him right here. Inside me. Inside this field.

Grannie say ain't no in between. Everything either black or white. I mostly believe everything Grannie say. But in this case, knowing what I know about me, about Ev, I ain't for sure.

About the Author

J. Marie Darden was born in Cincinnati, Ohio, but was raised in Maryland. She spent many summers in Kentucky. She holds a bachelor's degree in English from Morgan State University and a master's in English education from The Johns Hopkins University. She is a professor of English at the Community College of Baltimore County in Maryland. She lives with her husband and son in Columbia, Maryland and London, England.

AND HERE'S A GLIMPSE AT THE EXCITING SEQUEL TO ENEMY FIELDS:

Finding Dignity

BY J. MARIE DARDEN

Time marches forward to 1992, and Dignity is coming of age. Her lineage makes her feel like a mixed bag of tricks, a gray jigsaw in a puzzle of black and white. She has been deserted by her mother; she is puzzled by her dead father, and raised by her strict, religious Aunt Lette and Uncle Sam. She is loved and cared for, but something is missing. No one wants to tell her why her mom stays drunk and gone and why her father is dead.

To escape from a complicated family history that she barely understands, Dignity leaves Kentucky to accept a scholarship at Morgan State University in Baltimore, MD. Unfortunately, along with her college credits, she also acquires an identity crisis. Because of the way that she looks, her pale complexion and her fiery red hair, she still has a hard time "finding her niche" in the historically black college. And having an Italian boyfriend with a racist father, along with a dark and lovely nemesis who hates "redbones" and who is plotting her demise on campus, does not help her dilemma.

On her road to self-discovery at college, Dignity begins to realize that the past she has been trying to forget just might be the key to her future. A pilgrimage back to the South helps her to find the truth about her drunken mother, her dead father, and herself. And the truth may set her free.

It's a story that is an odyssey of self-discovery. It's about finding friends and finding family. It's about finding the courage to understand the past and to undertake the future. It's about *Finding Dignity*, and dignity is something that everyone needs.

AN EXCERPT FROM

Finding Dignity

In Media Res: Just after Finals Junior Year
Morgan State University 1994

DIGNITY JACKSON—THE PREMISE

Strong as the bond is, much as you may love and cherish someone, and even though you might need an anchor to cling to in this hostile portal that is life, there are deal breakers. You can know someone for years. Develop so closely together with them that the two of you can play "remember when" all day every day and never run out of material. And you can come through for someone again and again in intangible ways that require something other than language to express—distant drums, gossamer bubbles, or the beating of dragonfly wings on cool summer lakes—and even still, even still! There are deal breakers. The concept is simultaneously maddening and intriguing. It is the hardest lesson I have learned so far in college.

For me, this idea of deal-breaking is a principle that proves true over and over again. Eventually, inevitably, loved ones come to a blockade, a forceful wall that neither can penetrate. When that happens, when you can no longer walk forward, the obvious choice is to go backwards. Cut and run. Happened to my mom, Sister Rebecca, with, well, practically everyone that she was close to, including me. To my Aint Angus and her sister, my Grandma Pearson . And now to me and my estranged, Italian boyfriend, Sal. I wonder if there is any way to overcome this dilemma.

Either way, this deal-breaking is a good reason to leave town. Because bonds, living bonds, the ones that people read about and dream about and leave about, these are the only things in this life that really matter. They are safe harbors against incompatible truths. I'm beginning to realize that breathing brings paradox, that to exist is to contradict; so close relationships, then, inevitably end in escape. That's why I am going back home to Kentucky.

This morning, right after finals, I couldn't stop to pack up the whole apartment. There'd be time for that later. All I knew was I had to get the hell out of Dodge. I had already called Aint Angus to tell her I was coming, although I didn't have to. Ever since I could remember, Aint Angus's door had always been open. Literally. Any time, day or night, I could show up at her door and just walk in. She was always glad to see me and encouraged me to stay, and very often I took her up on it. Before I left for college at Morgan State in Baltimore, back when I was in high school and got bored over winter break, or if I had a tough time with Aunt Lette and her "holiness" rules about church all day every day, and always for the majority of the summer, I would pack my bags and go stay with Aint Angus. She was the closest thing I had to a mama, next to Aunt Lette, the one who raised me.

Of course I talked to Mercer that morning. He's been my best friend since I was three years old. He's always had my back. He is one of those extraordinary people. Couldn't wait to see him, tell him all about me and Sal, and hear about his latest antics at Kentucky State. He'd be able to tell me what to do. When I talked to him, he said he had some interesting news to share. Tried to pump him for details, but he said I'd understand when I saw him in person.

Once I found out my final grades (four A's and a B, just enough to blow my 4.0, son of a biscuit!), I called Sal and gave him my Aint Angus's phone number and address. I didn't want to totally cut him off, just in case I was making a mistake. Then I packed up two suitcases, one of clothes and shoes, and the other full of my cosmetics and hair stuff, stopped at the 7-Eleven on Cold Spring and bought two bean pies, a huge container of Gatorade and a pack of Capri menthols, and I headed for 70-W to get some serious road before dusk. By 10:30 A.M., I was well on my way. It would take me eight hours to get to Lexington if I drove non-stop. If I played it right, I'd get there well before dark.

❁❁❁

Junior Year
Morgan State University 1994

DIGNITY JACKSON 1

It was our junior year at Morgan State University, and I was nominated by *The Quiet Revolution (QR)*, a group of passive-aggressive anarchists who thought globally and acted locally, to run for Ms. Morgan during senior year. I was at first flattered by the group's show of support, counting it as proof that they accepted me and believed in me. And I thought it would be groundbreaking to have an "independent" candidate, someone unaffiliated with a sorority, run for this contest. Soon, though, my obligatory neurosis set in. I began to strangle myself with a subconscious "what if" pattern that I could not turn off.

What if I run but I lose? What if the race gets ugly? What if they find out that I am a fake? What if they finally see that I am a completely neurotic quasi wanna- be revolutionary with a bag of compulsions the size of east Baltimore?

Yet my friends thought I was the obvious choice. And they knew that we had some capital saved up from our fund-raisers and other activities, so they thought I actually stood a chance of winning. In my mind, I wanted to take a shot at it, to make a statement that you don't have to be a right-wing sorority girl to make a name for yourself at Morgan. But, in my heart, I felt nauseous, weak, and confused. Still, I officially accepted the nomination, so that meant I would have to be ready to speak at the rally that coming Friday, on stage, announcing my platform and intentions, with a world of judging faces in front of me. I swallowed down my anxiety and felt it mix with my intestines to create a thick rope in my middle.

By this time, Salmon and I had been together since the middle of freshman year, and we were still going strong. Unless you count the fact that I literally went into conniptions whenever he tried to touch me. Or the fact that his family had practically disowned him for choosing a dark-skinned girl of questionable lineage rather than a wholesome Italian one, and that this family dissention gave him nightmares. Between my intimacy issues and his nocturnal freak-outs, neither of us was sleeping at night. But we did it together, and we did it lovingly.

I spent at least a portion of most evenings with Sal, unless I had a meeting with The QR or the Art Club. I had a million acquaintances, but no really close friends. I carried a steady supply of emotional bricks in my countenance and built nearly tangible walls whenever would-be friends tried to get close. There were only two people that I confided in: My boyfriend Sal, and Kiko, the Japanese girl who lived upstairs and did my hair and nails.

That day, after I accepted the nomination for Ms. Morgan, I walked across the campus and over to my apartment in Northwood. Sal wouldn't be around until after basketball practice, so I went upstairs to visit with Kiko. I felt like I needed to talk.

That's when I ran into Stacy Smithe. We used to be girls back in the day, but then she played the backstabbing ho card. Went after a dude that I was supposed to be seeing. If that wasn't bad enough, she tried to front and say that she did it because I am a redbone, so I must think I'm all that, so she took my man to protect the purity of the black race. To me, she is the one who thinks I'm all that, because she is the one who always has something to say about it.

For real, she is underhanded. Ever since that whole thing with Khalil, the guy she skeezed from me back in freshman year, she had it in for me. When I was rushed during sophomore year, she went around badmouthing me to the sorority sisters to tell them I was not a worthy pledge, meanwhile kissing their behinds so that she would get on line. Not that I was pressed—I wasn't the type for sororities. Then she tried to get Khalil to bad mouth me to Salmon so he wouldn't want to be with me. Khalil and Sal have been thick for years, even after 'Lil started seeing Stacy. Finally, she tried to get Khalil to stop speaking to Sal, saying she didn't feel comfortable doing things with Sal if I was going to be around. That girl has been taking witch pills since early freshman year!

That day she greeted me with the usual grimace and scowl.

"Dignity! Girl, when have I seen you?! What you into these days?" She put on a fake smile that she pressed in my face on her way down toward the parking lot.

"Minding." I can't stand somebody who tries to sabotage and hate on your life behind your back, then wanna grin up in your face later.

Stacy walked two more steps closer. "Umm. I see you still got that nasty attitude! So unbecoming for a girl like you. Did you hear about the Greek breakfast on Saturday? Oh, that's right! You're not a Greek, are you?" She ran her fingers through her freshly permed hair.

"No, Stacy. I guess I don't need a circle of elephants around me to feel secure. But eat some eggs for me, huh?"

"To be sure. I guess you heard that I'm running for Ms. Morgan. Can I count on your vote next term?" Stacy looked over her shoulder at me, like she hoped to see envy in my eyes.

"That would be silly, Stacy. Only a moron would vote against her**self**!" This time it was my turn to see the jaw drop.

"You? Oh, really? Did you pledge sometime and I didn't know about it? I didn't know you were one of us, Girl!" She oozed with fake enthusiasm.

"No. It's all Greek to me. I was nominated by an independent group. So let's wish each other luck!" I tossed my wavy mane, a feature that I knew she envied, and continued toward Kiko's apartment.

Stacy did not turn around as she continued through the lot of parked cars. "Good. Then I'll see you at the rally on Friday! Good luck, Girl! I know independents can have a hard time!"

When I finally reached her apartment, Kiko did her best to console me, although she never really agreed when I would say that Stacy was a pig. She didn't want to bad mouth a steady client. But she did reassure me about my nomination for Ms. Morgan.

"You beautiful, Dig. You much prettier than many other, Girl! You do fine, you see! I do your makeup—remember how we do with gold and brown? Eyes look like sunset? And pile your hair up like model—you be beautiful!" Kiko patted my hand while we sat at her table drinking green tea sweetened with honey.

I tried to explain to Kiko, and to myself, why the whole thing was so scary for me.

"It's complicated, and I haven't completely figured it out. Maybe, maybe it's that Ms. Morgan stands for something that I'm not sure I can be..." I looked into my green tea, and my reflection was distorted—how fitting.

Kiko broke off a corner of the toast she was eating and nibbled and listened. "Why? Ms. Morgan—— she a queen, right? Smart, pretty. You perfect!"

"No! That's just it. I don't feel smart or pretty! I feel...like a fake!" I played around with the loose leaves that had eased around the bottom of my cup and pouted.

"Silly! You no fake, Dig. I know you, and you not no fake. See, Mother used to say, feelings is funny. You no can trust feelings. They change like quick silver! You make a decision, and you go, you do, but no trust feelings all the time!" She finally swallowed the toast corner she'd been gnawing.

"What do you mean? Don't trust my feelings?"

"Feelings change, okay? Decisions you make, they don't change. See, one day, I wake up, look in mirror, I feel like the pretty goddess. Hair feel shiny, skin feel pink and full of color. Next time I see mirror, I feel like the monster! Why I got sunken cheek? Why my hair seem brown instead of black? No. Feeling change too much; you can't keep track. So, I make decision: Me, Kiko, I am beautiful. Inside I shine, so outside I shine, too. No feeling, Dig. Decision."

What she said seemed so simple and made so much sense that I rather believed her. Or, at least, I wanted to. I swished my index finger through the tea to see if it maintained any heat after all my sulking. It was tepid, but I took a sip. "Ah-hah! So, if I just ignore my feelings, maybe I will feel beautiful, too!"

"You almost see but not all the way see. You say you ignore feelings and feel beautiful—no! You ignore feelings and *be* beautiful. Beautiful mean smart, Dig. And sweet in the heart. And wanting to work for good. That's why maybe you win!" Kiko ate the last of her buttered toast, scraped the crumbs from the table into her hands, and took both of our cups to her kitchen sink. Kiko was forever eating buttered toast. It was her favorite thing.

While Kiko was in the kitchen rinsing out our cups, in those moments while I didn't have to look into her simple face or splinter her trusting eyes with my fearful truths, I cut to the center of what I was feeling.

"You have pictures all over your apartment, Kiko. Your mother, even though she is passed to another plane, your grandparents, sketches of Okinawa. I love all the jewelry you kept from your paternal grandmother and the kimonos from your great aunt! I mean, even if you live here in Baltimore, and many of these people are still in Japan or gone on before, I look around here and I know you're connected. Me, I have nothing. No real clues as to who I am!" I had to blink away tears quietly, quickly, before she finished rinsing and came back to the table.

"I mean, I have Aint Angus, my auntie, and Aunt Paulette and Uncle Sam, who raised me, but it's like all this messed-up patchwork that doesn't make any sense together. At holidays, I see all of these folks that look just alike. Same hair, same skin color, same eyes. And then me, like the one patch of blue in a basket of red cherries. I don't seem to belong to any of them. They're always so careful around me, like they are hiding the fact that I am completely different. They don't have any stories to pass down to me, and I won't have anything to pass down to my children. I feel like I have no identity! It sucks!" I wiped the wetness from around my eyes, but there was no way to erase away the red puffy pillows that formed around my lids whenever I started crying.

Kiko sat down at the table and pulled the silver chain from around her neck. She passed it to me. I noticed the silver and jade locket on the bottom, and I opened it up. Inside there was no picture, no trinket like what I am used to seeing. Just an inscription in a straight, Roman font. "Kiko." I looked at the locket with a puzzle in my voice and questioned, "Okay...?"

"It is me. It is who I choose to be, the name I choose for myself. Not Papa. Not Mama. They hold their share in picture, in memory. But, me, Kiko, I keep inside my own heart and decide every day and choose every night who I will be. You the only one who can decide that. You alone have power to decide who you will be."

Sounded like a plan to me. I just had to decide who I would be, make a decision about it, and stick to it. With this revelation on hand, I went down to my own apartment to write my nomination acceptance speech and to wait for Sal to come.

Also Available from Strebor Books International

All titles are in stores now, unless otherwise noted.

Baptiste, Michael
Cracked Dreams (October 2004) 1-59309-035-8

Bernard, DV
The Last Dream Before Dawn 0-9711953-2-3
God in the Image of Woman 1-59309-019-6

Brown, Laurinda D.
Fire & Brimstone 1-59309-015-3
UnderCover (October 2004) 1-59309-030-7

Cheekes, Shonda
Another Man's Wife 1-59309-008-0
Blackgentlemen.com 0-9711953-8-2

Cooper, William Fredrick
Six Days in January 1-59309-017-X
Sistergirls.com 1-59309-004-8

Crockett, Mark
Turkeystuffer 0-9711953-3-1

Daniels, J and Bacon, Shonell
Luvalwayz: The Opposite Sex and Relationships 0-9711953-1-5
Draw Me With Your Love 1-59309-000-5

Darden, J. Marie
Enemy Fields 1-59309-023-4

De Leon, Michelle
Missed Conceptions 1-59309-010-2
Love to the Third 1-59309-016-1
Once Upon a Family Tree (October 2004) 1-59309-028-5

Faye, Cheryl
Be Careful What You Wish For (December 2004) 1-59309-034-X

Halima, Shelley
Azucar Moreno (December 2004) 1-59309-032-3

Handfield, Laurel
My Diet Starts Tomorrow 1-59309-005-6
Mirror Mirror 1-59309-014-5

Hayes, Lee
Passion Marks 1-59309-006-4

Hobbs, Allison
Pandora's Box 1-59309-011-0
Insatiable (November 2004) 1-59309-031-5

Johnson, Keith Lee
Sugar & Spice 1-59309-013-7
Pretenses 1-59309-018-8

Johnson, Rique
Love & Justice 1-59309-002-1
Whispers from a Troubled Heart 1-59309-020-X
Every Woman's Man (November 2004) 1-59309-036-6
Sistergirls.com 1-59309-004-8

Lee, Darrien
All That and a Bag of Chips 0-9711953-0-7
Been There, Done That 1-59309-001-3
What Goes Around Comes Around 1-59309-024-2

Luckett, Jonathan
Jasminium 1-59309-007-2
How Ya Livin' 1-59309-025-0

McKinney, Tina Brooks
All That Drama (December 2004) 1-59309-033-1

Quartay, Nane
Feenin 0-9711953-7-4

Rivers, V. Anthony
Daughter by Spirit 0-9674601-4-X
Everybody Got Issues 1-59309-003-X
Sistergirls.com 1-59309-004-8

Roberts, J. Deotis
Roots of a Black Future: Family and Church 0-9674601-6-6
Christian Beliefs 0-9674601-5-8

Stephens, Sylvester
Our Time Has Come (September 2004) 1-59309-026-9

Turley II, Harold L.
Love's Game (November 2004) 1-59309-029-3

Valentine, Michelle
Nyagra's Falls 0-9711953-4-X

White, A.J.
Ballad of a Ghetto Poet 1-59309-009-9

White, Franklin
Money for Good 1-59309-012-9
Potentially Yours 1-59309-027-7

Zane (Editor)
Breaking the Cycle (September 2004) 1-59309-021-8

9 781593 0902